A HEALTH CARE MYSTERY

DEATH WITHOUT CAUSE

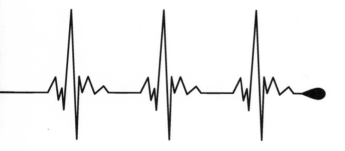

A HEALTH CARE MYSTERY

DEATH WITHOUT CAUSE

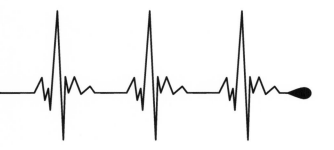

PAMELA TRIOLO

Death Without Cause

Pamela Triolo

F I R S T   E D I T I O N

HARDCOVER ISBN: 978-1-939288-09-7
eBook ISBN: 978-1-939288-10-3

PAPERBACK ISBN: 978-1-939288-06-6
Library of Congress Control Number: 2013931497

Published by Post Oak, An Imprint of Wyatt-MacKenzie
postoak@wyattmackenzie.com

For Peter
My forever love, my inspiration.

Man has made many machines,
Complex and cunning,
But which of them indeed rivals
The workings of his heart?

Pablo Casals

PROLOGUE

The human heart is a highly sophisticated pump. Protected by the ribs, it lies deep in the chest cavity. Though scientists have created prototypes, successful replication has failed.

The adult heart is roughly the size of a man's fist and weighs about a pound. It pulses an average of one hundred thousand times a day, over two billion beats in a normal lifetime. In one minute, this magnificent muscle pumps about five liters of blood. The heart sustains life in two ways. First, it siphons oxygen-rich blood from the lungs, circulating it to the brain, kidneys, and other vital organs and tissues of the body. Then it recycles waste products, like carbon dioxide, back to the lungs for exhalation. The work performed by a heart over a lifetime is comparable to a single man lifting thirty tons to the peak of Mount Everest.

Heart performance is a delicate, synergistic balance of anatomic and physiologic factors. Fluid and electrolyte balance provide the electrical conductivity necessary for the heart to beat. Hypothalamic cells affect the rise and fall of blood pressure, stimulating an increase or decrease in cardiac output. The complex and elegant interfaces that occur at the cellular and organ level are unknown and taken for granted, not even given a thought by the average healthy person.

The heart is a living paradox—strong yet fragile. Subtle changes within this system can trigger a cascade of events that, if unrecognized, will kill.

CHAPTER 1

TEXAS MEDICAL CENTER, HOUSTON
Early October

Santos Rosa raced up the stairwell on the tail of his long white coat. Her heart pounded and her mind raced. *One more to go ... we're almost there ... will we make it in time?*

"Patrick, you're a maniac, wait up!" Patrick Sullivan's long legs took the stairs two at a time and he burst through the door and ran down the hall toward the polished brass entrance of the VIP unit—the unit that housed headliners from rock stars to international royalty. She caught up with him as he punched in the security code. The doors flew open. Santos and Patrick, experienced CCU RNs, rushed in side by side. She looked up and down the hallway. Every sense was on full alert, fueled by the adrenaline of anticipation. She spotted a staff member who pointed down the hall to the left. On reflex, she reached into her pocket, grabbed her stethoscope, laced it around her neck, and ran.

"Code Blue, Jones 6 ... Code Blue, Jones 6," the overhead paging system repeated.

Santos and Patrick were rotating on the code team. She looked up at Patrick and saw concern etched on his face. *Who was it this time?* The lavishly furnished unit had hosted a string of who's who for decades. The crash cart was next to the door, drawers open and supplies littering the floor. Staff spilled out the doorway, waiting to assist.

Entering the hallway of the spacious suite, she wove through the crowd of residents, medical staff, pharmacists, and nurses in search of the patient. Before she could see what was going on, she could smell it—sweat and blood.

What she saw was shocking. Sheets of shiny, wine-red blood cascaded off the bed and dripped onto the floor. The tile floor was stamped with bloody footprints. The woman on the bed, a well-known and respected public figure, was still, her skin as pale as her hair. Dr. Richard Whiting, CCU medical director, was doing CPR, and the bed rocked with the force of his chest compressions.

"More plasma!"

"Coming!"

"No pressure, no pressure! We're losing her," shouted the anesthesia resident monitoring blood pressure, oxygen saturation, and cardiac rhythm. The attending anesthesiologist, OR mask still hanging around her neck, bagged the patient forcing in oxygen. Every heart in the room pounded rapidly. Every heart but the one they had come to save.

"Come on, people," Whiting shouted. "We can't lose her!"

Whiting briefly looked up, and his eyes locked on the newcomers. His ruggedly handsome face was wet with the sweat of exertion, and his long gray ponytail had come loose. Hair was plastered to his face and neck. Deep green eyes, ringed by dark circles of exhaustion, reflected his worry and sadness.

"Patrick, get your butt over here. Take over for me."

Patrick quickly navigated around the equipment and people and smoothly transitioned chest compressions, relieving Whiting.

"Santos, take a look at the record with me." Whiting headed over and stood by her side, looking down at her. Everyone towered over her. "How could we let this happen?" On the portable computer, she swiftly pulled up the EHR, reading over the electronic health record for clues.

"She was here for a knee replacement, a simple knee replacement. We should have put her in CCU as a precaution," Whiting commented while scanning. His eyes darted back and forth between the patient and the record.

"Labs look normal, her INR looks normal. She was getting routine enoxaparin injections and Coumadin by mouth," Santos reported.

"That can't be right. That INR cannot be right. It's too low … it's normal. She's hemorrhaging! We need to recheck it now … where's that Vitamin K? Move it people!" he shouted.

"Injecting now. More plasma on the way."

Santos read from the record, "She has a history of some internal hemorrhoids, some pretty serious bleeding episodes. Admitted to the ER twice for rectal bleeding. She's on beta-blockers and Coumadin for atrial fib. Looks like her INR fluctuated quite a bit." Her heart was sinking with worry, and she stopped, looked at him, and waited for his response.

Whiting raked his hand through his wet hair, looked down, and muttered under his breath, "What a mess! God help us."

Three long seconds passed.

Decision made, Whiting turned around.

"Call him," Whiting said quietly to the tall man standing nearby, telltale corkscrew wire threaded into his ear. The man's tailored black suit and tie stood out in stark contrast to the sea of blood-splattered white coats and rumpled, faded blue and pink scrubs. His face was a mask of emotion, but the eyes were alert, constantly scanning the area. "He needs to be here. Be sure that someone is with him when he hears. This could kill him."

The man nodded, lifted his hand toward his face and

softly spoke a few code words into the radio. Then he returned to watching the unit, the flow of clinicians coming and going, and occasionally his eyes would rest on the still figure of the woman on the bed.

⌐⌐

Outside the circle of the code, a tall man in a pristine white lab coat carrying a collection of tubes and vacutainers passed by the open door of the room. He looked at the organized chaos, but kept his distance. Then he stopped, turned around, and shuffled out of the unit as quietly as he had come.

CHAPTER 2
Two Months Earlier ... August

He could not breathe.

The weight crushed his chest. He struggled in agony to draw in just one lifesaving breath, but his ribs felt squeezed in a vise. He tried to inhale again ... break loose ... nothing ... he was paralyzed. Fully alert, his brain super-charged with the adrenaline of fear, he knew he was suffocating. Within moments, he saw black and white dots swirling. Losing his grip on consciousness, he plunged into the abyss.

He shot up in bed, gasping for air, drinking in deep breaths of cool air. His heart hammered, threatening to explode in his chest. Blood pounded up his carotids and throbbed into his jaw. The sheets were wet and cold with the sweat of his fear.

Fresh memories flooded back as if it had been yesterday, when in fact it was nearly thirty years ago: suffo-cating, then waking up intubated, alert yet unable to move a muscle, eyes fixed on the cracked and peeling ceiling in the Cyprus hospital, alive only because a machine breathed for him. Tears burned his eyes, tears that he would never weep, and he swallowed hard, choking back the bitter taste of bile.

He had suffered the humbling, grueling, and never-ending journey of rehab as he struggled to strengthen wasted muscles. The attack of Guillain-Barre forced him to regain the stamina to walk, to rediscover the dexterity to eat, and to rebuild the neural pathways that had forgotten how to do the simple things in life—hold a fork, brush his teeth. The humiliation of going from decorated military pilot to helpless baby as others washed him, fed him, and cleaned up after him was still raw.

He lived in a prison not of his making. They had let him down, crippled him for life, and robbed him of his hopes and dreams. The people who had taken an oath to protect and cure had destroyed the man he was, the man he had hoped to be. He had lost everything: his career, the woman he loved, and any chance of ever becoming a father. *Bastards!*

He had chosen the path of anger for years, and anger had carved deep lines in his forehead and the downward creases of his mouth, sculpting his face into a mask of bitterness, his mouth a sneer. Nearly succumbing to the depression of self-pity, he stopped himself before drowning in the black hole of despair. He breathed more evenly now, his heart slowed, and he looked around at the tranquility and order of his bedroom and remembered. Today would be different.

⌒

After the usual slow struggle of shaving and showering, he limped into his kitchen, a crutch supporting his weak right leg. His hand tremors decreased a bit when he poured thick black coffee into a heavy white stoneware mug. Juggling the mug in his left hand, he headed over to the kitchen table, spilling some of its contents on the floor. Sighing, he put the mug on the table, went back to the counter, pulled off a length of paper towels, and mopped up the small mess.

He had no close friends and lived alone. His house was meticulous in its order, a clue to his military past.

There was not a speck of dust on the minimalist space; magazines and books were stacked on the coffee table, corners matching and titles in alphabetical order. The white dishes on the open shelves were arranged with such symmetrical precision that even Martha Stewart would approve. His shrine of a computer alcove held the latest high-tech gadgets, with cords neatly wrapped and everything in place.

These days, everything seemed to tick him off. His anger, simmering for decades, had moved closer to the surface after his new supervisor had recently moved him with other MTs—medical technologists—to remote, windowless cubicles away from the general bustle of the hospital laboratory. Instead of covering all functional areas of the lab, the redesign clustered MTs into work groups: chemistry, hematology, stat lab, etc. His new assignment was chemistry, not his favorite. His preference was the stat lab, where the sense of urgency and variety kept him pumped. The stat lab was the epicenter of medical decisions, and the techs who worked there were adrenaline junkies.

He doubted the suits had any idea that the real source of power in health care was the laboratory. Physicians, nurses, pharmacists depended on lab results to provide crucial pieces of the clinical puzzle. Unlike forensic experts who searched for answers after death, health care clinicians searched for real-time biological clues—clues vital to discovering the cause of illness. Lab tests revealed secrets and told truths. Lab results could bring patients incredible joy and unspeakable sorrow.

With the local TV news on in the background, he ate a simple breakfast of instant oatmeal, his head buried in *The Houston Chronicle.* He glanced up and a rare smiled played on his lips. *If I did it right, would I read about this in the papers?* Anonymously, of course—this would be a perfect crime. His Google and other Internet searches had yielded long-ago references to his heroism. Now he was just another vet lost in the mainstream of life. Maybe finally, he would get some recognition for his IQ of one-fifty-five and the precision of his planning. He was about to begin a deadly game where he would write the rules, others would unwittingly play, and he alone would know the score.

CHAPTER 3
Late August

In the early morning darkness, Santos rode The Woodlands Express into Houston, drinking in the relative quiet of the dim interior. She was dark and striking, a petite young woman of twenty-five with streaks of natural russet in her thick, mahogany hair. Her hair swung shoulder length, framing an olive-skinned oval face with hazel-rimmed brown eyes. Her eyes appeared to change color depending on her emotions, from warm coffee to black that could shoot sparks of amber when angry. Right now, they were clear and bright, sparkling with anticipation.

Named for the day she was born, *Dia de los Santos,* All Saints Day, Santos was a first-generation Texan. Her family had emigrated from Mexico some thirty years ago, and she was the youngest of seven and the first to be born in the United States. Though not the first in her family to graduate from college, she was the first nurse, and that achievement was the pride and joy of her parents. Her cultural background had turned out to be a career boon as well: bilingual in Spanish and English, she was much sought-after for her ability to translate for families who came from around the world for care.

She reflected on the past two weeks and smiled at the memories of her vacation in Telluride. The drive up through Texas, New Mexico, and then the winding mountain roads of Colorado had allowed her to decompress. She loved to travel and explore. The spectacular mountain peaks, crisp mountain air, and the wonderful aromas of cedar mulch and juniper trees had made for a welcome escape from the oppressive heat of the southern summer. The dry heat, nearly cloudless mornings, and afternoon cooling showers were lovely. She had happily slept with the windows open at night while temperatures dropped into the forties. The public transportation system was amazing. Gondolas connected Mountain Village with the village of Telluride. The only one of its kind in the US, the ride down to Telluride showcased a spectacular view of the valleys. When the gondolas got close to the tree line, they nearly grazed the foliage, and then soared high into the sky. The ride was so quiet that she could hear the sounds of birds and the distant laughter of families.

Refreshed, she was ready for the never-ending challenge of work.

As the bus drove down Montrose under the arched canopy of gigantic live oaks, she could see the lights from the sprawling Texas Medical Center, the largest medical center in the world. The brightly lit twin needles of St. Luke's Towers stood out in relief against the backdrop of night. The TMC, composed of over fifty organizations employing some one hundred thousand faculty and other staff, covered an area about the size of the Chicago Loop. Created as a nonprofit mecca for health care over sixty years ago, it now included a cluster of nationally known Magnet hospitals recognized for the high caliber of their nurses. Riding in and seeing the exciting complex still gave her a thrill. With six million patient visits a year, the TMC had been her first choice for work and education. Yet, until 2011 when US Representative Gabby Giffords had come for rehabilitation from a traumatic brain injury, few people outside of Houston seemed to know of its existence.

The bus pulled up to the Holcomb stop, and her mind jolted back to the present. She stood up with the rest of the early risers to move off the bus. After good-byes to some of her regular riding friends, she briskly walked the short distance to work. The air was cool and breezy, heralding the onset of fall, the much-awaited respite from the scorching and humid heat of summer. The route took her along outdoor paths bordered by huge mounds of colorful vincas and petunias, then inside to air-conditioned skywalks that connected most of the buildings.

As she walked, she noticed people eating in restaurants, new seasonal clothes in some of the shops, and a sale in the jewelry store. She was constantly amazed by the buzz of activity even this early in the morning as patients and students from all over the world came for health care or education.

Three years out of college, Santos had quickly earned the title and role of clinical mentor in the thirty-bed CCU. She felt privileged to work at Medical Center Hospital, where the nursing beacon burned bright and there was a waiting list for employment. Nursing was her mission and her passion. She had chosen nursing as a career because she knew it would challenge her intellectually. Naïve going in, she had discovered that it tested her in every way, stretching her to grow. She knew that every day she could make a difference in people's lives.

She moved purposely through the maze of corridors, smiling and exchanging greetings with colleagues from Food and Nutrition Services, Housekeeping, and Pharmacy. At 6:30 a.m., the halls were already crowded and bustling with people and equipment. The thousands of employees in the 450-bed academic tertiary hospital made it more like a small town. Staff considered their coworkers part of their family, generally spending more time at work than they did with their families at home. Teamwork was one of the reasons staff stayed and the patients received some of the best care in the city.

She guided a lost couple to the east wing pre-op area, walking and talking with them to allay the husband's obvious fears about his wife's imminent surgery. Then she swiped her badge through the electronic time-and-attendance recorder, avoided the slow elevator bank, and walked up the two flights of stairs, jostling the backpack on her back and the casserole in her arms.

Approaching the entrance to the CCU, she punched the red button on the wall with her right elbow. The double doors swung open, revealing a sea of patients organized in circular pods around the centralized workstation. The noise and bright lights of the unit assaulted her senses. Having been away for two weeks, she stopped and looked with fresh eyes at what new patients and families saw every day. It struck her how the cavernous architecture and tile floor amplified the noise—the constant beeping of IV pumps and heart monitors as well as the whooshing rhythm of the ventilators. The unit was alive with movement and energy. Change of shift. The unit was crowded with doctors in long, white coats, accompanied by exhausted medical students in their distinctive short white jackets. At least ten clinicians stood clustered around the workstation. She headed toward the conference room wondering as usual how patients could ever rest and heal amidst the cacophony.

Though just five feet, she felt taller as she walked with confidence into the conference room bearing gifts. A cluster of nurses, both men and women, were finishing work and chatting. Everyone looked up with smiles when they saw her. Not only was she new energy back from vacation, but she had brought a casserole of breakfast tortillas to feed the forever-hungry crew of nurses and residents who rarely got off the unit to eat. She unzipped the red-quilted insulated cover and lifted the lid from the still warm dish. The aroma of scrambled eggs, sautéed onions, green peppers, potatoes, and sausage filled the room. The conversation shifted from patients to food.

"How do you stay tiny when you cook like this?" asked Emma with a Southern drawl and a roll of her eyes as she opened a foil wrapper and bit into a soft, warm breakfast tortilla. She sighed deeply with pleasure. "Mmmmmm … your Mamma taught you well."

Emma Perrine, RN, had been Santos's mentor since she started on the unit. A beautiful woman with skin the color of creamy milk chocolate, Emma's dark eyes were warm with compassion and deep with the wisdom of experience. At forty, Emma was an expert practitioner who was also the mother of three active teenagers. Like Santos, Emma was multilingual, fluent in both French and Creole. Her body, graced with generous curves, was testimony to her love of food and her reputation as a fabulous cook. Santos smiled as she watched Emma eat, remembering the story of her friend's delight when nurses went from white uniforms to comfortable scrubs with elastic waists.

Cody Patterson, the RN administrator on duty, stopped in while on rounds.

"For once, I'm in the right place at the right time." He sat down at the table and quickly reached for one of the rapidly vanishing tortillas. "There's nothing in the world like homemade breakfast tortillas! Santos, you're the best! Why don't we do this more often?"

Santos shook her head, then smiled and pointed her finger. "Cody, your turn next time."

"Hey, now that we have you back, when is your *Abuela* going to make tamales again?" Patrick Sullivan smiled, winked at her, and then leaned over to pluck a tortilla from the casserole. Five years her senior, he was tall, with a strong athletic build and youthful good looks. He was one of the best and brightest nurses on the unit; in fact, in the entire hospital. Well-known for his consistent performance, great interpersonal skills, and strong clinical diagnostic aptitude, Patrick was constantly encouraged to move into management. Yet he had told Santos that the real place to make a difference was in patient care. He was consistently in demand as a mentor for seasoned nurses as well as students and new staff. His energy was boundless, he always had some new project going, and he had just finished his graduate degree. He was on Santos's case to get started on hers.

Santos smiled at Patrick then frowned. She looked around the room with concern at the crowd that had gathered, counting heads and tortillas. Would the supply of food hold out? These people were her work family. This was a real treat, and she only hoped it would go around.

Patrick ate with relish, attracting another envious comment from Emma. With the chiseled jaw and lean look of a marathon runner, he was able to consume tons of calories and never gain an ounce. Santos watched him finish his first tortilla in three big bites and reach for another. She felt warm all over thinking about Patrick and smiled at his obvious pleasure. She had tremendous respect for him; she could always count on him for great clinical advice or help. Besides, he was so cute with his blond buzz and those few freckles.

"Abuelita hasn't been feeling well recently. I really need to go and see her."

"Abuelita" was Santos's special name for her grandmother. Wishing for tamales was one thing. Making them was another. Tamales were an ancient food, dating back to the pre-Columbian era, and a holiday favorite of her family. The preparation of this labor-intensive comfort food began with soaking dried corn husks for hours, braising beef or other filling, creating the sauce, preparing chilies and grinding them to powder, and making *masa,* a cornmeal dough. The multistep process took hours and many hardworking hands. Santos's job in the production line was lining the corn husks with masa.

"I'll be sure to bring some in when the family gets together again over the holidays. Ya'll come! We can always use an extra set of hands."

"I heard that the cooking school in The Woodlands had tamale classes," Emma piped up. "Bet they can't compete with your family recipe, but that would be fun to do as a group sometime."

"Let's do cooking school before I start classes next semester," Santos replied. She had just registered for her first course at the University of Texas Health Science Center School of Nursing. She was excited not only about the challenge of graduate work, but also about meeting new people from other hospitals. She loved learning, was always hungry for new information.

The quick conversation around school and food abruptly ended with the departure of the night shift and the need to get to patients. Santos sat down, logged in, and began to review the electronic records of her patients. She had much to review, as all the names were completely new. Pausing in her work, she looked over her shoulder at the casserole of tamales, thinking she should put the leftovers in the refrigerator. Too late—devoured.

Before she went back to the records, her mind skipped ahead to Kimberly's wedding this weekend. Santos met Kimberly at a seminar on quality improvement. It turned out that Kimberly worked in physical therapy at Medical Center Hospital. They knew many of the same colleagues and quickly found common ground. Over the years, they had forged a relationship that grew into a strong friendship. Kimberly was from the country-club set and Santos's family—well, no one owned a set of golf clubs or belonged to a country club. She was excited about the evening, but had mixed feelings. *So many weddings, and I go alone.* It always felt a little awkward and lonely. But she smiled, happy for her friend. Back to the present, Santos squared her shoulders and dug into the patient records.

CHAPTER 4

While Santos was working her first shift in two weeks, keeping up with patients and the constant churn of medical students and residents, he completed a set of blood tests and verified results. *Will they ever label these specimens right?* The health care system was full of potholes and riddled with mistakes—mistakes that could misdiagnose or kill.

A smile quirked at the edge of his mouth.

His mind worked rapidly while he processed specimens. His conscientious side was energized by the precision required. In spite of the constant repetition, doing it right required discipline. The job was dangerous: it involved constant exposure to blood and body fluids, viruses and bacteria. Measuring the right amount of a specimen, usually blood, diluting as needed, adding the appropriate reagents, and mastering the technology were all a part of successful testing.

A raw sense of power throbbed through him as he analyzed samples. Patients knew their lives were in the hands of doctors and nurses, but did they ever give a thought to the people behind the scenes? He could change lives in an instant, and no one would ever know.

Absorbed in his work, his thoughts rarely strayed from the boundary of the specimen. Analyzing specimens brought him peace and calm. The potent sense of control, knowing that the outcome of his professional work affected people's lives, combined with the tranquility of the detailed work, had kept him engaged for nearly three decades. Consumed by the process, he was free of his lower-body physical weakness. His hand tremors eased up with voluntary movement, and he felt unencumbered.

The hours flew by, and his subconscious worked through the puzzle of his plan. He would fine-tune each step, yet leave room for improvisation. The plan was a game, an intellectual challenge. It had been percolating under the surface of his psyche for years and was nearly ready to put into play.

He pulled off his latex gloves, heaved himself up out of the chair, and lumbered over to the computer cubicle to review the latest set of lab results for outliers before posting to the patients' electronic records. As he scanned the lab results, he remembered that tonight he had an appointment at the health club. He worked out three times a week, twice on his own and one night with a trainer who was also a physical therapist. He kept his upper body strong, using free weights at home between the health club workouts. As a result his upper-body strength was formidable, a source of great pride for him.

The weekly check-in with the trainer helped to keep up the flexibility and mobility of his legs, particularly the right one. Even though the workout was often painful, he knew, after years of rehab, that it kept him strong and active.

Returning to the centrifuge, he picked up a fresh specimen. Specimens came into the lab via pneumatic tube or personnel walked them down to the Processor. The Processor would log in the specimen, scan the bar code with the patient's ID, and run it in the centrifuge where it would stay until picked up and analyzed by the MTs. Then the MT would scan the patient's bar code pasted on the specimen into the scanner and manually enter the test results, or the computer would analyze and record them.

Focus helped the hours fly. He smiled. Soon it would be time for him to launch the game.

CHAPTER 5
Labor Day Weekend

Saturday morning dawned cool and clear, with periwinkle skies. The haze of humidity had lifted, and the passing "cold" front brought relief from the heat, dropping the temperature to a gorgeous eighty degrees. Santos sat on her small sheltered back patio, drinking jasmine tea, her favorite, steeped exactly two minutes. She loved the soothing fragrance of the tea. Wind chimes played softly and melodically in the distance.

Without warning, a wave of melancholy washed over her. Her index finger traced the rim of the fine bone-china cup, one of her late mother's, and she felt a small chip. Lifting the still warm cup to her cheek, she remembered the times she had watched her mother drink from this very cup. She felt a strong spiritual connection with Marianna, and cherished using her mother's things, liking wearing her pearls, as it made her feel closer ... the sadness blew away, passing just as quickly as it came.

The first falling leaves of the season swirled and danced across the lawn. She reflected back on the week's events. The slightly detached vacation sense of perspective lingered. Tonight was Kimberly's long-awaited wedding. Santos had errands to run, groceries to buy, and she desperately needed new shoes. The racing of her mind stopped when a vague feeling of envy surfaced. It seemed as if most of her friends were either married or getting married. Right now, she focused her time on career and school, too busy to think about marriage. Besides, work consumed her and she had little energy to devote to a relationship.

Her cell phone rang. Reality returned.

She took at a look at the caller ID, saw that it was Patrick, and wondered what might be going on with work. Santos always kept her phone close, anxious to be available for work and family. Her brother, Santiago, had teased her about what he had called her "addiction" to communication devices.

"Good morning! You're up early," she said, smiling. "What's up?"

"Lots to do. You know the drill. I've already been out— great three-mile run. Thought I'd call and see if you needed a ride to the wedding."

Patrick was going to the wedding, too?

She exhaled, caught off guard … confused. If she said yes, this would be a date. Their first date. Going to a wedding with someone was a big deal. She really liked Patrick, but they rarely had time to talk outside of work. Twelve-hour shifts did little for your social life. She had no idea how parents with kids juggled nursing shifts, much less how singles found time to date. Logistics rushed through her mind—travel time and the distance between their two homes. Then the more important question: was she ready for this?

She took a deep breath.

"Patrick, it sounds like a good idea, but I have to get some new shoes. I thought I'd come into town a little early, shop, and then head over to the wedding."

She paused. He was quiet.

She broke the silence. "I'll see you there? Save a dance for you?"

"I'm going to hold you to that! Sure I can't pick you up?"

She could hear disappointment in his voice.

"Patrick, I'll see you there. It'll be fun. We need to

have some fun. Work has been crazy, hasn't it?"

"Yes, it has. Okay, I hear you. I'll see you there. Have fun shopping." Then he hung up.

She sat for a moment, staring at her cell phone, wishing her mother were still alive so she could ask advice. *Why did that make me anxious? What do I do? Many women would love to be Patrick's date for a wedding. Why am I hesitating?* She believed in destiny and timing in love, though choice would always play a big part. Now was not the time. Glancing at her watch, she got up and went inside.

Chapter 6

That same Saturday morning, he sat glued to the computer engrossed in a web search. Searching for ... he was not certain yet. It had to be something that would confuse yet not raise a red flag. It would have to be difficult to diagnose and impossible to trace. It had to be ordinary and every day, yet lethal and quick so they were helpless to stop him. Take them out of control for once.

His head throbbed.

Employee morale in the lab was at an all-time low. Their new manager, a young MHA, wet behind the ears with no clinical experience, had an office in another building. He was just another suit; might have been on another planet, he was so invisible. Obviously, he was a climber, another administrator on his way to the next job who would never learn their names or stop to listen to their issues. Unless you have been in the trenches on the clinical side, you have no idea what it is like.

These days, it seemed as if the only hospital communication, other than reading about something in the newspaper, was from the highly developed staff grapevine, where rumors of another five-percent cut fueled his discontent and paranoia. It would be typical of the bean-counter administration to terminate the most senior people with the highest salaries. The recent knee-jerk boardroom decisions that had reduced supplies and personnel fueled his resentment. Then he thought of the salaries those "suits" made ... and his anger nearly blew him off track.

He took several deep breaths to calm himself. Then he refocused on the game plan. He felt like a cat toying with a gecko. He wanted to taunt them and play with death. Come in and out, quickly and quietly, put those arrogant snobs in white coats in their place. Show them real power … the power to kill. They deserved to be humbled. Nothing ever seemed to faze those docs, not even when they let healthy people crash into disability—a disability that would plague them their entire lives. They could walk away; go home in Jaguars to fancy West University or River Oaks. He had seen some of them in the society pages of the paper, partying in Aspen, of all places. They were all smiles, trophy wives dripping with ostentatious bling. Trim pretty boys. Aging icons. Unlike them with the constant rounds of parties and balls they attended, he was always alone … feeling lonely, damaged and incomplete.

Rage coiled in his gut like a serpent ready to strike; contempt energized him, sharpened his senses, and intensified his efforts. He obsessively searched through laboratory sites, E-Medicine.com, and other sites looking for something that would morph the spark of an idea into a flame of action. *What laboratory test is routine, ordinary, done every day that if not done right could be life-threatening?* He went through the screens he knew by heart: hemoglobin and hematocrit, platelet counts, differential screens, electrophoresis tests, reticulocyte counts, blood chemistry.

He thought back on his organic and biochemistry background and pulled out an old textbook, opening it to a well-worn section. As his finger traced down the page, his hand stopped at a bold heading. All of a sudden, it was clear. He sat back in his chair and smiled the smug smile of success. Revenge was sweet.

CHAPTER 7

Santos arrived at the cathedral that evening thirty minutes before the ceremony. She quickly found a parking place and followed others into the nearly empty church. She had chosen to wear a black, raw-silk sleeveless sheath that skimmed her curves and showed off the remnants of her vacation tan. She carried a small, black-beaded clutch, and a black wool shawl, essential for survival in chilly, air-conditioned Houston. She was anxious to snag a seat on the aisle so she could shoot great pictures of the bride.

She entered the church and was swept away by the heady scent of tropical flowers and beeswax. Dozens of white arrangements of roses, gardenias, and calla lilies were strategically placed on the altar. The heat of the evening intensified the perfume of the flowers. At the end of each aisle were tall glass hurricane lamps, circled by greenery, and tied with huge satin bows. The lamps softly glowed with white tapers. The candlelit aisle marked the journey to a new life for a committed couple whose story had begun on a blind date three years earlier.

She paused in the vestibule of the church, feeling a bit unsure in such a grand setting. This was a lot more formal than the weddings she usually attended. She looked around to see if she saw anyone she knew.

"Santos, are you ready?" She turned around to see one of Kimberly's much younger brothers. He looked smart and grown-up in his black tux with white boutonniere roses. He held out his right arm, and she gratefully accepted. "I don't have to ask 'bride's side or groom's' with you, do I?" he smiled. "You look great tonight, Santos. Different from your usual jeans and T-shirts."

"Thank you, Andy. You don't look so bad yourself."

Andy guided her to a perfect spot on the aisle in the middle of the church. Santos knelt down in the quiet of the church to offer a prayer for the couple. Then she slid back in the pew to watch the parade of fashionistas. She was not disappointed. The church filled quickly with young and old, all well-dressed for a Houston evening wedding. She was pleased that she had carefully chosen her clothes for the evening. *Better to be overdressed than under,* her mother had always said. Marianna had felt it was a sign of respect to dress for the occasion. The church was overflowing with the multicultural community, men in their dark evening suits and sophisticated women wearing everything from black cocktail dresses to glittering St. John knit suits.

"Hi there…."

She was so busy watching the parade of well-dressed family and friends that she did not see Patrick slip into the pew on her left side.

"Hi yourself … where did you come from?"

"Andy told me you were here."

She smiled up at him. "You clean up nicely." He looked handsome in a dark, tailored suit, white shirt with silver cuff links and a blue tie. His face had a healthy glow from the sun.

He sat down next to her and gave her a long look. Then he reached over and gently took her hand … she turned to look at him. Patrick's blue eyes turned deep sapphire with warmth.

"Santos, you look beautiful tonight."

His words touched her soul and rekindled a fire long asleep. Her breath caught in her throat. At a loss for words, she looked away from his eyes, and touched the cuff link on his wrist, rubbing the fine polished metal with her thumb. Her heart fluttered ... she felt warm all over. *Am I blushing?* Something shifted inside of her. It had been a very long time since someone had told her she was beautiful. After a few moments, she found her voice.

"Thank you, Patrick ... thank you ... you are very sweet."

The people in the pews next to them began to whisper and look toward the back of the church. She squeezed and released his hand, then checked her watch. It was time. The congregation rose to attention when the organist at the huge, three-keyboard pipe organ began to play the wedding classic Clarke's "Trumpet Voluntary," heavy on the bass pedals. The pipes thundered, and the church vibrated from floor to rafters as the glorious music filled the church.

Weddings were important; the sacrament of matrimony was the beginning of a promise of commitment to one person, a commitment made every day for the rest of life. Santos's eyes filled with tears at the sound of the music. Patrick put a clean, pressed handkerchief in her hand and nodded. She gratefully took his handkerchief and used it to blot the corner of her eyes, then clutched it in her hands, hands that had suddenly become sticky with perspiration. Patrick nudged her, handing her the camera. She was so flustered she almost forgot to take pictures.

Santos waited, listening to the music, leaning into the aisle to watch for the bridal procession. Finally, Kimberly, statuesque blond, a third-generation Houstonian, appeared, gliding down the aisle. The bride's long hair, elegantly pulled back into a loose-fitting crocheted chignon studded with pearls, gave her a medieval look. She wore her mother's princess cut wedding dress of ivory satin. Kimberly clung to the arm of her distinguished, gray-haired father. Her dress, heavily beaded with pearls, sequins, and crystals, caught the light just so and sparkled softly. Her twelve-foot veil fanned out behind her. Santos smiled as she watched her friend walk down the aisle. *Every woman is a princess, but especially on her wedding day.*

⌇

The River Oaks Country Club was the scene for the lavish reception and a first for Santos. William Hogg and Hugh Potter had developed River Oaks, a prestigious neighborhood near the heart of Houston. She had checked out the history prior to the wedding. In 1923, they bought two hundred acres around the country club, and in 1928, sold lots for $2,200. The area was famous for classic homes built by lauded architects, with stunning landscape designs that featured azaleas and magnolias as well as other Southern horticultural treasures.

Flutes of sparkling champagne awaited guests as they entered the club. Champagne was Santos's favorite, a taste acquired during her college years. An upbeat swing melody floated into the foyer from the big band playing in the ballroom. Well-dressed guests moved into the candlelit ballroom, glittering with magnificent Austrian crystal chandeliers. Dramatic arrangements of yellow roses towered over guests, and she watched as guests stopped in awe to gaze and admire.

Santos laughed and thought, *Some of those flower arrangements probably cost more than one month of my salary!* The reception in the main ballroom consisted of tables surrounding the dance floor. Each table featured a different ethnic feast: Middle Eastern, Mexican, Asian, and of course, Texas barbeque. Guests moved from table to table sampling chef-inspired savory specialties. The setting fostered mingling and tempted sumptuous tasting. The five-tiered wedding cake was decorated with white buttercream frosting, yellow roses, and a huge bouquet of yellow roses crowned the top. The two-tiered groom's cake was the classic chocolate cake with fudge icing.

The dance floor filled quickly with young and old, toddlers in their fathers' arms and groups of young women line dancing. Santos found herself swiftly snatched up by one of Kimberly's four brothers. They all took turns dancing with her.

"When are you going to marry me?" asked Andy, at least ten years her junior, as they moved to a rhythmic salsa on the crowded dance floor.

"Oh, Andy, I'm too old for you."

He smiled. "I'll wait."

The music shifted from salsa to a slow dance, giving the dancers a breather. Andy thanked her and headed off to make a younger conquest. The band began to play "I Will Always Love You," and she walked to the edge of the dance floor looking around for the ladies' lounge to freshen up and rest her aching feet. Patrick came up behind her.

"No, you're not leaving now." He grabbed her hand and pulled her back onto the dance floor. "This is one of my favorite tunes. You owe me at least one dance." He held out his arms to her. "Come on, Santos."

"Patrick, my feet are killing me. I need to sit down for a few minutes."

"Take off your shoes."

"I can't! This is the River Oaks Country Club."

"Why not? Everyone else has." Patrick motioned to the piles of women's shoes stacked around the edges of the dance floor.

She glanced around, noting many of the women

dancing without shoes.

"Good idea!" She walked off the dance floor, pulled off her shoes, and walked back to him. "That feels much better … you can certainly be persuasive, Patrick."

She looked at him and smiled wryly, and then with a slight hesitation stepped closer to him and said, "I love this song, too."

Patrick continued, "My mother was hooked on the movie *The Bodyguard.* She loved hearing Whitney Houston sing. Can you believe Whitney is dead? At forty-eight? Such a great voice."

She nodded, and Patrick kept talking. "Dolly Parton actually wrote this song before we were born. Bet you didn't know that."

"Really? I didn't." She still had not moved to dance. It was such an intimate song.

"Come on," he said and pulled her gently in his arms. "I won't hurt you."

She sighed, touched the fine wool of his dark suit, breathed in the subtle woodsy scent of a man's cologne, and found herself surprised to feel shelter in the warmth of his arms. After a few minutes she began to relax. He held her close, his hand on her waist, and they moved as if they had been dancing together for years. He towered over her; her head rested in the center of his chest. She could feel his heartbeat, and she surrendered to the tenderness of the moment, gently rocking to the music.

She looked up for a moment to watch the dance floor, a stage for lovers and long-married couples who glided gracefully all around them, the bride and groom joining in. The music inspired powerful emotions, bringing back memories, creating new ones. For a brief time, the couples on the dance floor escaped the technology-driven, frenzied world of data phones, texts, and Twitter and lived in the moment, cocooned in the music.

The music ended, and Santos quickly stepped back from Patrick.

"Thank you, Patrick. Not too bad for our first dance."

"There will be many more," he said, looking down at her. He was still holding her hand.

She blushed again. "Right now, I must get off my feet," she said. "Or I won't be able to walk on Monday."

"Okay, I'll let you go—for the moment. But will you promise me one thing?"

He reached down to grab her other hand. She was trapped.

She laughed and played along. "Another dance?"

"No, promise me that this is just the beginning."

She looked at him, once again surprised by his directness. Here in this beautiful place, celebrating the promise of love and commitment in marriage, surrounded by family and friends, her heart began to fill with joy and hope. The sudden wave of emotion caught her off guard. She was speechless. She looked up at him, and then the words spilled out.

"Yes, I do believe that this could be just the beginning."

Stunned dizzy at her words, she stood immobile for a few seconds. His smile spread wider than she had ever seen it, and he looked deeply into her eyes.

"I've got to go," she said, breaking the spell of the moment, looking for an excuse to escape. "My feet are killing me, Patrick."

"Go, go!" he said.

What have I done? I cannot believe I said that! she thought as she walked gingerly on her blistered feet to the ladies' lounge. *Can one glass of champagne do that to me?*

She shook her head, embarrassed, wondering what she had done, and let a small, nervous laugh slip through her lips. *Will he remember this on Monday?*

You bet, she thought. *Patrick remembers everything.*

Chapter 8

Santos woke up late on Sunday. She lingered in bed, feeling lazy and a bit tired.

It had been a fun, fairy-tale evening, but different from the weddings of her childhood. Growing up in a big family, she had enjoyed the camaraderie and warmth of Mexican weddings, full of children and celebration. Children came dressed in their best church dresses, pants, and jackets. *We knew everyone. There were no VIPs, just family and close friends. Never felt alone or intimidated, like last night.* The events around a wedding might go on for days, with the actual ceremony and reception only a part of the celebration. *Such fun we had,* she thought.

If she did not go the reception, her mother would always bring her back a piece of wedding cake in a napkin.

"To put under your pillow and dream of your future husband," Marianna would say.

Her mother's death a year ago still left a raw, gaping hole in Santos's heart. Though her mother had died peacefully, on her own terms and supported by hospice at home, Santos missed her terribly. All life events, from her achievements at work to celebrations of life, were bittersweet since her mother was no longer there to share them. But her spiritual roots were deep, and she felt close to her mother even though she was no longer living.

What a night, she thought, smiling. Her feet, punished by dancing, screamed for attention. *What was I thinking, wearing new shoes?* Then she reran the evening in her head. Now that it was over, the short but intimate conversation with Patrick made her anxious. He was so thoughtful, bringing the handkerchief. It had been so comforting to dance with him—comforting, but not much more. They had chemistry, but no sparks. She closed her eyes, trying to think that one through. *What did that mean?* They were good friends and worked together well as clinicians. She had great respect for him. Yet she knew little about him outside of work. *This could be complicated. Not sure I am ready for this.*

She sat up, got out of bed, threw on her cotton robe, and went to the front door to pick up the newspaper. Returning to her small, organized kitchen, she ground coffee beans and started the coffeepot. Craving fruit, she opened the refrigerator and grabbed an orange. She loved the smell of citrus. Inhaling deeply the fragrance of the skin, she peeled the fruit and dropped the skins into the small compost tin under the sink. Then she popped a juicy wedge into her mouth, piled everything onto a tray, and opened the door to the patio. She sat down next to a small table and opened up *The New York Times Sunday Edition* to get her dose of great writing and current events, check out the book reviews and travel specials. *The Times* was a luxury she indulged in once a week.

The sky was clear again—not a cloud in sight. The wind blew gently through her wind chimes, creating a melodic tranquility. She was grateful it was not last year at this time. Then, her daily reality had been grief and anxiety. Was this really the time to get involved? Was she just setting herself up for more pain? Conflicted, she put *The Times* aside, got up, and walked inside.

CHAPTER 9

On the inaugural Monday, "Game Day," he arrived hours before his shift. His enthusiasm was sharpened by an edge of paranoia. He would carefully plot the chain of events that would lead to the kills, build them into his normal pattern of activity so as not to draw attention. There were a number of questions floating around in his mind. *Where to begin? What unit?*

After thinking about it nearly day and night, he had decided to use several different methods to avoid detection. With his clinical background and knowledge of biochemistry and pathophysiology, he knew exactly what to do. The methods and mechanism of death were clear, but the actual unit or units were not. Insulated by distance, housed in the basement lab plus access to the computer in the privacy of his remote cubicle, he felt that he could commit the crime by remote control.

He picked up a set of samples from the centrifuge and ran them through the Vitros 350 analyzer. After a few minutes, the results were visible on the 350's computer screen. He smoothly rolled his chair over to the computer linked to the hospital electronic patient record and reviewed the patients in the CCU and their previous results. He focused on one patient in particular with a diagnosis of heart failure and then checked the medical record. The patient had been on diuretic therapy, common for heart failure, and had a recent bout with diarrhea. There was an order for a nutrition consult as the patient had not been eating well prior to admission and during this hospitalization. He noted discharge orders pending normal lab results.

Absorbed in his review, the minutes flew and activity in the lab picked up. *Looks like a "frequent flier,"* he thought as he scanned the medical record. Frequent fliers, admitted many times over the course of a year, had very complex medical problems and often multisystem issues.

He looked around the room ... empty ... the coast was clear. He carefully navigated his rolling chair to the computer screen of an MT who had stepped out to go to the bathroom. The absent MT was still logged in. He pulled up the new lab values in the batch of blood samples. Then he looked around the room again ... still clear.

The tips of his fingers tingled with erotic anticipation as they lightly stroked the keyboard, and he felt adrenaline surge through his core. He made a quick keystroke, adjusting the dangerously low value to a normal level, reviewed the remainder of the lab results, and transmitted the information to the hospital patient electronic record. Now he was past the point of no return. An anonymous puppeteer, he had the power to pull the strings of doctors and nurses. He felt in complete control. They would not have a clue. Amazing how tweaking one little variable could end a life.

CHAPTER 10

That same Monday arrived too early for Santos.

She boarded the 5:15 a.m. Woodlands Express at the Sawdust Park and Ride. Though the commute to the TMC was long, it allowed her to escape to a lovely wooded community in an affordable patio home in Auburn Lakes instead of living inside the Houston Loop. Plus, she saved money and time since the bus dropped her within a block of the hospital, avoiding the shuttle from remote parking.

She settled back in the dimly lit interior as the bus began its journey into Houston. Most of the people on the bus caught another hour of sleep, but she used the time to read and highlight some recent articles on advances in heart disease she had found in *Dimensions of Critical Care Nursing, New England Journal of Medicine,* and *JAMA.* She would post the best articles on the bulletin board in the staff lounge for this month's Journal Club.

The hour flew, and she walked the short distance to the hospital in the predawn light. Multidisciplinary rounds began at 6:30 a.m., and she wanted to get there on time for the briefing on the work ahead and to talk about what had not gone well in patient care the week before. The conference room on the unit was crowded with medical students, residents, staff physicians, the social worker for the unit, and other nurses. Rounds had been in place for years as the team constantly worked on improving care with a patient focus.

Someone had brought donuts and made Starbucks coffee for the crowd, and Santos, along with the others, eagerly converged on it.

"How can the combination of coffee and donut taste so good, yet be so bad for you?" she asked as she cut a glazed donut in half. "If I keep eating like this and going to weddings over the weekends, I'll blimp out again."

"Some wedding, huh?" Patrick commented as he slid his long legs into the last available chair by Santos. "Must have cost a bundle."

"It was beautiful. Wasn't Kimberly gorgeous?"

Other colleagues who had attended agreed. She looked at Patrick and smiled. "I did have to do CPR on my feet, though. Never again will I wear new shoes to a wedding where there is dancing."

"I'll remind you of that next time," teased Patrick.

The conversation ended when the nursing director, Dr. Heather Lewis, a nurse with a PhD, and medical director Dr. Richard Whiting came in to begin the review of patients from the previous week and to plan goals of care for the current census. Dr. Whiting, in his sixties, was the spirit behind the unit. Santos managed a smile at Dr. Whiting's signature look, his long, thick silver hair tied neatly back in a long ponytail. Few who met him today would have guessed his past. His first career was as a studio rock musician who not only recorded with the best but also toured with the best. His instrument was bass guitar. He had collected guitars since he began playing in the sixties. Highly gifted, he played by ear.

Though he had dropped out of college to pursue his passion for music, when he was ready, he had reapplied. He began his second attempt at college on academic probation, but graduated with a 4.0 GPA, earning admission into medical school. After his residency, he was rapidly board-certified in internal medicine and cardiology. He credited his wife of over forty years, a nurse who put him through school, for his wake-up call. He had fallen in love with her when he met her through mutual friends at a gig. She had refused to marry him until he got a "real job" with a solid career.

Richard and Heather were partners in the leadership of the unit. Richard was a master at navigating the challenging and occasionally contentious relationships with his medical partners, translating for the nurses and patients, negotiating with board members, and advocating with administration. Santos had heard him say, "If I could work with musicians, I can work with anyone."

Heather, on the other hand, was the reason Santos and the rest of the team loved working in the CCU. While in school, Santos had heard a speaker on careers discuss the research on job satisfaction. She learned that the most important factor in job satisfaction was not your salary, but your boss. Many of her classmates had chosen a place to work for their shift or specialty preference or for fifty cents more an hour. She chose her job because of Heather. A great boss was priceless.

Heather was dressed in a dark business suit and freshly pressed white lab coat. Her long dark hair, touched with gray, was tucked into a bun at the nape of her neck. Heather's eyes, graced with fine wrinkles, sparkled with intensity and a sense of humor. Never one to take herself too seriously, she was a role model for every member of the staff.

As the unit director, Heather led with firm compassion. She advocated for staff when it was needed, justifying her budget to support raises and development of current staff as well as the addition of new staff. She valued education, encouraging her employees to go back to school. She gave feedback on performance on a regular basis, both good and bad. Heather believed in catching people doing things right and reinforcing that with praise. Her standards were high, and she was consistent and predictable. Heather was the glue that connected the team together, and the CCU had a reputation across the hospital for giving some of the best patient care in the city.

Santos waited for Heather to initiate rounds. The group, used to the routine, settled down to listen and engage in the dialogue regarding patients and families. The unit had emptied out over the weekend, and the census had dropped to sixty percent occupancy. It was rare that the staff had time for a breather.

꙰

At 8:00 a.m., rounds were over and morning labs were posted in the EHR. Heather would triage them: identify lab results that would require immediate action, labs to watch, and labs within normal limits; then review the pending transfers and a few discharges and finally alert the RNs on her team that they should begin the transfer or discharge process. During one day, there could be as many as twenty-five ADTs—admissions, transfers, and discharges—on this unit. They were time-consuming, and smooth handoffs required good communication, not only among the unit nurses and other professionals but also to the transferring units.

After checking in with Heather, Santos walked to Mrs. Adams's bedside and smiled.

"Good morning! I have great news for you. Your lab results are normal."

Mrs. Adams dropped her counted cross-stitching and clapped her hands with glee. She looked like a little girl with her long, thin braid of gray hair neatly wrapped around her head.

"It isn't that I don't like ya'll, but I have work to do back home."

Mrs. Adams was well-known and loved by the CCU staff. At seventy-two, she was lean and petite, her skin deeply weathered from the sun and from her history of smoking a pack a day. Though she had kicked the habit when she got pregnant with her son, Roger, in her late thirties, the damage to her lungs was already done. Roger was Mr. and Mrs. Adams's surprise baby and the joy of their lives. Now that Mrs. Adams had been widowed for ten years, it was Roger who took care of her.

Mrs. Adams was and in and out of the hospital regularly due to her chronic congestive heart disease. Despite her frequent hospitalizations, she was friendly, had a great sense of humor, and was always appreciative. She had a great memory and called every staff member, from housekeepers to dieticians, by name. Mrs. Adams had picked up a bug this time and had diarrhea during nearly her entire hospitalization. This had embarrassed her no end, and she was anxious to get home to her little cottage in the Village of Tiki Island, near Galveston.

Santos knew the story of the cottage: Mrs. Adams had moved into her home with her husband right after their honeymoon in Niagara Falls. That May, the freak snowstorm that hit the Falls area brought travel to a standstill and frightened Mrs. Adams who had never seen snow before. She was not going back.

Over the years, her cherished home had survived many hurricanes and tropical storms. She was anxious to get back and put in her cool season annuals like snapdragons and sweet alyssum. Mrs. Adams loved gardening and pushed herself to do it, even though she had to stop every few minutes to catch her breath. The cycle of life in gardening energized her. She studied the horticulture of the subtropical climate and enjoyed the challenge of growing plants in the sandy soil of the Bay Area.

"Santos, you should see the pink and white verbenas I planted. They are just gorgeous! Roger made window boxes. I painted them red—can you believe that? They look so cheerful. We have lots of tourists walking in our neighborhood ... because we are so close to the canal, you know. The verbenas smell so good the tourists stop and ask what they are. And my bougainvillea ... they are huge! The drought has really been good for them."

"Then let's get you out of here," Santos said and reached over to grasp Mrs. Adams's cool delicate hand in her warm one. "When is Roger coming to pick you up?"

"As soon as I call him, he said he'd be here in a jiff. He wanted to stop by that Rice Market and see if they had any specials on meat. So he's in the neighborhood."

"Okay, why don't you give him a call, and then you can start packing up."

While Mrs. Adams placed the quick call to her son, Santos got ready to remove her patient's IV and disconnect the heart monitor. She always liked to take off the adhesive patches and clean the area, since the adhesive was so sticky that if she did not use a little mild acetone on it, patients would be scrubbing it off at home for weeks.

Before she could get started, she got a phone call. She listened attentively to the clinical request for assistance and replied, "I'll be right there." She turned to her patient. "I'm sorry, but I need to care of something. But I'll be right back. Can you get around and start collecting your things with all of this stuff," she motioned to the monitor, "connected to you?"

"Sure, honey, don't you worry. I'm an old pro with this equipment," Mrs. Adams replied. "You go on and do what you need to do. I'll be just fine."

CHAPTER 11

He waited, uncertain of what to do. Waiting was the hardest. The bustle of the lab activity went on around him, yet he felt completely alone, in a vacuum, in a world of his creation. He knew that he would have to be patient, especially with this one. He had taken his first step over the line. He longed to be present in the CCU to see if anything had happened.

He felt a degree of separation anxiety from his project. Wondering what, if anything, would happen, and how long it would take. Would the kill happen in the hospital? Would he ever know? Would it ever occur to them that something out of the ordinary was going on? He wanted them to know something was wrong, yet he did not want them to know. The risk of discovery was seductive yet dangerous. No, discovery was not an option. He would win this game.

Agitated with his escalating frustration and anxiety, he pushed back his wheeled chair from the computer screen, heaved himself up and out, picked up the crutch that was propped against his desk, and hobbled out of the lab. Doing something was better than doing nothing. He took a few deep breaths to calm his anxiety and headed to the cafeteria for a cup of decaf.

Chapter 12

Mrs. Adams scooted her tiny bottom to the edge of the bed, sat up, and felt a bit light-headed. She paused, feet dangling over the edge of the bed, feeling cold. She wanted to get out of the hospital gown and slip into her softly worn, comfortable blue jeans and sweatshirt. Put on warm socks and her clogs. Feel like a real person again and put this hospital episode behind her. Mrs. Adams had faced her own mortality many times now and always felt grateful for every moment she was not in a doctor's office or hospital. She wanted to breathe fresh air and feel the sun on her face. Anxious to leave, she wanted to push herself to get dressed and pack her things but thought better of it.

Sit back, she thought. The nurses had warned her repeatedly not to get out of bed if she felt unsteady or light-headed. "All I need is a broken hip," she muttered under her breath and pushed herself safely back into the bed. The last thing she thought as she began to feel her heart beat rapidly was *I'm so tired.*

CHAPTER 13

The high-pitched wail of the heart-monitor alarm sliced through the buzz of unit activity. The monitor tech at the workstation saw the beginning premature ventricular contractions of ventricular tachycardia explode into the lethal arrhythmia ventricular fibrillation. VF, the rapid, chaotic, and irregular quivering of the heart ventricles, would lead to certain death. The tech called a preemptive Code Blue.

Within seconds all available RNs, MDs, and respiratory therapists rushed to the bedside of Mrs. Adams. Emma, first on the scene, followed the rule, "Treat the patient, not the monitor," and quickly assessed her. She was unresponsive, with no palpable pulse. Her respirations were rapid and weak. The aberrant heartbeats were mere quivers, not the forceful pumping of the heart muscle needed to circulate oxygenated blood to her brain, lungs, kidneys, and liver. Death would occur within minutes.

Santos rapidly rolled the crash cart to the bedside and broke open the locks. Full of dread, she watched Emma apply the quick combo patches to the patient, turn on the defibrillator, and set the energy level for 200J. Charging took seconds, but it seemed like minutes as the patient's life slipped away. They would only have a few minutes before irreparable brain damage set in. The code team arrived, and cardiology resident Dr. Nicholas Landon began CPR with chest compressions. Cody Patterson took over ventilation with the Ambu bag pumping two quick breaths of oxygen-rich air into her lungs. One of the other nurses administered Epinephrine, 1 mg IV push, then an amp of bicarb.

"It's ready," Emma said.

She looked around the bed area and said loudly, "All clear!"

Everyone backed away from the bed to avoid being shocked. Emma delivered the electric charge to Mrs. Adam's chest. Her back arched and lifted off the bed with the strength of the charge, then bounced back down—limp and lifeless.

"Come on, Mrs. Adams. Come on back," Santos encouraged, believing that her patient could still hear. The words caught in her throat, and she fought back tears.

All eyes went to the monitor above the bed. The VF continued. The rhythm was still shockable. If they were lucky, the next shock would knock out the VF, and a normal sinus rhythm would appear. Santos administered the dose of Amiodarone to manage the arrhythmia. The rotating drug sequence would continue by protocol as long as Mrs. Adams was unresponsive.

Nick continued chest compression with Cody ventilating for two long minutes.

"Let's do it again," Emma said with authority.

"All clear!"

Once again, the team backed away from the bed. They moved quickly, smoothly, with a common goal: save the life and minimize any brain damage. Again, Mrs. Adams's back arched as the brutal shock ripped through the fragile frame. The VF that reappeared on the monitor triggered an audible sigh of disappointment.

The minutes flew by as the team focused on saving her life. When the anesthesia resident, a tall, lovely blonde, arrived, she took over for Cody. All business, Dr. Nancy Nathan, hair pulled back from her face in a ponytail, quickly gloved and slid an endotracheal tube down Mrs. Adams's throat. She removed the face mask from the Ambu bag and connected the ET tube to oxygen. The two residents adopted an alternating rhythm that allowed Nancy to push air into the lungs while Nick paused between chest compressions. Santos sustained her role, administering medications by protocol, while one of the other nurses kept an eye on the clock and recorded every action performed by the team.

Santos, eyes moving from patient to monitor to crash cart looked across the room at Patrick. He nodded to Santos, and she followed the direction of his eyes. Roger was standing there, paralyzed with shock, his ashen face crushed with devastation. In one hand he held a bunch of freshly picked flowers, several of which had fallen to the floor. She immediately handed off medication administration to another nurse and went over.

"Roger, I'm so sorry." She took hold of his arm then paused to give him a long look, carefully gauging his response.

"Your mother went into ventricular fibrillation, a serious heart arrhythmia. We are trying to knock it out and have to shock her."

Roger said nothing. Distress and stunned concern were visible on his face. There was a flurry of activity, people moving in and out of the area, so many tubes and so much equipment surrounding Mrs. Adams's bed. Trash and open supply containers spilled off the bed onto the floor. Looking into the area surrounding the code, Santos could not even see Mrs. Adams, just the tips of her toes.

"Are you okay? Can I take you to the waiting room?" She looked up at Roger, but he hardly seemed to hear her. She quickly changed gears. "Or are you up to being with her?"

After a moment he said, "I want to help," and paused.

Then he looked at her and asked, "Maybe if she knows I'm here she'll come back?"

She guided him to a position near his mother's head opposite Nancy, who continued to oxygenate the patient. Quietly, she explained the process to him and the dangers of shock.

She quickly leaned down and said in her patient's ear, "Roger is here. Your son is here. He wants you to come back." She looked up at him, hoping her gaze was encouraging. "Come on, Roger, talk to her."

"Ma ...." He choked up, backed off, and composed himself for a few seconds before he continued. "You're a fighter. Come on back. Come on back, Ma."

Roger was a trooper. He fell into the rhythm of the team's work, stepping back when someone needed to get in, touching his mother and talking to her for nearly thirty minutes while CPR continued. His mother continued to be unresponsive.

Finally, Dr. Whiting, who had been observing for the last twenty minutes of the hour-long code, said gravely, "Stop. Time out. We need to let her go. This isn't working."

He paused, looking around the room at the team that was not ready to give up. Conflict was etched across his face, but his voice was certain. "We're only prolonging her suffering."

Though Santos wanted to disagree with his decision to end the code, she knew that it was highly unlikely that Mrs. Adams would live. The strain on her heart had been tremendous. Heather had pulled up the living will, where Mrs. Adams had stated that if there was no hope and her prognosis was terminal, there should be no extraordinary care.

Heather walked over to Roger, who was still at his

mother's side.

She touched him on the shoulder and got his attention. Then she quietly but firmly said, "Mr. Adams, your mother is not going to live unless we put her on a machine and artificially breathe for her. Even if we put her on the machine, it will only keep her alive for a short period of time. Her heart is tired …." Heather looked at Roger and paused. He nodded. "We've looked at her living will. She did not want this if she was terminal. She is terminal, and we should stop now." Heather looked over at Dr. Whiting and then back to Roger, "Do you understand?"

Roger, still in shock, was silent. He looked at his mother and took her cold hand in his, then kissed it. "Mom wouldn't want this. This isn't Mom. She would be upset with me if I let this continue … I know she will be going to a better place … go ahead."

Heather conferred with Richard, then the team.

CPR ended. Nancy carefully deflated the balloon that sealed the trachea and gently pulled out the ET tube. *Would she breathe on her own?*

The once frantic pace now appeared to be in slow motion. The minutes dragged as they waited. Carts and equipment were wheeled away from the bedside. Most of the team left to return to their patients, but Santos and Nick waited with Roger. She knew that the dying process could last from minutes to hours. She had pulled up a chair, and Roger sat by the bedside, continuing to hold his mother's limp hand. Silent tears slipped from his red eyes and ran down his cheeks.

The heart monitor continued to read a ventricular fibrillation for a few more minutes. Mrs. Adams's shallow breathing became more and more labored and then slowed down. She took a long last breath that was more like a long, tired sigh and then stopped. There was no electrical pattern, just a flat line on the monitor. No one moved. No one said a word. In the background, they could hear the beeps of other monitors and voices in soft conversation, but around the bed, there was silence.

Roger began to weep. He continued to hold his mother's limp hand and then leaned over to try to embrace her, and his tears spilled onto her chest. Santos put her hand on his shoulder and said nothing, just supported his grief with her presence. Emma slipped up beside them and gently suggested that, if it was okay with him, they could say a prayer for his mother.

He nodded yes. They held hands and prayed over her body silently. As Santos prayed, she not only prayed for Mrs. Adams, but for the family and all people affected by the ripple effect of death. With a heavy heart she sighed, wondering, *how could we have let this happen?*

Chapter 14

At dawn, the lightly loaded helicopter flew a serpentine path, dodging and weaving, crisscrossing the jungle, hugging the tree line. The turbulence generated by the rotors flattened the dense foliage below. Mist rose from the tropical floor, creating low-hanging clouds, obscuring visibility. The thud of the huge rotors and the drone of the engine could be heard long before the aircraft was seen. He was flying the airship everyone dreamed of flying, the Bell HU-1 Iroquois, the "Huey."

He focused his attention on the instrument panel and went through the drill from flight school: *needle, ball, airspeed.* It was automatic now. He managed the pitch of the aircraft while listening through headphones for the voice of his commander flying ahead, his crew through the intercom, and the two emergency channels. Though he had made runs like this hundreds of times, he was hypervigilant, scanning the sky for other aircraft, the ground for landmarks and activity, and the instruments for changes in terrain. He felt a heightened sense of danger, and his gut rocked and rolled, cramping with anxiety. Something was out there. Something always was. *Would it find them today?*

Sweat trickled under his arms and rolled down his back, saturating his combat fatigues. His headphones were clammy, glued to his ears. The hot, humid day made the air density high, giving them less than normal lift. He adjusted the controls. Pumped, adrenaline throbbing through his veins, his every sense was on full alert.

He heard the high-pitched hiss first. It came out of nowhere—a high, explosive ground-to-air rocket roared through the gigantic main rotors, shredding them, crippling the forty-eight feet of metal lifting power.

"We're hit! We're hit! We're hit!"

The Huey groaned and began to shudder violently, then spin wildly, quickly losing altitude. He braced himself, both hands on the vibrating stick, desperately trying to regain control. A second rocket blasted through the ship, exploding into the soft targets of his men. Blood spattered the windshield. He heard screams. When he looked back over his shoulder, he saw one of his buddies without legs, body parts crushed, and fire. He coughed, choked by thick, black smoke, and watched helplessly as the jungle below rushed up to greet him.

⌇

He shot up in bed. It was completely dark in his air-conditioned bedroom. He was disoriented and freezing. His T-shirt and shorts were wet with sweat, the sheets saturated. His heart pounded. Fear and memories jolted through him like it was yesterday, and tears flowed silently down his face. He brushed them away, remembering how, when he had returned from 'Nam, the subconscious memories and depression had made his left eye tear for well over a year. He was furious with himself for this weakness, for the fact that he could not shake these memories. They came when he least expected them and shattered his relative peace. Post-Traumatic Stress Disorder lingered and haunted his nights.

Breathing deeply, he looked at the time on the digital clock on his nightstand. It was three in the morning. Too early to go to work, yet it would be impossible to go back to sleep. He felt lost and lonely to the core.

He had let them down. It was his job to protect his men.

There was no one to talk to about his feelings, his experiences. He was his own shrink—and a damn worthless one. Still shaken, he turned on the light, and artificial day flooded the room. He took a few deep breaths, then reached over and picked up his crutch. He longed for relief from the torture of his painful memories.

He trudged slowly over to his computer alcove. It was time to work on the game wall, his cyber-trophy case, and his private version of Pinterest. He created Mrs. Adams's profile, cutting and pasting information and pictures; he would add her obituary later, now that he had photos from Facebook and Google. He could not believe she was on Facebook. Quickly, he became absorbed in his work. The game held the promise of success, maybe not for his men, but for him.

CHAPTER 15

He got to the lab before the Processor began her shift. He would have to work fast, multitasking, completing his required work and then launching the kill method *du jour* before she arrived. He tackled the backlog of specimens that had come in from the 5:00 a.m. blood draws. The results required posting between seven and eight.

He would target the CCU for the time being. There were always plenty of bloods. In addition, it would give him an opportunity to study the patient population, hunt for the next victim. Best to stay away from the VIPs for now—their electronic records were under constant scrutiny and routinely swept for inappropriate staff access. He had the right to dig through the records in the CCU. It was a part of his job, like any of the techs. He checked the orders, ran a set of bloods for chemistry, and selected two samples for his use.

He took the target tube and attached a new barcode. Then he entered the lab results and completed the remainder of the samples in the lab. Only then did he allow himself to scan the CCU census. He noted that Mrs. Adams was no longer on the unit. His curiosity piqued, he could hardly wait to find out what had happened to her. She had been very sick for some time. Maybe he had actually done something good by helping her to leave this world.

CHAPTER 16

In the CCU, interdisciplinary rounds were wrapping up. Santos listened carefully. She was always eager to learn from her mentor, Emma. Every patient had a story. She enjoyed learning not only the clinical picture, but also the rich tapestry of life found in each person. Yet, that was the very thing that made death difficult. Every patient left an imprint on Santos. When they died, their deaths left a hole in her heart. The sudden death of Mrs. Adams was so sad, so unnecessary. *Why?*

"Mrs. Verona has really progressed well post-MI. She hasn't had any arrhythmias; her vital signs are stable. Family's been supportive, and she's walking without discomfort. No chest pain since admission. We'd like to DC her IV before we transport, but we're waiting for lab tests. We can put in a saline lock, which will be more comfortable for her ... she's a little anxious about being transferred off the unit."

Santos smiled. Emma looked after her patients as if they were her own family, treating them with deep respect and getting to know them well, including their families.

"I'm not really concerned about her anxiety ... she's not talking about a premonition ... now that would worry me. I think she's just uncomfortable leaving people she knows," Emma continued.

She had learned over the years from Emma's role modeling that the nurse's role was to create a healing partnership with the patients and families that crossed her path. The connections forged with patients through times of pain, suffering, and uncertainty made the long hours and intense work worthwhile. The bonds that were created sometimes lasted for life.

Emma continued report. Underneath the older woman's warm yet tough maternal exterior was an incredible repository of clinical knowledge and instincts developed over decades of experience with all kinds of situations. Patients liked and trusted Emma so much that she was the frequent recipient of cards, flowers, and candy. In fact, one patient so valued Emma that he had contributed to starting a scholarship in her name so other nurses could be educated in cardiovascular nursing.

Today, Sheila, a senior nursing student precepting with Emma, attended rounds. Sheila had confided to Santos that she was thrilled to be working with a leader like Emma, since many of her student colleagues had trouble finding staff nurses willing to teach.

"Why don't I get the lab results from this morning and we'll get her transferred over to Brown 11 early before they get slammed with afternoon transfers?" Sheila offered.

"Sounds like a plan. Just let me know if you need anything," Emma commented as she continued to look at the goals of care for her patient.

‍﹏

Sheila walked to Mrs. Georgia Verona's bedside. She needed no introduction, having cared for her since admission.

"Are you ready to leave me?" Sheila smiled warmly. "If everything in your lab work looks okay, we're going to transfer you to Brown 11 today. You should be able to get some sleep there." She reached down to squeeze her patient's cool, slim fingers. The punctuating beep of the cardiac monitor alarm had plagued Georgia day and night, disturbing her sleep.

Sheila bonded easily with most patients, and Georgia was no exception. Patients when admitted were frightened and confused, often in pain. They became totally dependent on strangers who made them take off their clothes and dress in flimsy gowns with open backs, wired them to beeping machines, and stuck them with needles, drawing endless tubes of blood. Even the private functions of emptying the bladder or having a bowel movement became a public event, subject to measuring and recording. The fear that comes with a heart attack does not dissipate easily, often lingering for months. She anticipated that Georgia would be feeling vulnerable and anxious about moving off the critical care unit where patients felt protected and sheltered, and she did her best to assuage the worry.

"What if I don't want to move?" Georgia replied. She looked away, wringing the bed sheet in her hands. Then she turned back to Sheila, her eyes pleading.

"Can't I stay here another day?"

Sheila smiled, admiring this woman who, even while hospitalized, dressed "company ready" in pretty cotton and lace nightgowns. Georgia was a strong and gracious Southern woman who had raised five children. This morning, Sheila could smell a touch of perfume, and Georgia's long neck was draped with a soft, pastel scarf.

"You're doing so well. It's time to move you to inpatient where you can begin rehab, build back your strength to return home."

She sat down by the side of the bed, grasping both of Georgia's hands in her strong, warm grip. "You want to go home again, don't you?"

"Of course I do."

Georgia turned her head away from Sheila. Tears streamed from her eyes.

"This is so embarrassing. I can't stop crying! Thinking about moving from this unit, from you and Emma, scares me to death ... there, I've said it. I'm terrified that I will die. Not of death, I'm not afraid of death. I'm afraid of the dying part."

Without saying a word that might further distress or diminish this steel magnolia, Sheila grabbed a tissue and gave it to Georgia.

"I'm sorry," Georgia said after blowing her nose. "I'm acting like a baby, and you have better things to do than listen to my whining."

"You aren't whining. It's normal to feel anxious. Most patients are. Better to talk about it. Let it out."

Georgia nodded and blew her nose again.

Sheila smiled. "Have you looked outside today? When I came in, we had a beautiful blue sky. I think we might even have a real fall this year. I'll talk with Joanie on Brown 11 and see if we can't get you outside for just a few minutes today. Or would you rather have Sheppie come in for a visit?"

Sheppie was Mrs. Verona's golden-and-black miniature collie. She talked about the dog often, about how much she missed the comfort of the six-year-old dog's unconditional love. CCU had been a pioneer unit in the hospital for pet visitation. Research results had demonstrated that blood pressure dropped and many patients actually perked up after contact with their pet or another animal. The CCU used a service that regularly brought in well-behaved dogs and cats to visit with the patients. Everyone looked forward to those days.

"I would love to see Shep!" Georgia said, looking up

with a smile. "Can you really do that?"

"We sure can. When will your husband be coming in? Either he can bring her in, or we can wait until you move. We won't move you until he arrives. And I'll take the IV out. But before I do that, I need to check your lab results."

Sheila helped Georgia out of bed and into a recliner to eat breakfast. Georgia lifted the plastic cover and wrinkled her nose at the cold dry toast, scrambled egg substitute, and fruit cocktail. There was no hot coffee on her tray this morning—or any morning in the CCU.

"Eat. It'll give you energy. I'll be back in ten minutes and will help you get cleaned up."

As she left the room, she glanced back over her shoulder to see Georgia picking at her food.

CHAPTER 17

"Oh damn, her potassium is low," Sheila muttered, reviewing Georgia's lab tests.

She looked up to see Emma's signature disapproving raised eyebrows. Sheila blushed, realizing that her voice had carried quite loudly in the workstation. Though always warm, Emma had very high standards with her students—language included.

"Sorry, it just slipped out. What do we need to do?"

"Remember, patients can hear us out here," Emma said quietly. "What is her level?

"It's 2.8."

"Hmmm." Emma frowned. "That's on the border of a critical value callback ... Remember what that means?"

"Yes, I think so ... critical value callbacks are set by hospitals to reduce errors. Since so many decisions rely on lab test results, it is important that we evaluate the accuracy of lab tests as a safety step ... right?"

Emma nodded and smiled ... paused for a moment, then continued.

"Has she had any symptoms of hypokalemia? Bradycardia? Arrhythmias? Any other lab tests abnormal?"

"No, everything looks fine. She's been off her diuretic for two days. "

"Let's go check her out together," Emma said, "before we do anything else."

Emma and Sheila walked to Georgia's bed on a mission. Georgia looked up at them with alarm.

"Is something wrong?"

"Your potassium is on the low side of normal. How

are you feeling?" Emma asked, taking into account Georgia's color and monitor strip, as well as reviewing the latest vital signs on the computer terminal. "Let me quick run a strip here to check your heart."

Georgia nodded. "Other than being anxious about leaving, I feel better today."

"Sheila, let's play it safe and run a twelve-lead on her. It won't hurt."

Sheila ran the twelve-lead EKG quickly, and they both reviewed the results.

"I don't see anything unusual here," Emma reported. "There is no prominent U-wave or flattened T-wave that you see in hypokalemia. You could be tolerating your low potassium well. But since you are borderline, Dr. Clifton has a standing order for KCL."

"That's potassium chloride, Mrs. Verona," Sheila translated. "We're going to need to use your IV for a little while longer to give you a dose. If we don't, you could begin having problems with your heart."

"What kind of problems?" Georgia's vocal pitch rose with anxiety.

"Nothing we can't handle," Emma reassured her. "Your heart muscle needs the right amount of potassium to contract properly and pump blood. Coming into the hospital can radically change your diet, and that can really mess up your body chemistry. When you go home, you want to make sure that you eat fruits high in potassium like oranges, bananas, and peaches."

"Sheila, I'm going to hang the KCL and set up the pump for twenty mEq for an hour. We can recheck her blood after that and see how she's responding."

Emma turned back to Mrs. Verona and placed a hand gently on her shoulder.

"I'm sorry, Mrs. Verona, but we are going to have to keep you here just a little while longer."

CHAPTER 18

He felt trapped in his windowless, frustrating world. The clock read noon. It was okay to escape and eat. He would learn soon enough if anything had happened. Better not to be at the scene of the crime. He rocked back in the chair, stretching his legs, then leaned forward, and grasping the table with both hands, heaved his body out of the chair. Then he leaned over to pick up his crutch, limping over to the refrigerator to retrieve his lunch. He was unusually stiff today. *Must be the low pressure. Going to rain.* He headed for the outdoor patio, hoping to catch some of the cool and dry weather of an early Texas autumn.

When he reached the patio, the wind had started to kick up, swirling the dust on the concrete. A line of dark clouds formed on the horizon. Looking at the clouds in the still-blue sky and feeling the change in temperature, he guessed he had about twenty minutes before rain would sweep through the area. He sat down, opened his rumpled brown bag, and pulled out a sandwich of white bread and leftover meatloaf. Cooking for one person was always an effort, but after years of being alone, he would either make a full meal and freeze individual portions for dinner or use them for lunch. It almost made the effort worthwhile.

His sense of isolation deepened with the gathering storm clouds. He felt the discomfort of eating alone in public. The hollow feeling of being all by himself, detached, without purpose, crept over him. The depression that was always on the edge of his psyche almost overcame him. A sense of sadness overwhelmed him, threatening to suck him down into the well of despair. Surrounded by staff laughing and talking at nearby tables, he stood out as the only solo diner on the patio. The colorful umbrellas that shaded the tables began to billow out with the wind as the storm approached. His appetite left him. He stuffed the half-eaten sandwich back into the bag and tossed it into the trash container five feet away.

Lifting himself out of the metal chair, he adjusted his crutch under his arm and walked into the hospital. He made it to the glass automatic doors just as huge drops of tropical rain splattered on the patio.

CHAPTER 19

Horizontal sheets of black rain pelted the windows of the CCU. The bright sky had turned dark as night. Houston weather, famous for producing three seasons in a day, had rapidly changed from partly sunny skies to deep rolling rumbles of thunder and flashes of lightning.

"Code Blue—CCU, Code Blue–CCU, Code Blue–CCU," sounded over the page system in the practiced monotone of the operator.

Clinical staff ran the crash cart and defibrillator to Mrs. Verona's bedside. Sheila watched, immobilized, her hand covering her mouth and tears streaming from her eyes. Emma's face glistened with sweat as she worked. She knelt on the bed, her outstretched and locked arms pressing deeply and rhythmically on Mrs. Verona's sternum, compressing her chest, manually pumping her heart. Dr. Nancy Nathan, tendrils of long blonde hair escaping from her surgical cap, pink scrubs spattered with blood, bagged the intubated, lifeless woman.

Bed sheets were scattered on the floor, and miles of clear tubing filled with meds bisected the bed. Pumps beeped, and the heart-monitor alarm screamed. Trash piled up on the floor. Oblivious to the noise, physicians shouted for medications while nurses rummaged through the crash cart for syringes and equipment or hung new medication-filled drips. Everyone was talking and moving at the same time, yet there was rhythm to the response of the adrenaline-fueled team.

"We're losing her, folks. We're losing her. BP seventy over forty," cried Nancy. "I need more pressors."

"We can't. We've got the drip running as high as we can," Santos called out.

"Damn ... Emma, keep going. We can shock her again in two minutes."

Santos looked up from her work and saw Sheila crying on the fringe of the action. Recording the code in progress, she handed off her responsibility to Patrick and walked over to Sheila. She wrapped her arm firmly around Sheila's shoulders, held her close, and handed her a clean tissue. She could feel Sheila shudder against her, struggling to contain her sobs. First codes were always difficult. You wonder if you did everything that you could. Santos remembered her first code like it was yesterday. The passing of time did not make them any easier.

She saw Dr. Whiting enter the cubicle. He watched for a few minutes, walked over to Patrick, and reviewed the notes. The team had done CPR for nearly an hour without any heartbeat returning.

"It's time to let her go," he said with compassionate authority, his voice cutting through the noise. "Sorry y'all, she's not coming back. She's suffering ... we're prolonging her suffering. She's not coming back. Let her go now."

The room went silent except for the steady beep of an IV pump.

The team stopped, slowly, one by one. Emma, perched on the bed, sat back on her heels with a deep sigh of disappointment. Nancy stopped bagging and turned off the oxygen at the head wall. Then everyone stopped. The monitor beeped. The team, motionless for a moment, looked at Mrs. Verona. Their efforts had failed.

"You did everything you could," Whiting said. "Sometimes it isn't enough."

The clock ticked by as sad moments of silence passed.

Nancy gently peeled off the tape that had secured the endotracheal tube to Mrs. Verona's face. Her long, elegant gloved fingers deflated the balloon, and then she slid the tube out of Mrs. Verona's mouth. Emma respectfully covered Mrs. Verona's nearly naked body with a sheet, and then brushed Georgia's hair back over her forehead. Santos kept a tight grip on fragile Sheila. *It was just yesterday that Mrs. Adams died—now this.* She looked at Sheila, still weeping and staring at the lifeless body in the bed, and remembered how emotionally devastating these moments could be to a young nurse.

Chaplain Smith, watching on the edge of the once-frantic scene surrounding Georgia's bed, stepped forward.

"Why don't we all say a silent prayer for Mrs. Verona?"

He bowed his head, the clinicians bowed theirs, and he offered a short impromptu meditation. The group huddled, some holding hands. Disappointment and grief were palpable throughout the CCU. When one is lost, everyone feels the pain.

The cubicle was silent again, and clinicians started to clean up or leave.

"Why don't we go take a little break together?" Santos suggested. "Emma, okay with you if I take Sheila out of here for a moment?"

Emma nodded. "Sure ... I'll work with Karen, and we'll bathe Mrs. Verona and get her ready for the family visit. Not to worry." Then she gave Sheila a long, firm hug.

Santos put her arm around Sheila, and they walked away.

Sheila stopped abruptly and turned to Santos, panicked.

"Who is going to call her husband? He could be arriving any moment."

"We'll take care of it. Let's just get you settled, and we can talk." Santos guided Sheila gently, but firmly. *Another loss.* She pushed her feelings of sadness aside to focus on supporting Sheila. They walked into the lounge, and closed the door behind them.

Chapter 20

Santos had worked nearly forty hours in three days. She woke up drained, the promise of a headache throbbing at the edge of her right temple. She dreaded attending the funeral of Georgia Verona. Yet nothing could keep her away. Though she had tons of errands to run, and was just about out of clean scrubs, she needed to go to the service. She had called and canceled her volunteer work at the community center. Heather had given Emma release time, and Sheila, crushed by the experience, planned to attend also.

Driving in to Houston, heart heavy, she pondered the two recent deaths. Sometimes a run of deaths happens, but with new technology and treatments, the mortality rate in the CCU was going down every year. People did not die as frequently as they used to in the unit—not usually.

When she arrived at the church on the bright and sunny day, Emma and Sheila were already there, waiting for her outside the main entrance of St. Paul's United Methodist. Emma was dressed in scrubs because she needed to go back to work; Sheila wore a trim black suit with pearls.

"Sheila, how are you holding up?" Santos grasped Sheila's hand and looked into her eyes. Sheila had obviously been crying, and her lip quivered. "I know this must be very hard on you."

"I feel terrible … like a failure. She didn't need to die."

"Oh, Sheila, I'm so sorry." Santos's heart melted and she folded Sheila into her arms. "I know this hurts bad, and I wish that I could tell you it gets easier, but it doesn't. This is the part of the job that we didn't sign up for, death and dying. We knew it would be part of the picture, but never that it would hurt this much." She held Sheila, patting her on the back, then turned to Emma.

"Thank you for being here, Emma. You are such a rock. I need a hug," she said, and reached out to Emma.

Emma smiled sadly, then pulled her in and crushed Santos in her arms for a few moments. Santos felt safe in the warm arms of her friend.

Emma pulled back and held Santos at arm's length.

"Thanks for coming, honey, I know it's your day off." Emma gave Santos a long, appraising look. "My, my ...."

"What are you looking at?"

"You look exhausted ... and you're losing weight. Time for you to find something else in your life besides work ... time for a man ... now, that Patrick, he's a good one. I see the way he looks at you."

"Emma, don't start, not now," Santos said, exasperated. "I don't have the time or the energy for a relationship."

"Amazing what givin' a little gets you, Santos. When you love someone, everything gets easier."

Santos saw one of the Verona daughters coming up the walk to the church. "Emma, the family is coming."

Emma walked over and said very softly to the daughter, "Mrs. Graceffa, we are so sorry for your loss."

The daughter, tall and elegant like her late mother, had carefully coiffed dark hair pulled back from her thin face. She raised her perfectly arched eyebrows, and then glared and spewed, "I still don't understand what happened to Mother. How could you let this happen?"

Emma paused, took a deep breath, and exhaled. Making no effort to defend she responded, "We feel your loss, Mrs. Graceffa. We are so very sorry. Your mother was a wonderful woman. We will miss her."

The daughter gave the three a long, bitter-cold look. Then she shook her head and said, "I can't believe we'll never know what happened," turned on her heel, and walked up the stairs into the church.

"I feel so awful," Sheila said.

"You know, I don't want to be defensive about this, but they could have let us do a post on her," Santos commented. "I'm really getting concerned about the number of deaths we've had, sudden deaths. With a post, we might have some clue about why this is happening."

"I agree," Emma replied and turned to Sheila. "Sheila, you'll find that families are often reluctant to grant permission for an autopsy. They feel violated by being in a hospital. They feel as if they've had no control. They're tired and don't want to go through the process. They want it over."

"What they don't realize is that what we learn might help them come to some closure, as well as help other families," Santos added. She glanced at her watch. "We'd better head inside. The service is about to begin."

CHAPTER 21
October

Santos and Patrick sat perched at the top of the large, tiered classroom, watching people enter and waiting for the meeting to begin. It had been three weeks since Georgia Verona's death, and there had been two additional unexplained, sudden deaths in the CCU. The atmosphere in the room was hushed and somber, thick with tension and riddled with questions, as the room filled with professionals and administration. The customary friendly chatter was absent. They had been called together to hear the results of the root-cause analysis, a quality improvement tool that methodically searches for the "why" behind the "what" of a situation.

Hospital security, flanked by two men in dark business suits, entered the room.

"You know," Santos leaned close and whispered to Patrick, "Sheila blames herself for Georgia's death. She's worried about going it alone after graduation."

"That's every student's fear, I think … we're all wondering what we could have done differently. What did we miss?" replied Patrick.

"There's got to be something else going on," she said quietly as they watched people look up to find empty seats in the already filled-to-capacity room. "I'm not usually paranoid, but my gut tells me something strange is happening here. We need to find out, Patrick." Their eyes met, and he nodded.

"Do you see what I see?" she nudged him and looked across the room.

Patrick leaned close and whispered, "Secret Service?"

She nodded. "Looks like it. See the wires in their ears?"

"Do you think this has something to do with the VIP we coded?" Patrick asked.

"Do you think it could be connected?"

"Obviously, someone thinks that's a possibility," Patrick replied.

Emma walked in with Sheila. Santos waved to get their attention. Emma managed a weak smile before heading up the stairs in their direction with Sheila in tow. Santos spoke to the hospital administration residents near her, and they bustled off to grab seats on the outer rim of the room.

"Emma, this is your day off!" Santos stood up to move and make room.

"Wouldn't miss this ... Sheila wanted to come. I'm stickin' by my girl," Emma smiled, hugging Sheila by her side. Emma and Santos jockeyed seats so that Sheila was between them.

Finally, the vice president for the Heart Center, Yasmin Kazan, stepped into the doorway. She was wearing a short, bright red jacket with her Magnet pin, a trim black skirt, and Feragamo pumps. Her usually warm smile was replaced by a concerned and serious look. She brightened up for a moment and walked up the tiered stairs, stopping at each row of chairs to shake hands or touch the shoulders of the many colleagues in the room, attempting to ease the tension.

Yasmin walked by Santos, leaned over and said, "Don't forget."

"I won't," Santos replied.

Yasmin was a beautiful young woman of thirty with dark, short, curly hair. Though the chic haircut that framed her heart-shaped face made her look French, she had been born in Iraq of a Greek mother and an Iraqi father who had met at the University of Texas in San Antonio. Yasmin had come to University Hospital right after completing her masters in hospital administration at St. Louis University and her residency program at Methodist in Dallas.

Yasmin had immersed herself in operations on the front lines, learning the people and systems, progressively seeking challenging leadership assignments, with her efforts finally culminating in her new role as VP. Respected not only because of her intelligence, she led through the many relationships she had established over the years. She had also worked hard to learn the language of the health care team as well as the language of finance and administration. Yasmin often found herself serving as a translator, bridging the disciplines for the greater good of the patients.

"How're you doing Sheila?" Yasmin hovered near Sheila.

"OK … I need to be here."

"We need to get to the bottom of this," Yasmin replied.

"Nutcracker Market again, you two?" Emma asked looking back and forth between Yasmin and Santos.

"Maybe," Santos looked down.

Yasmin and Santos had met during Yasmin's hospital administration residency. Assigned to work with an RN, she shadowed Santos for nearly a month, side by side on every shift. Yasmin developed not only a deep appreciation for the work of nursing, but a strong relationship with Santos that bloomed into a friendship. Though they did not see each other often, they had an annual tradition, the Nutcracker Market. It was coming up, and they both looked forward to it every year. This year, Santos was having second thoughts. She did not feel she would be much fun since she was so preoccupied with the deaths.

"Gotta go … Santos, I'm not going to let you off the

hook," Yasmin replied as she quickly headed down the stairs to the front of the classroom. She spent a few moments talking with the presenters, scanned the audience and began.

"Let's get started," Yasmin started and paused, waiting for the room to settle down.

"What we would like to accomplish during this time is three agenda items: first, a review of the root-cause analysis. We need to determine if this is a pattern of serious events or if these deaths were isolated incidents. Second, we need to agree on an action plan to increase the safety in the unit. And finally, though I hesitate to bring this up, we must be prepared if the media get wind of this. Jaime, can you present the overview of the root-cause analysis now please?"

Jaime Grant, one of the quality improvement specialists, stood up from her chair and walked over to the laptop. While Jaime brought up the PowerPoint presentation, Santos leaned over to Patrick and said with conviction, "This is a pattern. They are not isolated events. Something is going on here."

"If you could all follow along with me, let's briefly go over the facts. I hope I don't need to remind anyone that the material presented at this meeting is confidential and protected by Texas law. It is important that we approach this process in a blame-free manner. So let's be as open to the possibilities as we can."

Santos quietly continued her sidebar conversation with Patrick. "Glad they are taking this seriously."

Yasmin continued, "In the past four weeks, we have had three sudden, unexplained deaths in the CCU. All of them had a number of things in common. First, the patients were all ready to transfer off CCU to either telemedicine at home or another unit in the hospital. Second, all three patients, two men and a woman, had sudden, fatal episodes of syncope or ventricular fibrillation which were unresponsive to defibrillator shock and administration of lidocaine. All patients were in normal sinus rhythm prior to the incident, were up and about, and lab values were within normal limits or at the lower range of normal."

Santos, concerned, whispered to Patrick, "What about Mrs. Adams? Doesn't she fit the profile? Why aren't they counting her?"

"They aren't bringing up the VIP either," Patrick responded.

"This gives me chills," Santos replied. "If I let my imagination run wild, the possibilities are terrifying."

"Santos, right now, we've got to stick with what we know."

She nodded and listened.

Jaime continued, "All deaths occurred on the day shift, and the patients were being cared for by three different nurses, all experienced: Patrick Sullivan, Santos Rosa, and Emma Perrine, who had a student with her at the time. All three patients had different attending physicians. We have no autopsy results, since none of the families agreed to posts."

While Jaime finished up, Santos jotted down notes. She knew something was very wrong here. She did not believe much in coincidences—not in health care, anyway. Santos began to draw a diagram of arrows and events, following along with the root-cause analysis, retracing her steps, looking for patterns. Patrick saw what she was doing and reached over to draw on the same page with her, adding facts.

"Any questions … comments?" Jaime asked.

Santos considered the symptoms and patterns of the CCU deaths and reached back into her knowledge of biochemistry. Quickly it came to her. Her hand shot up.

"Could we consider this for a minute?" She paused. "What do we know about blood chemistry that can show up as either V-Fib or asystole? Could we talk about that?"

CHAPTER 22

Patrick and Santos left the conference room and said good-bye to Sheila and Emma, who went their separate ways.

"That was exhausting," she said with a long sigh. "We have to figure this out, Patrick. I can't believe the group would *not* consider the possibility that this may be related to blood chemistry. Or maybe it's something in the drips—wrong dose?"

"Do you have time for a cup of coffee or a soda? We could talk this over a bit and maybe begin to put the pieces together," Patrick said, looking down at her with an encouraging glance and placing his hand lightly on her shoulder. "Come on, you can do it. Let's see that gorgeous smile again. Don't you know that smiling increases your endorphins?"

"No, it doesn't!" she said and gave him a playful swat across the arm.

"Patrick, I don't think I can find a smile in me."

She paused for a second and said, "Does it really?"

She tilted her beautiful head of auburn hair and looked up at the tall professional she respected and trusted. There had been no more talk of a relationship, but their friendship had been growing over the past few weeks, the times of trouble binding them. Just looking at him and knowing that he was there to help was always such a comfort. She wondered, *how long can I continue to resist him?* Yet her energy was at an all-time low. *Do I have the energy for a relationship?*

He laughed back at her. "Who knows? Maybe it does."

"I'm tired and frustrated. But I'll take a break with you."

Patrick left for a few minutes and checked with Heather who said she would cover for thirty minutes. The two clinicians took the escalator down from the second floor to the cafeteria on the main floor of the hospital. They picked up their respective cups of tea and juice and headed for the seating area by the windows that overlooked the green, park-like setting. Though tall buildings consumed most of the real estate in the Texas Medical Center, a number of institutions protected small pockets of green space. Patients and families, students and staff enjoyed the ever-changing floral landscape of pink and white azaleas in the spring, lantana and petunias in the summer, mums in the fall, and cyclamen in the winter.

"I'm glad I'm wearing my lab coat." She shivered, cupping her hands around the hot cup of tea. "What is it about air-conditioning in the south? I'm always freezing!"

She made a beeline for a seat where the sun streamed in through tinted windows. Patrick sat down across from her. He broke apart a huge chocolate-chip cookie, still fragrant and warm from the oven, and offered it to Santos.

"Eat this. Chocolate always makes you feel better."

She could not help but smile and reached over, like a greedy child, to take a piece of the crunchy, gooey cookie.

"How did you know I was a chocoholic?"

"Oh, you'd be amazed what I notice about you." Patrick leaned in closer. She felt his deep blue eyes look right through her. Her defenses fell. His look touched her soul. She leaned back in her chair, warm all over. Her heart beat faster.

Any observer in the cafeteria would have thought they were an attractive couple of contrasts. They were a sort of "salt and pepper" combo: he was tall and fair, with athletic, boyish good looks. She was petite with a café au lait complexion and a smile that lit up her whole face.

Suddenly shy, she searched for words but could find nothing. *What is he doing to me?*

Patrick broke the silence. "Let's consider the facts: three deaths, all apparently preceded by cardiac arrhythmia; all unresponsive to CPR; three different nurses; different doctors; all patients apparently on the road to recovery. Unexpected demise. This is too weird. We are very close to calling this a Joint Commission sentinel event."

"There's been no new staff in CCU over the past month," she added, quickly recovering her composure. "We have no agency nurses. No one floated on the shifts where patients died. All of us are experienced; Emma carefully supervised even Sheila—and Sheila's good in her own right. There doesn't appear to be mistakes in terms of drug dosages or medication administration."

"Santos, too bad we can't dig into the VIP case. With the Secret Service present today, they must be suspicious about something."

"Patrick, she must have made it. That would be a miracle!" She smiled and reached across the table to grab Patrick's forearm. "Amazing ... I don't remember hearing anything about her death ... it would have been all over the media ... but we can't look into her record. We have no legitimate reason and couldn't do it without permission."

"I'll see what I can find out about her ... ethically. And yes, you're right. We'd better stay with the deaths in the CCU. We don't have any right to go through her record. In fact, we could lose our jobs if we do—even with a legitimate reason. Others have ... besides, her code was triggered by something else ... not cardiac."

She took a sip of warm tea and another bite of the

cookie. "You know what I think we should do? Get all of the CCU charts together and take another look at them. Maybe there's something in common, maybe there's not. But there has to be at least one clue in the medical records. We've got the symptoms, we need the cause."

Patrick nodded in agreement. "We could create a matrix of vital data."

"Then match symptoms, regardless of what the chart says, to potential causes—whether the cause could be pharmaceutical, blood chemistry, whatever … if we just go by the chart, we could be missing something. We can do a Med-line or Pub-Med search as well as a web search to see if we've covered all the causes of V-Fib."

"Why don't we form a multidisciplinary team to work this together? You know, people from the lab, a resident or medical student, perhaps a pathologist, some nurses?" Patrick suggested. "We're only going to achieve good results if we involve all the disciplines around the table."

"Great idea. Makes me feel better," she said with enthusiasm. "I know a medical technologist—Wendy. I met her during orientation. And I'll bet that Nicholas, that new cardiology resident, might be interested."

"Good idea. I liked Nick right away when he told me that he learned everything he knows from his mother who was a nurse!"

She took a quick look at her watch. It was an old Timex with a second hand, one of her mother's. She unconsciously rubbed her thumb across the crystal. "Time to head back up."

The pair pushed back their chairs and stood up. She popped the last crumb of cookie into her mouth and wiped the chocolate from her fingers on a paper napkin.

"Thanks for dragging me off the unit. Clears my head.

I'll feel a lot better if we take accountability for thinking this through instead of waiting for someone in administration to figure it out."

The man in a white lab coat sat alone by the window. He sipped a cup of coffee that had long ago gone cold. He had been listening closely to their intense conversation.

This is getting interesting, he thought. *I'm going to have to keep an eye on those two.*

After they left, he got up, stretched his legs, and ambled out of the cafeteria. *The stakes were going up.* His mind was already working on the next move in the game.

CHAPTER 23

Santos was working nights, reviewing computer notes in the workstation. Night shifts could be quiet and peaceful. Overhead lights were dim to help patients sleep and prevent ICU psychosis, the disorientation that happens with the disruption of circadian rhythms by the lack of daylight and darkness. During nights, there was none of the hustle and bustle commonly found on days. Family members were usually home or in bed in their hotel rooms, and the student traffic was gone. The relative serenity gave her time to think and reflect on the three deaths that had so profoundly affected Santos as well as morale in the CCU. Sleep evaded her, she wasn't hungry, and even when she rested she woke up tired.

The unit was so quiet that she could hear Mrs. Dajani moan. She logged off and purposefully walked over to the patients' area. Honed by years of routine, she quickly scanned the monitors. The Phillips monitor showed Mrs. Dajani's heart rhythm in two leads, III and VI. Her heart rate of fifty-eight, though a bit low, demonstrated that the beta-blocker she was receiving for the ST Elevation MI was working. The last blood pressure, transmitted thirty minutes ago, had been 112/65. The IV pump was running smoothly, the bag half-full. Pulse oximetry was displaying good waveforms with an SP02 of 98 percent.

In seconds, Santos had assessed the safety basics.

She leaned over the bed and studied Mrs. Dajani.

"Everything okay?"

"Oh, I had a nightmare. Dreamt that Jim and I bought this house, and it needed a lot of repair work—and we like new houses. We'd been talking about building a house until I got sick. The dream was so vivid. The carpet in the master bedroom was in shades of blue and pink, sort of Floridian, like you might see on the seashore. And there were boxes and boxes of presents that had been stored in the closets, never used. There was a lot of dark paneling, and instead of doors on the closets, there were these heavy brown drapes."

Santos smiled in the darkness, wondering why the dream would take on the characteristics of a nightmare. She restrained a chuckle when Mrs. Dajani finished, "When I woke up, I was relieved I was here! I thought, my God, why did we buy this house? It's so unlike us!"

Santos pulled up a chair by the bed and sat down. "Sounds like it's time to get you out of here so you can dream in your own bed at home."

～

While Santos worked, weary and worn down, he was lying in bed, hands behind his head, his mind scrolling through possibilities, energized. Not since Vietnam had he felt such a sense of purpose. He finally had a mission again.

Unlike in 'Nam, there was no one to please now but himself. He went to war to serve his country, yet what did that get him? Even his country seemed ungrateful, and he had returned to the States a mere shadow of the man he had dreamed of becoming. Everything was different. None of his training could prepare him for the reality shock of coming home. No one remembered the battles. No one could see the horrific scenes that vividly replayed in his dreams. Grief lingered and survivor guilt shadowed him every day. The vets who returned home, changed forever, were rarely understood by a self-centered, youth-driven America that had no empathy for the experience of war. The game was his salvation.

CHAPTER 24

The November day had finally arrived. Santos anticipated the Nutcracker Market every year, marking the next year's date on her calendar as soon as it was scheduled and requesting the day off. She had read in the *Chronicle* Ken Hoffman's column describing the Texas-sized three-day shopping extravaganza, a fund raiser for the Houston ballet, as "Houston's answer to Pamplona's 'Running of the Bulls.'" *How true!*

This year, Santos had almost canceled her annual date with Yasmin. As much as she loved the market, the deaths in the CCU stalked her days and haunted her dreams. She felt as if she were in a constant state of grief, saddened by the loss of patients she had grown to care so deeply about. Her mind worked overtime, thinking, w*hat caused this chain of deaths? Why?*

The nurses were seriously depressed. Though they had access to counseling and did critical incident debriefs, it was still tough. A young nurse, already disheartened by a breakup with her boyfriend, had tried to commit suicide. People were worried about their jobs, their licenses. A complaint lodged by one of the families had resulted in an unscheduled inspection by the Department of State Health. The unit was becoming unglued with uncertainty.

Santos had called Patrick the night before to vent. She had told him she was thinking of canceling her date with Yasmin. He encouraged her to go, telling her the distraction would make her feel better. She decided to follow through with her plan. Time away in a happy place would help heal her resilient spirit.

That morning, after a quick shower, she made herself a breakfast of yogurt, fruit, and granola, gathered a pen and paper, and sat down in her robe at the little kitchen table gazing at the sunshine outdoors. Not hungry, she knew she needed to eat. She made a list of the things she needed and gifts she might buy. She was hoping to find some more of those holiday embroidered towels for Christmas gifts, and the mint hot chocolate mix was great for stocking stuffers.

She drove into Houston through rush hour, looking forward to catching up with Yasmin, though she was not sure she wanted to talk about work. She parked at the Texas Medical Center where she and Yasmin had agreed to meet then take the Light Rail to Reliant Center. Knowing the scope and size of the event, she had dressed for the occasion in comfortable walking shoes, cowboy-creased dress jeans, and a simple white cotton embroidered blouse with her forest-green suede jacket. She had finished her look with a festive silver bell on a long red cord. It jingled with her every step.

"Love those shoes!" Santos greeted Yasmin, who was waiting nearby at the light rail stop. "Look at you, don't you look pretty," she continued. "Didn't wear your blue snakeskin shoes, I see."

"My shoe fetish only goes so far!" Yasmin looked down at her red ballet flats covered with sequins. She was dressed in a classic black sweater and slacks, a strand of fresh water pearls circled her neck. "These should be okay, don't you think?" Yasmin said looking down at her feet.

"I hope they hold up—your feet. We have lots of walking to do."

The train pulled into the station. Yasmin had already bought tickets and they found seats.

"How's your mother? Dad?" Santos asked. Though their styles were as diverse as Texas, the time working together had led them to discover that they had much in common. Both Houstonians, they were from strong, ethnically diverse families. Santos was Catholic, and Yasmin, Muslim; yet spiritually, they were like sisters with similar morals and values. Though their schedules did not allow much time together, they made the time for special events and monthly lunches. Both families had become close.

"Good, all good," Yasmin replied.

They chatted as the train traveled south to Reliant Stadium, the home of the Houston Texans. Santos was still stunned by the size. Gigantic Reliant Center had a two-story wall of windows and spanned over seven hundred thousand square feet of exhibit space, divided into eleven halls. The Nutcracker Market consumed all of it. The festive fundraiser attracted over three hundred vendors selling everything from candy to leather jackets and holiday decorations. It was the only place to buy the coveted, delicious Donne Di Domani marinara sauce. In over twenty years, the forty-some women who made up the Italian sorority that created the sauce had donated all of their proceeds, well over a million dollars, to charity.

When they arrived at Reliant Center at 8:30 a.m., there was already a line of women armed with plastic shopping bags snaking their way through the lobby.

"Wow, it gets bigger every year," said Santos.

"Definitely a girl thing," Yasmin remarked. For every man in sight there were at least fifty women waiting for the doors to open.

"Look at that!" Santos nodded and smiled in admiration at a tall and slim, striking blonde wearing a tan suede cowboy hat, skintight red leather snakeskin jeans, and full quill boots. As she walked by, her waist length curly hair swung with every sway of her hips.

"Wish I was in that great of shape!"

"Love those jeans! Certainly a great place to get fashion hints," remarked Yasmin. Women were dressed in everything from simple jeans to denim skirts with Native American silver and turquoise Concho belts. "People watching" was half the fun of the market.

When the doors finally opened, the army of shoppers mobilized to crush through the entrance. The crowd noise was deafening. They wove their way through the throngs of focused, serious shoppers in the crowded aisles. The vivid colors of the booths and the sounds of music and voices were an instant assault to their senses. Yet, in spite of the din and commotion, she was glad that she had made the effort. It was the perfect escape from work, and as she walked, she saw the anticipation and joy on the faces of the shoppers. It reminded her that it was good to be alive and healthy.

She was relieved that she had made her shopping list. There were rows and rows of booths with huge red and white signs overhead marking the aisles. Christmas music played over the loudspeakers, and the children's choir was getting ready to sing. They stepped back, almost run over as a group of women on a mission stampeded to the location of their favorite Christmas decorations. Some women had already found the cocktail bar and were strolling down the aisles sipping glasses of wine.

Santos and Yasmin exchanged glances.

"Little early for wine, don't ya'll think?"

"If I drank wine now, I'd be asleep in five minutes!" Yasmin concurred.

"How about we walk down the aisles together for the

first thirty minutes then maybe split up?" Yasmin nodded in agreement and pointed at a vendor selling Texas candied pecans.

A few minutes later they headed to the back of the exhibit hall, stopping to sample some warm and moist cowboy biscuits, dripping with honey butter. Once they reached the back of the hall, they were delighted that there was actually room to walk and an area quiet enough that they could talk.

"This is really a relief for me. I need an escape from work these days." Santos sighed. "I've never felt this way before."

"With all of the deaths, the uncertainty and scrutiny, it must be really hard on the staff," Yasmin replied.

Santos was quiet for a moment and then said, "If it's okay with you, I'd rather not talk about it. Sometimes I feel worse rehashing the details. I just need a break today. *Comprendez?*"

"*Si,*" Yasmin replied and gave Santos a quick but warm hug.

"Ah, exactly what I needed," she replied with a sigh.

Santos paused for a moment, struggling. "On the other hand, maybe we *should* talk about work ... and, I may have another problem."

"I understand about work, but what else is going on?"

Yasmin guided them to empty chairs at the back of the hall. There was no one near; they would not be overheard.

"I don't know where to begin."

"Let's sit down. I'm listening. Talk to me girl!" Yasmin reached over to grab her hand.

"I don't know what to do about Patrick ...."

"What do you mean? I thought he was your friend?"

"He is ... he is ... but I think he wants more ... he looks at me with those crystal blue eyes—they look right through me. I turn to mush. Makes me crazy ... I don't have time for this!"

Yasmin laughed. "Oh Santos, I think your time may have come."

"Give me a break. I will choose the time. I don't have the energy for a relationship ... not now, maybe ... maybe later."

"He's a great guy, Santos. He's smart, professional, your friend ... and awfully cute ... what are you waiting for?"

"I don't know ... I only have so much capacity right now and these deaths are constantly gnawing at me. It's all I can think about."

"So what do you think?"

Santos was quiet, composing her thoughts. "We don't believe this is something random. We believe that something or someone is causing these deaths."

"You're serious. What do mean something or someone? Mechanical error? You don't think that someone is deliberately doing something to kill patients?" Yasmin leaned in.

Santos nodded. "Who knows? Something is terribly wrong. Yasmin, I was there. I saw them happen. There was nothing we could do to bring them back. Nothing worked, not CPR, not drugs, nothing. We were powerless. One moment, they were fine. The next ... gone. Who knows who is next or why? It isn't safe. The CCU isn't safe. We're all worried, wondering when the next bomb will drop. That's why we called you about the team meeting idea. We've got to work fast ... I can't sleep, I'm so worried."

"Well, the team meetings start tomorrow, right?"

Yasmin asked.

"Yes."

"Then we have a plan. I'll do whatever I can to help," Yasmin added.

"We need to pray," she said. "Something dangerous is killing patients in the CCU. I may be jumping to conclusions, but I don't think I'm wrong. We have to find it ... soon."

CHAPTER 25

Santos merged into the traffic during the dark early morning on the already busy Hardy Toll Road, eager to get to the first meeting of the multidisciplinary team. She felt cocooned in the relative safety and quiet of her car. Seeking distraction from her obsession with the deaths, she toggled the radio dial back and forth between NPR, the local weather, and traffic reports. She was on the road very early since the team had decided to meet prior to their shift while they were still fresh.

They had scheduled four meetings, twice a week beginning at 6:00 a.m., with a deadline of two weeks to conclude their work. Patients' lives were at risk. Her mind was constantly working, searching for pieces of the puzzle; as a result, she was not sleeping well. Emotional fatigue compounded the lack of sleep. She felt as if she was running on vapors. Her only hope was that this new team would discover essential clues to what was causing the deaths of their patients.

When she walked into the unit, she ran into Dr. Stuart Yudsky and stopped to say hello. Dr. Yudsky, a psychiatrist, had volunteered to meet with traumatized staff. He was tall and thin, with graying hair and glasses balanced on the tip of his nose, and he smiled when he saw Santos.

"How's it going?" she asked.

"While I can't name names, Santos, you know that, I could start a whole new practice up here with these staff. This is a good group; they care. Caring hurts."

She nodded.

"Heather and Richard are increasing the staff meetings to once a week, round the clock. I'll attend every week, one shift, just to take the pulse of the group and see how we can help."

"Thank you so much," she replied. "Do you have a moment?" He nodded. "I have a wild idea. I'm almost embarrassed to bring it up."

She paused to look around then guided him over to a quiet corner. "Has it ever occurred to you that there might be some psychopathology involved?"

"You mean the staff?"

"No," she continued, "not the CCU staff. Maybe I'm crazy, but sometimes I wonder if someone else might be causing these deaths ... besides us, I mean."

"Interesting thought. We've talked about the prevalence of mental health issues in the workplace, remember? Sometimes as high as twenty percent .... But Santos, be careful. Look objectively first, backtrack through the records, talk with staff, do the root-cause analysis before you let your imagination get the best of you and try to pin this on some serial killer."

He smiled and continued, "If there is a serial killer at work, we have serious problems. Not just in CCU, but in the entire hospital." He paused, grasped Santos's arm, and whispered, "If there is a serial killer involved, and I very much doubt it—that would be a worst-case scenario— everyone needs to be extremely cautious. Serial killers don't have a conscience. Be careful, Santos, slow down. Keep your thoughts to yourself. By all means, don't become a target."

She smiled shakily, almost surprised at how seriously he was taking her suggestion. "Thanks, Doc, I know we can count on you. Can we keep this conversation private? I'm feeling a little funny about even bringing it up."

He patted her on the shoulder. "Stays between us."

She walked into the conference room where the grateful night staff had made the team coffee. The small team that would be co-led by Patrick and Santos was already busy talking. She looked around, satisfied, at the assembly: Wendy Mark, MT; Nicholas Landon, DO, Cardiology Resident; Emma Perrine, RN; Chad Nash, a PharmD from Pharmacy; and Yasmin. Yasmin was doing this on the QT. Her boss did not see the deaths as much of a pattern. Yasmin disagreed and planned to participate and support as much as possible. They kept the team small for efficiency but planned to include other experts when they needed them. Patrick had invited a colleague from Quality Improvement, Susan Hendrick, who had trained with the well-known Donald Berwick, MD, to assist them with facilitation and quality improvement tools and techniques.

Introductions made, Santos passed out the agenda.

"In the future, at the end of each meeting, we'll evaluate where we stand, how we did, and what we could put on the agenda for the next meeting. We'll also talk about what we should and can communicate. For this meeting, we needed to get ourselves jump-started," Santos stated.

Patrick took it from there. "Our team mission is to deeply explore, without blame, what might be the possible cause or causes of these deaths. We are combining forces," he gestured with open arms, "to analyze medical records, to brainstorm, and to create a cause-and-effect diagram."

Susan, who had been briefed by Patrick and Santos before the meeting, added, "We'll be using a toolbox of quality improvement techniques and strategies designed to help us collect data, analyze, work efficiently, and focus. As much as possible, we'll start with data-driven decisions and then progress into some hypothetical causes."

"We need to accelerate this process because patients' lives are at stake," Yasmin commented. She looked around the circle of players. "And we need all of your help."

Santos rose to flip over a piece of paper on the flip chart with the list of ground rules. "Let's get down to business. We all agreed to the ground rules via e-mail prior to this meeting. Any issues?"

When no one said anything, she said, "We'll consider these approved. Let's begin with assignments."

"We need three people to do a chart audit and create a matrix of the patients who died," Patrick said. "We need admitting diagnosis and co-morbidities, meds and lab results during the twenty-four hours before death, and any significant cardiac events. Feel free to add in other areas as we need to see what all the deaths have in common … Nick, Emma, and Wendy, you are probably the best because you have the knowledge of medicine, nursing, and medical technology. Are you all okay with that?"

Seeing nods of agreement, he continued, "Can we talk about what type of information we might want on the matrix?"

"With the data you collect, can we also do an abbreviated process flow diagram of the steps that occurred within the twelve hours preceding death?" Susan suggested. "And we will need to put together a cause-and-effect diagram at our next meeting to look at possible causes once we have the data from the chart review."

The team continued to huddle, making assignments and starting to work. The hour flew by.

∽

He was up early on the unit, drawing some routine bloods. It provided him with a legitimate opportunity to collect information and make key decisions around timing and patients. The staff was very quiet, tired, and depressed. Even the patients seemed on edge, as though they could sense that something was going on. Everyone was so self-absorbed that no one paid any attention to him.

As he walked by the conference room, he noticed a group of people meeting in a circle with a flip chart. He thought that he recognized some of them, definitely Wendy, from the lab. And the nurses he'd seen in the cafeteria— they were in the room, too.

What was Wendy doing here? Especially this early? Meeting with those nurses—and were those doctors?

His anxiety, usually held in check, bubbled up, pumping adrenaline, triggering the paranoia that slept below the surface of his psyche. He was drawn to the action in the conference room. He moved in more closely, giving in to the dangerous but uncontrollable attraction. His pulse pounded in his throat. Staying out of sight, he inched closer to the door and thought he heard them say something about an "Ishikawa diagram." Now what was that? They were so intent on their discussion that no one noticed him.

Looks like they are planning war games, rookies! He would teach them, humble and confuse them. *Disable players. Take them out of the game. They think they are the hunters. They will be hunted.*

CHAPTER 26

One week later, the multidisciplinary team again clustered around the table. Laptops connected to the network, and pairs of clinicians huddled together, peering intently at the screens. The room was full of obsessed energy, and the faint smell of perspiration clung to the stale air.

Richard stood in the doorway of the conference room with Heather. They silently surveyed the scene of focused contemplation. The team was so intent on their work that several minutes went by and no one noticed their presence.

"Good morning." Everyone quickly looked up. Pausing, his tone softened and warmed with concern. "How is everyone?"

"Incredibly frustrated," blurted Wendy Mark.

"I feel as if we're working against the clock, not sure when, how, or what will bring on another death," said Patrick. "I'm with you Wendy, 100 percent."

"Humbled," said Nick. "We're all highly educated and experienced clinicians here, and I feel powerless to stop this."

"Staff is really hurting, and call-offs are up," Emma remarked. "This is really taking a toll on everyone."

"Okay, so we're frustrated and humbled, not a bad place to be," remarked Dr. Whiting with a thoughtful nod of his head. "Some of us are energized by failure. It will help us work harder. We need to continue to support the staff and let them know what we are doing to address this issue. Why don't we post some of our work on the unit intranet website just to keep them up to date?" Dr. Whiting sat down at the table. "This situation has brought us to our knees ... where are we? Have you finished the chart matrix?"

"Yes, we're finished," Nick began after a brief pause. "Guys, feel free to jump in anytime." The members of the chart audit team nodded. "We now know that every person died of classic SCD—Sudden Cardiac Death. We have one important piece of the puzzle. But though we know how everyone died, we don't know why. What caused the deaths? What was the trigger? All the deaths happened within one hour of symptom onset. We've gone through every detail in every chart, adding in Mrs. Adams at Santos's suggestion. We created a matrix from the chart review that demonstrates clearly that every patient who died had cardiac arrhythmias immediately prior to cardiac arrest. We know that the most common arrhythmia leading to SCD is V-Tach, accelerating into V-Fib, and then followed by asystole."

"We have also ruled out most of the organic causes of SCD, like aortic stenosis, endocarditis, congenital heart disease, and acute myocarditis, so we need to look at the noncardiac causes," said Patrick.

"We are about to work on a cause-and-effect diagram, a fishbone diagram, to dig deeper into the potential causes that will really unlock this mystery," Santos chimed in.

Susan, the team facilitator, asked, "Can you join us? We could really use your expertise. Not only will it help us, but you'll get up to speed right away if we find the potential cause."

"There is a lot at risk here, not just patient lives, but the hospital's reputation. If this continues, they could shut down the CCU; we could lose our accreditation and then our funding. The legal, regulatory and financial impacts are huge," Richard replied. "Of course we'll help."

Heather nodded her agreement. "These deaths have a huge ripple effect not just in the CCU, but the whole hospital. I don't even want to even think about what else could happen."

The team took out large pieces of flip-chart paper and taped them to the walls with masking tape. Susan drew the diagram of the skeleton of a fish. The box at the head was the problem—in this case, SCD. She then drew the long line of the body of the fish with a black magic marker and lines at 180-degree angles out from the body of the fish. Each line had a heading.

The fishbone diagram took a complicated issue and broke it down into parts that could potentially lead to a solution. The team had agreed that they needed to look at four Ps: procedures, physical plant, process, and people. In each of these areas, they would ask the question, "What is it about this area that might cause the SCD?" The team would then brainstorm everything about procedures that could potentially cause noncardiac SCD, from standing orders for drugs to lack of routine maintenance of monitors, then move on to the other areas. The whole idea was to brainstorm without blame or criticism of ideas, then drill down to a few key root causes.

"This methodical process is really frustrating. Can't we just brainstorm and get on with it?" asked Patrick.

"We could miss something, Patrick, a crucial piece. One more meeting and we should have this figured out," said Susan.

The team collectively eyed the "people" heading, which could mean unit staff, patients, students, and staff from other areas of the hospital. It was the one area where everyone hoped they wouldn't find anything.

"Let's get started," Susan said. "You can begin anywhere, but let's save 'people' for later."

CHAPTER 27

Regular meetings ... they met again. What is going on?

Saturday morning, he reflected on his progress as he sat outside listening to the drone of lawnmowers and the sound of children laughing next door. He had casually found out the nurses' names while up on the unit drawing bloods. After some quick research, he'd learned that the "Ishikawa Diagram" he'd heard them mention was a tool used to identify the potential causes of a problem. *If Wendy was up there with them, had they discovered that someone was tampering with lab results?*

The sudden rush of awareness brought his lurking paranoia to the surface, launching a full-blown panic attack. What if they discovered the cause of the deaths? Could they trace it back to him? Paranoia was a roller coaster ride of emotions. Confident in his ability to cover his tracks, he was usually able to keep it in check. But new information sparked fear.

His heart pounding, he began to sweat and his blood pressure rose, causing his chest to constrict and making him even more anxious. He started to get a splitting headache. The pain radiated in a tight band from the back of his head, squeezing. He could hardly breathe. He could hear his heartbeat pounding in his ears. Then his ears began to ring.

Settle down. Deep breaths. Get your act together, Soldier!

After a few minutes of deep breathing, the headache was still there, but his heart rate had returned to normal. He continued his positive self-talk. *You're smarter than the whole group of sissies. They've never seen war.* He realized that it was highly unlikely that they had figured out the cause of death, much less the trail to the lab results and then back to him. He was just nervous because of the dreams. He had another traumatic night, suffering through recurrent nightmares. This time he had suffocated and died. The dreams were vivid, painful. He pushed his memories deep within him during the day, but they surfaced all the stronger at night.

It seemed to be getting worse. Sleep deprivation was feeding his depression and his panic attacks. He had read a recent story in *USA Today* that stated the number of soldiers forced to leave the army due to mental disorders had increased by 64 percent. War was taking the usual emotional toll on the soldiers. "Just wait until they get home," he said to himself. "It doesn't get any better."

But he needed more information. Offense is the best defense. No way was he going to be the hunted.

He reached over, picked up his laptop, and connected to his secure wireless network. Once the home browser screen opened, he began scanning the Internet for information, particularly about Santos, but also Patrick. After a few minutes, he was able to acquire home addresses and phone numbers. He browsed for further information, finding several citations of publications, graduations, etc. After about fifteen minutes of research, he logged in to Facebook and found that Santos had a profile open to anyone. She had neglected to add privacy features. He saw pictures of her trip to Colorado, found her friends, where she went to school, learned about her hobbies. There were no pictures or comments about boyfriends or roommates.

People can be so stupid, he thought to himself, looking at the wealth of information available to anyone who logged on. *This is very helpful.*

Gaining new intelligence helped him feel more in control. Time had passed quickly, and it was time to go in, grab something to eat, and print out directions. It was a beautiful day. Time to go for a ride. Do a little reconnaissance. He longed to learn more about her. *At another time, I might have had a chance with someone like her.*

His final thought came from somewhere deep inside, somewhere dark where regret had turned into rage and bitterness. It almost surprised him as it bubbled to the surface. *If I can't have her, then no one else will.*

CHAPTER 28

The sun was streaming through her bedroom windows when Santos woke on Saturday.

Nine a.m. was sleeping late, but she was drained from work and the extra team meetings. She was also spending time away from work preparing for the meetings, staying up late and studying, trying to unravel clinical clues that would solve the mysterious deaths. Resolute, Santos kept circling back to blood chemistry. *What could be lethal that we would not see? High or low potassium could kill, but we would see symptoms. Wouldn't we?*

She sat up, found her robe at the foot of her bed, and slipped it on. Then she walked the short distance to the kitchen to make coffee. She had already planned to do something besides work on the case today. She needed a mental break and knew that the best medicine was physical activity in the sun.

Her home was small. Her sister, Maria, teased her saying that you could go from door to door in two steps. The house was really a great room with an open galley kitchen and a bedroom. Santos ground fresh coffee beans and started the four-cup coffeemaker. Then she began to boil an egg. *Need some protein,* she thought. She poured a glass of orange juice, doled out her vitamins, and started to toast a piece of nine-grain bread from Deb's Great Harvest Grain Bakery. The aroma of toasted whole grains made her kitchen smell wonderful, bringing back memories of home. Rarely did she have the time to make it to the bakery, and when she did, she stocked up. Her freezer was full of sliced loaves, ready whenever she wanted it for toast or a sandwich.

She loaded a tray with her blue calico dishes and carried it to the sheltered backyard patio, placed it on the table, and sat down. She had splurged on Texas fig jam at the Nutcracker Market and spread some on the chewy warm bread.

This is what I work for, she thought to herself as she gazed on the tranquility of her small but well-kept garden. She sat for twenty minutes, just letting her shoulders relax, sipping her coffee, and eating her breakfast. Then, brushing the crumbs off her nightgown, she got up and headed into the house. It was time to change into work clothes and get the yard ready for winter.

Chapter 29

It took just forty-five minutes to navigate the thirty miles to her house. Traffic was light on Saturdays, and he knew the area fairly well. Houston, known for its urban sprawl, covered over eighty-seven hundred square miles and was larger than the state of New Jersey. Families in the Houston area could travel across several counties to see each other. He had lucked out that she lived relatively close.

He drove slowly down her street looking for her address. He felt drawn to find her, to see her when she did not see him. The street was a quiet cul-de-sac of well-kept patio homes. Several people were out in their yards.

Before he could find the address, he saw her. Her size, walk, and mannerisms were distinctive, and he easily recognized her outside the hospital environment. *She's so pretty,* he thought, *I could watch her forever.* She was dressed in faded, torn blue jeans and an over-sized white long-sleeved shirt. She wore a wide-brimmed straw hat with a red ribbon. She was deep in conversation with one of her neighbors when the wind blew her hat off her head. It cartwheeled, rolling into the street. Santos made a dash for it and neatly scooped it up. He quickly slowed, hopeful that she would not see him. By the time he drove by, Santos was continuing her conversation with the neighbor. She did not look up as he passed.

There were no security gates, and the neighborhood appeared to be composed of retirees and families in their first homes. His envy resurfaced, and he thought of how he would never share his home with anyone. His neighbors never stopped to talk. He could not remember the last time someone had invited him to do anything. Santos was laughing, and she took off her hat to smooth back shoulder length hair that shimmered copper in the sun. *What a doll.*

CHAPTER 30

"Don't look now, but this is the second time that car is driving by," remarked Mrs. Banks.

Mrs. Banks was Santos's sharp-as-a-tack elderly neighbor. She headed up the neighborhood watch and knew more details about the goings-on inside the perimeter of their homes than in world news. Santos stopped laughing and held her position, feigning listening to her neighbor. It was uncommon to have any car in the cul-de-sac that they did not know. There were no houses for sale, and the neighborhood was well off the main roads.

"We can never be too careful," said Mrs. Banks. "Did you hear that two guys were caught digging up and stealing water meters around here? Can you believe that?"

Santos looked back at the car as it left the subdivision. It was a dark grey sedan, a Toyota Camry maybe? She did not know anyone with that kind of car, but she would remember it if she ever saw it again. It was too far away to get the license plate. "No, I didn't hear that," she replied.

"Good to talk with you. You work too hard, Santos. And you need a boyfriend. You aren't getting any younger, you know. Girl like you needs to have babies while you're young, like I did."

"Mrs. Banks, you're too much! I hardly have time for myself, much less a guy in my life. Good to see you, too. You're right, though, we can never be too careful. Thanks for all you do for us."

Santos gave her neighbor a warm hug, then pulled on her gardening gloves and headed back to her house. "I'd better get back to work!"

CHAPTER 31

On the Tuesday after his weekend field trip, he realized that he needed to focus on his primary role in the lab to avoid suspicion and detection. He was preoccupied with his "side job" and obsessed with Santos, but he could not let that make him careless. Since he was up early, he stopped and picked up donuts and freshly baked kolaches, still warm from the oven. Want to win a popularity contest? Bring in food. Besides, it would make him appear more like one of the gang, even though he was not. He would never be.

While everyone was in the break room eating, he got to work. He simultaneously analyzed the lab tests that had come in with the first set of blood draws and scanned the census looking for the next intriguing opportunity to kill. He quickly identified an easy target. He methodically diluted a small portion of the sample, ran it, and transferred the results over to the electronic patient record.

Finished with his most important work, he used his upper body to heave himself out of his chair and slowly walked into the break room. It was time to create a potential alibi. He picked up the last kolache, now cold, and ate it with relish. He made small talk with the techs in the break room and drank a cup of strong, bitter coffee.

He had tied up all the details. They would remember that he had been in the break room with them, but would never be quite sure about time. He wondered when the blood in his veins had turned to ice. He could not remember the last time he had felt any warmth about anyone or anything. Even heartbreaking stories of loss and death failed to faze him. He lived in another dimension, disengaged from life.

Every day that passed, his life felt more like an out-of-body experience. It was as if he were watching a play, writing it, and directing it at the same time. The pawns he cast to play the parts, clinicians and patients, were doing exactly what he wanted them to do. They had no clue that they were in a game for his amusement and revenge, manipulated by the master.

CHAPTER 32

Santos began her second shift in the CCU, with one more to go. The continuous emotional strain of the unresolved sudden deaths obsessed her day and night. This morning she had slept through her alarm. Skipping breakfast, she raced to the Park and Ride, nearly missing the bus. Fatigue clung to her. Her brain was cloaked in fog.

She wasn't the only one. The collective human empathy of patients, family, and staff was soft-wired together in a web of sadness and anxiety. Family overheard the whispers and noticed the meetings, and staff walked on eggshells wondering if death was stalking one of their patients. Just opening the doors into the CCU was like entering a low-pressure zone of depression.

She reviewed the lab results of her patients, paying careful attention to a patient who had arrived yesterday to rule out MI. Acting as charge nurse, she strove for continuity when making patient assignments. She had assigned herself this patient, and she smiled and shook her head when she thought of how much he did not want to be in the CCU. A big man, over six feet, he was tan and fit. Mr. Gideon had told her the whole story, in detail, of how he had landed in the hospital.

Liam Gideon had been out on the golf course enjoying the lovely cool day of late fall in Houston. He enjoyed swinging his golf club like a baseball bat, and he saw number nine of the course as a unique challenge. While most people were satisfied just to get the ball close to the water and then pitch over, he liked to try to drive the green some three hundred and fifty yards away.

He felt especially blessed because he was home for ten days from his current work assignment in China, where he was the president of a branch of an energy company. A devoted family man, Liam had found that living overseas had tested the limits of his commitment to a company that had employed him for over twenty-five years. He was looking forward to dinner that evening with his kids and grandkids. They were picking up classic Texas barbeque— brisket and ribs from one of their favorite restaurants, Dickey's. He could not think of a more perfect dinner than barbeque, washed down with an ice-cold Shiner Bock, surrounded by his family in his backyard shaded by gnarled, mature live oaks.

He had stood on the tee for number nine and looked at the pin on the green. It was a perfect day for golf, warm with no humidity. The flag on the green waved stiffly. He felt the breeze behind him and decided to go for it, with assistance from the prevailing wind. He took a practice swing, looked at the green one more time, then lined up, swung, and crushed the ball. The oversized driver hit the ball with a crack, and it shot like a bullet through the air, crossed over the water, and landed just short of the green.

"Dawg'on it," he'd said under his breath. He leaned over to pick up the remnants of his tee. As he stood up, he felt tightness grip his ribs. He sucked in a few deep breaths attempting to ease the tension. He had a history of back pain, but stoic by nature, he had a high pain tolerance. This did not feel like the excruciating pain of nerve pressure. Maybe it was heartburn and would pass?

He avoided saying anything to his golf partners and got on his cart to drive to the green. Halfway there, the searing pain began to radiate down his left arm and up his jaw. He knew the signs of a heart attack. He would have to act quickly. His beautiful wife, a nurse and now a teacher of nurses, would be furious with him if he did not take immediate action. So making apologies to the rest of the foursome, he drove the golf cart to the parking lot, got in his car, and drove himself to the hospital. He called his wife from the emergency room.

Though his EKG results and early cardiac enzyme results were normal, his cholesterol was elevated. Since he had a family history of sudden cardiac death, the nurse practitioner in the ER, after consulting with his internist, decided to admit him to the CCU. His stress test of a month ago was normal, and if his enzymes remained steady with no changes in his EKG, they would discharge him in the morning.

Santos knew how he felt. He was wasting a day in the hospital when he could be with his family. He had to return to China on Sunday. Frustration was his middle name. When she looked at his lab results, she knew that he would not be happy with the news.

Leaving the computer, she walked to his bed where he was sitting on the edge of the bed, waiting. He grabbed her gently but firmly on the forearm, smiled, and looked her right in the eyes.

"You're going to let me out of here now, aren't you?"

"Soon, very soon."

"What does that mean? I can see in your eyes that you have some bad news for me."

"Not bad news."

"Well, what is it then? Give it to me. I can take it."

"All your blood tests are normal except your potassium. It's on the low side of normal."

"So …."

"Low potassium can affect the beat of your heart."

"I'm listening."

"Potassium influences the electrical conductivity of your heart. It's an essential component of blood chemistry. You're an engineer; you understand how systems work. Everything works together. Biochemically, your electrolytes must be in balance for your heart to beat in a steady rhythm."

"So if I get up and leave right now, what could this low potassium do to me? Why can't I take a pill at home? Time's a-wasting here." He slipped off the bed and stood up giving her a serious executive look, questioning her authority despite his flimsy hospital gown.

Santos smiled. "You don't have to stay. You have choices, but you should make an informed decision."

"Okay. I'm listening," he said, standing tall, deliberately folding his arms across his massive chest. He towered over her.

"Didn't you tell me that you recently returned from very long overseas travel? And you had a strenuous workout before heading out to the golf course?"

"Yes."

"You could be dehydrated. Your electrolytes are out of balance."

"So I just drink a lot of water. Or is Gatorade better?"

"Since we don't know what happened to cause your chest pain, and since your potassium is low, it's possible that it caused your heart to go into an irregular rhythm."

"I don't understand."

"I'll say it again. Potassium affects the conductivity of your heart. Your heartbeat is *triggered* by electrical impulses at the cellular level. If you don't have enough potassium, it could be life threatening. You could develop an irregular heartbeat that could escalate into a fatal rhythm … you could die."

Mr. Gideon glared at her. She saw disbelief in his eyes. And mistrust.

"If Mrs. Gideon were here right now, she would tell you to stay."

A long sigh of capitulation escaped from Mr. Gideon.

"How low is my potassium?"

"Moderately. What we do is give you potassium through your IV. Then we'll draw your blood again."

"How long is this going to take?"

"To be realistic, you should be out of here by midafternoon."

After another impatient sigh and a long stare, he sat down on the bed, got under the covers and pulled the sheet up.

"Let's get this show on the road."

CHAPTER 33

After collecting her supplies, Santos returned to her impatient charge and found that his wife, Fiona, had joined him.

"Now you listen to her," Fiona said with an elegant Southern drawl, nodding at Santos. "She knows what she's doing, and you know nothing about this."

Mr. Gideon respectfully tolerated his wife's rebuke and looked lovingly at her; it was obvious to Santos that he adored her. Santos was touched to see a couple still in love after decades of marriage.

"I hope he didn't give you too much trouble," Fiona said apologetically.

Fiona Gideon looked fresh and beautiful in a cornflower linen dress that brought out the color of her eyes. She stood by the bed with a plastic bag of her husband's clean clothes slung over her arm. Tall and slender, Fiona had shoulder-length blonde hair. Nearly six feet tall, she and her husband made a handsome couple. Mr. Gideon had told Santos their recent life story. They had lived all over the world together. It was their dream that they return to Houston to be closer to her parents and surrounded by their family. Over the past year, another grandchild had been born, and Fiona had been thrilled that she was there to see baby Scott delivered.

"Not a problem," Santos said, and she gave Mr. Gideon a conspiratorial wink. "We worked it out."

She began to hang the IV bag on the preprogrammed pump. She took his vital signs as a baseline and looked at the monitor, seeing the normal sinus rhythm of his healthy heart. Finally, she connected the IV tubing to the port, opened the stopcock, and started the pump.

While the potassium chloride dripped slowly into his vein, she stayed at the bedside, systematically assessing his clinical response. Administration of the KCL would take a couple of hours. Though the lab results showed low potassium, he had no other clinical symptoms of hypokalemia. Still, she knew it was possible to remain asymptomatic. He could be suffering from dehydration from the recent overseas travel and his time on the golf course.

And yet ....

Her gut told her that something was not right.

She decided to stay longer and continue to observe him. They talked about the upcoming holidays and how much they missed spending Thanksgiving with family. The Gideons would be home again for Christmas. While they comfortably chatted, Santos kept an eye on her patient and the monitor. Everything seemed to be going smoothly.

"You know, I need some real food," he said, holding his stomach. "My stomach is starting to cramp a little. Maybe I am dehydrated. That could cause stomach cramps, right?"

She watched the monitor closely, assessing his pattern. "Yes, it could."

As she watched, she began to see a subtle change in his EKG. His T-wave started to peak, and his QRS complex was starting to widen. The electrical patterns of his heart were changing. She walked over to the monitor, pressed a button, and ran a paper strip to review more carefully. Her heart beat rapidly as she recognized the changes.

"Is something wrong?" Fiona asked.

She looked at Fiona and saw the reflection of anxiety.

"How do you feel, Mr. Gideon?"

"Fine," he replied.

She turned back to the monitor. Fiona moved closer to watch.

"I'm seeing some subtle changes in his EKG," she explained in an even tone. *What is going on here?* Her anxiety rose with her adrenaline, and she pushed down her feeling of panic. She had to stay cool in order to manage the clinical situation.

In seconds, the P-wave started to disappear. Her concern escalated. A code was imminent, and before she could move, the heart-monitor alarm shrieked and the normal sinus rhythm of his heart was gone.

"My heart ...." he gasped. Then he lost consciousness.

Ventricular tachycardia ripped across the screen of the monitor. Death was moments away.

She did not hesitate. "Code Blue! I need help! Call a Code Blue!"

There were only seconds to intervene before he suffered permanent brain damage or died. CPR alone would not be enough to save him. She had to know exactly what was causing the V-Tach. Santos quickly flipped a switch on the IV pump.

"Mrs. Gideon, please stand back. I'm sorry, but I can't explain right now." Fiona's face went pale. Fiona backed off and Santos saw her shock and deepening worry. There was no time to console.

On autopilot, she put the bed flat and began chest compressions. Before finishing thirty, Sheila, Emma, Nick, and Patrick rushed over with the crash cart.

"Emma, quick. Be sure the KCL is off. Run normal saline," she spoke with calm authority over the exertion of chest compression.

Something was terribly wrong. And it had to be the KCL.

He had all the symptoms of *hyperkalemia*. Looking up at the monitor, she saw the classic electrical response of the heart to an overdose of potassium. Her mind raced, remembering that high doses of potassium during bypass surgery would stop the heart from beating. Excess potassium causes cardiac cells to depolarize; eventually, the cells cannot recharge to trigger the heart to beat. The heart stops. Another systemic disaster was brewing, and Santos knew it. Blood was pooling in his quivering heart. The pooled blood might clot, leave the heart, and lodge in his brain, causing a stroke by blocking the flow of oxygen-enriched blood to the brain. Or the clot could become a pulmonary embolism obstructing blood flow to his lungs. Either could kill.

Mr. Gideon's heart was on a rapid and deadly track to asystole, complete stop. She knew if they did not stop the downward spiral of microscopic and anatomic events, he would quickly die.

Without questioning Santos's call, Emma verified the KCL was off, ran normal saline, and took a quick look at the monitor. She saw it as clearly as Santos: hyperkalemia. She began to hunt through the medication drawer of the crash cart.

"Calcium chloride coming," said Emma, opening the prefilled syringe.

"Mrs. Gideon," Emma looked across the room for Fiona. "I need his weight to calculate the dose."

"Two-ten," said Fiona without hesitation.

Talking while working, Emma continued, "Calcium chloride is the first line of treatment for hyperkalemia. It will help us shift the potassium from the extracellular to intracellular …." She stopped to make a quick calculation then inserted the needle into the IV port. "I'm going to push this antidote over two minutes … and we should be able to stabilize him … the aberrant beats should stop."

Mr. Gideon was breathing shallowly. Nick put a face mask on the patient and quickly connected tubing to the wall oxygen supply. He watched, ready to bag if needed.

Santos quickly briefed the team, recounting the events that had led up to the fatal arrhythmia.

Looking up at the heart monitor, she saw his heart pattern start to change again. It was stabilizing.

"Nick, okay if I stop the compression now?"

"Seems like he's coming out of it. Yes, let's back off for a while and see how he does."

"What else do you need us to do?" Emma asked as she moved over to Mr. Gideon's right side, opposite Santos.

"Mrs. Gideon, are you okay?" Patrick asked, turning to Fiona, who stood stunned and glued to the ground.

"Please let me stay. I won't get in the way," she replied, backing off further to allow the stream of health care providers and equipment closer to her husband's bed.

Heather, who stood on the fringe watching the code play out, walked over to Fiona. "I think he's coming around. Stay here," she motioned and wrapped her arm around Fiona's shoulders.

The minutes flew by, and Mr. Gideon continued breathing the oxygen-enriched air. Nick occasionally bagged him through the mask for additional support. The rest of the Code Blue team had arrived: anesthesia, the administrator on call, a chaplain, and the attending cardiologist. The area buzzed with conversation.

"Where are we?" asked the anesthesiologist. "What's his P02?"

"We're good," Nick replied, "stabilized at 98 percent."

The anesthesiologist nodded and continued to watch.

Everyone stood by, ready to take it to the next level. Each member of the team took a respective expert look at the scene, collecting data and evaluating the need for further action. Santos took deep, steady breaths, eyes glued to the monitor, waiting for his heartbeat to stabilize further.

Her mind was racing. *What just happened?*

After a few long minutes, the collective sigh of relief was almost audible when the monitor showed normal sinus rhythm. When Mrs. Gideon saw the conversion of the pattern, she covered her face with her hands and began to weep tears of relief and joy.

"Mr. Gideon, wake up," Santos said. "Time to come back now."

Minutes passed. Slowly, Mr. Gideon regained consciousness. He seemed anxious and terribly confused. Santos could relate. One moment he had been having a conversation, and then he blacked out. He would remember nothing.

He choked out, "What did you do to my chest? Oww, dang it. I feel as if I've been punched!" He looked down at his chest as if he might find the answer. Everyone looked at Santos, who was speechless for a moment.

After a brief pause, she replied, "Mr. Gideon, your heart essentially stopped. The heartbeats you had weren't circulating any blood to your brain ... or any of your other organs. I had to start CPR. You hurt from me crushing your chest, manually pumping your heart."

He rubbed his aching chest and looked with disbelief at Santos. "You did this? I haven't hurt this much since college boxing ... young woman, you're stronger than you look."

Santos watched Mr. Gideon take a deep breath. He looked around the area, absorbing the state of confusion, the equipment stuffed into the small space, people he did not know standing around him, meds on his bed, spent syringes and trash. Then he saw his wife, crying. He looked at her with concern.

Santos caught his look.

"You're going to be fine, Mr. Gideon. Your heart is back in its normal sinus rhythm." She stopped, unsure of how much to say to him. "You had a close call. I'll explain everything to you." As much as she could. "When your doctor arrives, we'll brief her."

"Dang it," Mr. Gideon said and pulled off the oxygen mask. "Come here, Honey." He reached out his hand to his wife. "Don't cry. Come on over here." Fiona stretched out her hand to his. He pulled her over to him.

"Don't you worry ... you'll get those beautiful eyes all red. Darlin', everything's going to be okay."

CHAPTER 34

Emma, concerned, went looking for Santos. Santos had stabilized her patient, finished charting in the electronic patient record, and then asked for a brief break. Emma found Santos sitting alone at the table in the tiny nurses' lounge, crying hard.

Emma paused briefly in the doorway and then slowly walked over, pulled out a chair, and sat down by Santos. Then she reached out, put her arm around Santos's petite shoulders, and crushed her close.

"Oh, honey, let it out. It's okay to cry."

"I could've killed him," Santos looked at Emma with terror in her eyes. "I could have killed him … this normal, healthy man; a husband, a father, a grandfather. I could have killed him! Oh my God!"

Emma sat back, then reached out and grasped Santos firmly on both shoulders.

"Look at me. Snap out of it. You didn't kill him. You did good. You stopped it. You did what every great nurse does—you assessed the situation, and you acted quickly and confidently. You did good! I'm so proud of you." Tears filled Emma's own eyes.

"Now don't *you* go and cry on me," Santos piped back, pushing Emma away. "They can't find us both blubbering in here." She let out a long sigh, followed by a little nervous laugh. "You know, my hands were shaking when I came in here. I kept my cool, but when it was all over, my hands started to shake … I'm so cold!"

"That's normal," Emma replied. "For a long time, my hands would tremble, and sometimes my knees would wobble after an emergency." Emma took off her lab coat and wrapped it around Santos's shoulders. "It kept up for years and then finally stopped. I had this GI patient one time bleeding out a river of blood, and we couldn't stop it."

Emma quickly caught herself and stopped, realizing this was not the time for war stories.

"Well, it's comforting to know that I'm not losing it," Santos said with a note of sarcasm.

"I want you to eat and drink something. Then go wash your face and put on some lipstick. Go and see the Gideons. They want to thank you."

"I'm not hungry."

"You will eat something before you leave this room. Nurse's orders. Now pull yourself together, and we'll see you in ten minutes. There's some of my leftover gumbo in the refrigerator. Heat it up."

"Yes, ma'am," Santos said, giving Emma a mock salute.

Emma stopped, thought for a moment, and gave Santos a long, searching look.

"Why are you looking at me that way?"

"Have you considered that what happened today may be a clue?"

"What do you mean?"

Emma took a deep breath and explained, "You thought you were giving him potassium for hypokalemia. But he didn't need it."

Santos paused. "Did I read the lab results wrong?"

"No, I double-checked. According to the lab results, you should have given him the potassium."

"So you're saying his lab results were wrong? That he didn't have low potassium?"

Emma nodded. "I think that Wendy, a long time ago,

told me they keep lab specimens for up to two weeks. We might be able to recheck his original sample. I'm not sure yet, but we need to consider this as a piece of the puzzle. This was too much like the deaths, Santos. He was lucky. You were there watching him. I can't figure this out yet, but let's not discount this as just a near miss. I don't think it was a lab error."

Emma pushed her chair back and gave Santos a quick hug, crushing her to her ample chest. "My late father-in-law used to say, it's not a mistake unless you do it twice. Let's not let this happen again."

"Thanks, Emma. What would I do without you? This has been really hard, probably the roughest patch in my life … other than Mom's death."

"Honey, I will always be here for you. Don't worry. Now get your act together, eat some food, and get back out there. Don't forget the lipstick. You're looking pale."

Emma got up and walked to the door. Santos still sat at the table.

"Move it, girl. Or I'll send Patrick in here. He'll snap you out of it."

"Don't you dare, Emma. I'm a wreck. I don't want him to see me like this!"

Santos obediently got up and headed over to the refrigerator. Emma turned around, thinking, *I ought to try that one again; that really did the trick. Maybe there is something going on* … Emma smiled.

CHAPTER 35

While Santos waited for Heather outside the conference room, she could not resist a quick look inside. Multidisciplinary rounds, where the critical incident involving Mr. Gideon would be discussed, were about to begin. What she saw made her nervous. It was nearly filled to capacity, and buzzing with conversation. She saw students, staff members, and a few people she did not know, all come to debrief the near miss of yesterday. *Probably some curiosity seekers,* she thought. Rumors had already spread; she had heard some of them, the hospital grapevine alive with misinformation. The "telephone game" of communication, information passed from individual to individual, had created all kinds of stories ranging from fact to science fiction.

She dreaded the Debrief. She would be the center of attention, and her peers would question her. Yet she knew it was important. The discovery process around this event might be a huge piece of the high-stakes puzzle they were trying to solve. Emma hadn't been wrong: this was too much like the other deaths to be a coincidence. They were still trying to track down Mr. Gideon's original lab specimen to retest it for potassium. Heather had advised Santos not to talk about the search for the original blood work since it might lead to catastrophic rumors that lab tests were inaccurate. Something or someone could be falsifying the lab results. *Could someone actually be tampering with results? But who, why? Or am I paranoid?*

"Are you ready?" Heather came up behind her, interrupting her thoughts.

"Ready as I'll ever be."

Santos looked into Heather's eyes and saw compassion and support.

Walking into the room, she was pleased to see that her team members from the root-cause analysis were present in the room. They had the most knowledge about all the cases.

Nick caught her eye and silently mouthed, "You can do this."

Wendy reached out, grabbed her hand, and gave it a quick squeeze then whispered, "You go, girl!"

She managed a rueful smile then quickly took her seat. The Debrief began.

CHAPTER 36

All the seats in the conference room were taken, and staff clustered around the doorway, spilling out into the hallway. Clutching his plastic carryall of vacutainers, butterflies, tubes, and blood specimens, he looked legitimate. He eased his way into a place where he could listen but not be seen by the people in the conference room. He watched Santos, who was deep in conversation with Heather. *She looks exhausted,* he thought. *My rules. My game, Little One.*

Feasting off their frustration, he was also anxious for information. *How much did they know? What were his chances of being discovered?* He was bursting with pride. Any information he could glean provided positive reinforcement, fueling his mania. His conscience had gone to sleep long ago. He had read once in a book about sociopaths by Dr. Martha Stout that the ultimate contest between conscience and authority is war. Obedience is passive. He had followed orders. He had to kill or be killed. His mind wandered back to 'Nam and surfaced his feelings of righteous indignation. *Courage was not following your conscience. Courage was killing when you had to kill.*

This was exciting!

Careful to mask his emotion, he pasted a serious look of listening on his face. It was hard not to smile. This was theater in the round, and they were talking about his show!

He returned his attention to the conversation in the conference room. Rounds began with the discussion of looking at process and facts about what had happened with Mr. Gideon and why, versus blame and speculation. The facts discussed in the Debrief were clear: Mr. Gideon had been given a lethal dose of KCL.

He overheard comments about tampering, wrong specimen, or pharmacy error. His anxiety began to rise. Listening intently to the discussion, he secretly hoped there would be paper outlines distributed, but there were none. The suits were in damage-control mode, trying to prevent this from becoming a lawsuit or hitting the newspapers.

Looking at his watch, he realized that it was time to get back to the lab. Rounds had not yet ended. Starved for more information, he would have to consider other sources of intel without arousing suspicion. He quietly backed out of the doorway and made his way, invisible, down the back stairs, just another figure in a white lab coat.

CHAPTER 37

After the large group left the room, Heather listened to the animated conversation of the small team. She had made the right decision to restrict detailed information about the deaths. Only the small root-cause analysis team would have access to everything. The rest of the information would have to be carefully managed. Further rumors could destroy patient trust and hospital credibility. In addition, the discovery process needed to be confidential. If there was a killer out there, as Santos had reluctantly suggested to her, or if they were administering tampered drugs, or if lab results were contaminated, the search and information collected would have to be kept under wraps. Right now everything was speculation. Heather knew the entire team well and trusted not only their confidentiality but their clinical wisdom.

In her mind, the near miss of yesterday had many facets to consider. It was vital to seek the truth no matter what the consequences. Health care was already in a firestorm of debate: cost, quality, how much was necessary, rationing. The public trust was eroding. She also knew that the hospital had become a place of grave danger when people were most vulnerable. Patients were susceptible to iatrogenic illnesses, bacteria that were antibiotic resistant, staff that were impaired by sleep deprivation and drugs, hundreds of thousands of errors, every year. Now this.

As the unit leader, Heather took seriously the accountability of being the front line of support to patients and families. She hired carefully, looking for nurses and other staff who were not only bright and educated, but who would live the values that she wanted to have flourish on her unit. The deaths had kept her awake many nights. Though she never took things personally, she suffered the burden of accountability. Her gut told her that these events were not coincidental or random. She had shared her thoughts in confidence with Richard, but she kept her own counsel with the rest of the team. She did not want to inject fear into the process that would fuel further rumors.

"Is it possible to recheck his potassium level?" Nick asked.

Wendy replied, "Already done. Many people don't know this, but we keep blood samples for seven days ... some two weeks. We retested the original sample, and Mr. Gideon had a normal potassium level—actually the high end of normal."

"Emma, you were right!" said Santos. She turned on Wendy. "How is it possible we would get a lab result that was inaccurate? We base so many decisions on lab results. I can't believe this!"

"Now don't put me on the stand here, Santos," Wendy pushed back. "Let me try to explain a few things before everyone jumps all over me."

The room was silent. Tension was high, nerves strung taut to the breaking point.

"I'm sorry," Santos said sincerely, looking apologetic and embarrassed by her outburst. Wendy sighed deeply. "It's okay, Santos. I know this is hard, particularly on you."

Wendy continued, "As I've thought about it, there are several possibilities for why we had an error. There could have been reagent issues with the sample tested. The original sample could have come down cold, chilled with another set of blood samples ...."

"You mean that if we chill a sample that shouldn't be cool, it could affect the results?" shot out Patrick, clearly skeptical.

"Yes, it could."

"Oh my God … sorry for the interruption, Wendy," said Patrick.

"In addition, if the sample is drawn out of order, it can be contaminated with reagents and lead to false results. Tubes should be drawn in a certain order for accurate lab results—for example, start with a blue tube, then a red, then a purple top, etc."

"Even I didn't know that," said Nick.

"If you have a battery of tests, there is an order in which the samples should be drawn," replied Wendy. She paused briefly. "Then there is the possibility of machine calibration causing the error. The med techs always review the lab results prior to posting on the patient records. But this lab test was not unusual, at least from the sample that we had in the lab. We aren't sure about the original sample."

"All of this is good conversation … we are learning. But we still don't have an answer," Heather summarized. "Wendy, can you and a trusted team in your lab take a further look to make sure that we're doing everything to make sure that this does not repeat?"

"Absolutely," Wendy replied. "We're already on it."

"I don't really want to say this, but I need to." Santos hesitated. "Is it possible that someone could be tampering with the lab results?"

Santos's words hung in the room. The implications were horrific. No one spoke for a moment.

"Okay, but before we jump to that conclusion, we also need to take a look at the bag of fluid and the dose of KCL to make sure that was accurate," responded Chad from

Pharmacy. Chad had joined the group at Heather's request to round out the expertise at the table.

"You're right. We need to look at process, not at people," Heather said firmly.

Susan Hendrick had been listening to the dialogue throughout the entire meeting, and she finally made a comment. "I think it's time to consider the possibility of human intervention here. We need to take this line of thought slowly and carefully. And this needs to remain strictly confidential." She turned to Heather. "It's essential we keep this off the record. It's great to involve the category of 'people' for learning purposes, but we can cover that later with some sort of conference where we protect the names and talk about process."

"I agree," said Heather. "And we are forgetting one of the most important decisions we have to make today … What do we tell the Gideons about this?"

After a round of dialogue, the team agreed that honesty was the only way to go. The family deserved to know the facts. Heather agreed that she and Santos would talk with Mr. Gideon's internist, and the three of them would tell the family what they knew of the truth. The key messages would be that they did not know the actual cause but would discover it and that they were deeply sorry for the incident. Fortunately, for the Gideons, Heather thought, all was well. Others had died.

CHAPTER 38

The near-miss rumors swept through the hospital, fueling a wildfire of speculation and creating new gossip around the mysterious deaths in the CCU. Where there was no information, people created their own version of the truth. The grapevine buzzed electric with communication. On the way to the executive boardroom, Santos overheard conversation from a group of three clinicians huddling together in the hallway. "I heard the entire lab needs to be recalibrated ... just like them not to tell us what's going on! Watch *The Chronicle,* that's where we'll hear about it first ...."

She shook her head and approached the boardroom. While clinicians and staff worked under a cloud of misinformation and silence, hospital and medical administration with board members, had gathered for a long overdue meeting to discuss the hospital communication strategy.

She saw Patrick waiting outside and smiled.

"Hey!" he said.

They walked into the room and she whispered, "Ever heard of leading from thirty-thousand feet?"

"I think I know, but tell me what you're thinking."

"Well, if you are on a plane, a pilot or passenger at thirty thousand feet can't see much—whether there are leaves on the trees, crops in the fields, or cows in the barns. If the weather is clear, they can only see outlines of roads, maybe a large building." She paused to look around the room. "Since we've never seen most of the people in this room, it's doubtful that they are really aware of what's going on in patient care. They can't see the docs who don't wash their hands between patients ... they can't see that some staff are sleep deprived and working impaired ... dirty floors ... messy utility rooms. They don't see the bullying that goes on sometimes with new grads."

"So you're saying these people are probably really out of touch?"

She nodded and said, "This should be interesting."

The executive boardroom was one of the few remaining symbols of a more opulent era in health care and reflected the century the hospital had been in operation. Portraits of board chairs and CEOs circled the elegant, richly dark-paneled room. Antique equestrian and land-scape oil paintings were softly illuminated by wall sconces. The focal point of the room was a huge oval table that seated fifty. Physician and nursing administration, directors of clinical areas, legal counsel, marketing, and public rela-tions occupied nearly every seat. Santos and Patrick snagged two seats against the wall of the conference room.

"Have you ever been in here before?" she asked.

"Yes, for a few meetings. But it's mostly reserved for the board and medical staff."

"Glad I'm not presenting today!"

The room was loud with conversation and vibrating with anticipation. The table was set with heavy, ivory linen place mats and napkins. The noise grew louder over the clink of china, silver, and glasses during the luncheon service.

The room suddenly became quiet. Jason James, CEO, walked in with the chief nursing executive, Elaine Schilling, followed by Yasmin. Santos had only seen James once or twice, yet she knew Elaine well. She wondered how many in the room traded in the currency of information. There was power in information, and they wanted it now.

She noted that Mr. James, with his movie-star good looks, was dressed as usual with impeccable style. She had heard he had his suits custom made in Hong Kong. He straightened his French cuffs and designer red silk tie, preparing to speak. His thick, wavy dark hair, gray at the temples, was carefully styled. It was impossible to read what went on behind those dark eyes. He appeared unflappable, even cold and calculated. The man was more feared than respected. He was still considered a "Yankee" by many in the room, even though he had lived in Houston for ten years.

Dr. Schilling, the CNE, was wearing her favorite color, Baylor green. Santos thought she had never seen her look so tired. Her suit hung on her tall, lanky frame. Unlike Mr. James, Dr. Schilling was the heart of the organization. Nursing, after all, was the heartbeat of all health care settings. Over the years, Elaine had worked hard to first interest the board and senior administration in achieving Magnet status and then had built the professional infrastructure essential to create excellence in practice. Nurses at Medical Center Hospital were some of the best in the city.

While serving on the hospital shared governance council, Santos had learned that Elaine was the lone upper-level voice of the patient and family, since she was often the only clinician at the senior table. As more business executives from the energy and banking sectors sought executive roles, administration had shifted from patient care as the core business to making money as the core business. Held hostage by legal issues and sometimes regulators, decisions were not always about what was right, but about how to minimize the risk of liability and maximize the bottom line. Many patients and staff had never realized that their future laid in the hands of a single nurse leader whose voice of wisdom and compassion might or might not be heard by her colleagues. She saw Elaine as a warrior nurse, always defending the mission, the best in patient care.

Yasmin looked somber yet fascinated by the whole process. She was one of the youngest in the group, yet she looked focused and poised, ready for action. Dressed in a deep rose jacket and black skirt, she was polished and composed. Santos caught her eye across the room and gave a quick wave of recognition.

"Obviously there was a meeting before the meeting," Patrick whispered, nodding to the three who had just entered the room. "Those three have a script and are ready to take the stage."

"If we could have everyone's attention, please," Mr. James requested as he stood at the head of the table.

He placed the tips of his long manicured fingers on the table, squared his shoulders, paused, and looked around the room, gaining attention. He began to speak with authority in a carefully moderated, low, and even tone.

"Thank y'all for coming. I appreciate that so many of you took the time away from your busy schedules and the care of our patients to meet."

He nodded to a colleague, who began to pass around a yellow sheet of paper.

"We are here to discuss two important things: our media strategy and what communication we need to provide both internally and externally. We're passing around a briefing document that we will collect when this meeting is finished. But I want us to all be on the same page with the same information."

He paused to make sure that everyone had a copy of the document. While some immediately bowed their heads to read, he continued.

"I'll get right to the bottom line. After we've done all the research, there is a possibility that we have as many as four unexplained deaths in the CCU over the past ten weeks, along with a near miss that could have resulted in a fifth death."

A shocked "What?" escaped the mouth of a physician Santos did not recognize. Simultaneously, a nervous dietary staffer dropped a loaded tray of water glasses, spilling them on the table, the floor, and down the back of an unsuspecting member of the medical staff. The physician jumped out of his chair, outraged.

"What the hell!"

The room erupted. James lost control as people began talking all at once while hands shot up for questions. The room boomed with conversation, and staff quickly shut the door to the hallway.

James paused and waited. He did not respond to the raised hands or the conversation in the room.

"If I could have your attention, please," he asked loudly.

"We have a crisis on our hands here that could escalate into a media circus!" shouted an elderly, board member sporting a bow tie, his face contorted, purple with anger. Santos took a long look at him, worried about the possibility of a heart attack or stroke.

"Why have you taken so long to share this?" charged the enraged chief of surgery. Santos had heard rumors about him. Evidently, he had been away at a professional meeting for the past two weeks. His assistant, who had also attended, had posted on Facebook smiling pictures of them drinking wine on the beach. His wife found out from a friend. He was already having a bad day.

Before the meeting got any more out of control, Mr. James held his ground and started to speak while others were speaking. The room began to settle down, and he continued.

"We have recommendations around our media strategy and what should be communicated to our staff and our external stakeholders. Right now, I'm leaning toward a conservative approach until we know more. If we have a sentinel event situation, Elaine has advised me that it must be reported to the Joint Commission. If that is the case, we will be front page news. "

"We need to shut down the CCU!" cried a department director.

Santos cringed, picturing the impact of that suggestion on staffing and patient care and wishing she didn't feel so personally attacked.

"We are here to dialogue about this," James continued. "I need to tell you, though I am open to your input, time is of the essence. We can't deliberate all day. That said, at the end of the day, the final decision will have to be mine. I hold the ultimate accountability for the quality of care in this hospital."

"We'll see about that!" challenged a member of the medical staff known for his temper and public outbursts.

"This is a very complicated communication issue," Dr. Schilling's voice cut through the chaos with a nod from Mr. James. The room quieted and zeroed in on the new target. "We have obligations to consider. There are obligations to our staff and clinicians, to our patients and families, to our community, and to our regulators. These obligations are not just about information, but about what we are going to do administratively that demonstrates to our public what we believe, our values."

"As a group, we've had conversations before this meeting about what we believe in," began Yasmin. "We've agreed that we want to foster a culture of safety, free of blame, where staff will speak up. We believe that it is important that we share our concerns, that we are open with families, but also that our administrative actions and due diligence around discovery of what is going on be kept confidential for both legal and," she paused, searching for the right word, "investigative purposes."

"What do you mean, 'investigative'?"

"We are still working to determine the cause of the deaths," replied James. "We have a team of clinicians combing through the data, and we're hopeful that we'll discover what happened."

"You mean this has been going on for months and you're just now getting down to business?" shouted a board member who stood up and faced James. "You'd better start thinking about packing your bags if we don't get this thing buttoned down fast!"

～

Outside of the meeting room, a small group huddled, whispering to one another about what they had overheard. Walking by, he noticed the group and stopped.

"What's up?" he asked, gesturing to the door. "Another board meeting?"

"Not just another board meeting," replied one of the staff. "They're talking about what to do with the deaths in the CCU."

"There's a lot of shouting in there."

"Interesting," he said, nodding thoughtfully. "I'd be careful about being caught with my ear to the door." They got the message and scattered, returning to work.

"I need more intel," he said to himself and noticed a yellow piece of paper sitting on the bureau in the hallway. Looking around to be sure he was alone, he walked over, picked it up, and quickly tucked it into his notebook.

CHAPTER 39

"I can't believe they won't let us talk about this!" Santos said much too loudly. Everyone looked at the door of the break room. Thankfully, it was closed. "It is so unlike Yasmin to just give in. She knows better. She knows how serious this is ... how important it is that we nail this down. I can't believe she was a part of that decision."

Patrick jumped in. "Yasmin might have nothing to do with the decision. You heard James say that a team was working on the data ... and you heard his concern about the media, if this gets out."

A few members of the team had huddled for a quick caucus.

"It's got to be attorneys worried about the hospital being sued," countered Emma. "You know how litigious Texas is. Something goes wrong, everybody wants to sue."

"I heard that Heather got her hand slapped because we were honest with the Gideons," Wendy said as she walked in unannounced. She closed the door behind her.

"That's partially true," Patrick replied. "James didn't want her to say anything, but Elaine stood behind her."

"Our policy is to be open and apologetic to patients and families," Santos said. "The more I learn about James the less I respect him ... we just followed policy. You know, it's not just policy. It's the right thing to do!"

"What I've heard is that they don't believe this is anything but isolated situations. There's no proof that anything's wrong," Nick responded.

"Oh, come on, Nick, you know better than that,"

Patrick snapped. "We've never experienced sudden, unexplained deaths like this. To my knowledge, we've always been able to figure out what went wrong when we lost a patient. And we have the lab specimen from the Gideon case."

"You heard them, Patrick, there is to be no internal communication since it was decided that this was one isolated incident. There is no proof, right now, according to administration, that we've had a series of unexplained deaths," Nick said.

"Patrick, I agree with you, but Nick is right, too. The only evidence we have that something isn't right is that lab specimen. And that could be an isolated error," Santos responded.

"Santos, follow your gut. Don't be naïve," said Emma. "You can't just cave in to administration. They don't work at our level ... see what we see. Use your head and follow your heart."

"They want us to stop," Nick said. "No more meetings, no more discussions."

Patrick stood. "That ticks me off. Nick, what are you thinking? That everything's okay? That it's okay to stand by and let patients die?"

Frustrated, Patrick turned to Santos. "And you ... what about you? Remember thirty thousand-foot leadership? What are you thinking? What are you afraid of?"

Nick grabbed Patrick by the forearm as his temper flared. "Now wait a minute. Don't get on my case, Patrick. I've been with you all along. Just airing some of my concerns, that's all."

"It's a cover-up ... designed to protect administration from the media. This could potentially hurt more patients." Angry, Patrick paced around the room looking at each one of them in turn. "I can't stop. I'm not going to stop. My conscience and my gut tell me that something is very wrong here. I became a nurse to protect and care for patients. I don't know about you, Nick, or you, Santos."

"So what are we going to do? I'm confused," replied Santos.

"It's up to each of you, but I'm going to continue the search."

Ten seconds of silence went by while Patrick looked at each of them in turn.

"Come on, Santos, you have good instincts. You want the truth … are you with me?" He grabbed her hand, squeezed, and locked eyes with her. She hesitated for a moment and then smiled at him.

"I'm with you, Patrick. I don't know exactly what that means, but I'm with you."

He smiled back, moved toward her, and stopped himself.

"That's my girl!" said Emma.

"I'm not going to let you guys solve this without me," said Nick.

"Count me in. I think I can help here," replied Wendy.

"We really need you, Wendy," said Emma. "You're the only one who's been able to find us anything so far!"

"We'll have to do this under the radar," said Santos. "So what are we waiting for? Let's do it!"

CHAPTER 40

Santos lay awake. Once again, she was tired but wired. Her mind raced through the events of the past twenty-four hours. *Everything happens for a reason.* This situation was in her life for a reason; though she did not choose it, she was to learn from it. *That is why we are on the planet. That is why we meet the people we do and why we are given what we need if we open ourselves to the possibilities. It is the choices we make that create the pathways through our lives. The people we need come into our lives, and if we notice, they are there for a reason.*

This was a crossroads in her life, and she knew it—a developmental opportunity to lean in and solve the horrible problem that plagued her unit and the unsuspecting patients who came in believing they would be safe in the hospital. The deaths were devastating not only to the unit and immediate families, but they cascaded out, touching the entire community. They had to end.

She reflected on her own behavior. She was disappointed, embarrassed even, when she suggested that it had been an isolated incident. She felt as if she was letting the team down with her fear of rocking the boat. All this time she had a feeling there was something serious going on with the string of sudden deaths. *Why stop now?* It was important that she channel her passion and brainpower to help the team find the cause. They were such good people, the patients and the team. This was their problem. It was their unit. They owned it.

She wondered how her behavior, holding back when Patrick wanted to continue to dig deeper, to go against the grain of administration, was viewed by the some of the people she respected the most. She hoped that she had not lost their respect.

As was her pattern, lying on her back in the dark of her room, she asked for help. She silently reached out to her mother in spirit and to her other family who had passed, to her favorite saints, and asked that they give her the energy and courage to do the right thing. Holding her rosary, she fell asleep as the full harvest moon rose. It lit up the dark sky, and the night noises of the woods around her finally became still.

CHAPTER 41

Up at "o-dark-thirty" once again, he walked out to the driveway of his small, well-kept home to pick up *The Houston Chronicle.* Looking up, he lingered, captivated by the glow of the full orange moon just beginning to set in the early morning sky. *Full moons do wild and crazy things to people,* he reflected. He had learned from a medic years ago that the full moon brought the loonies into the emergency rooms and that babies were often born during them.

Carrying the paper into the house, he placed it on his Formica-topped kitchen table. Shuffling over to the kitchen counter, he filled his regular mug with strong black coffee and eased his way into the single chair at the table.

Quickly scanning the front page, he noticed a column heading: "Unexplained Deaths Rock Medical Center Hospital." He leaned back in his chair, sucked in a deep breath and whistled. He could not help but smile. He went on to read that *The Chronicle* had received an anonymous tip that up to ten patients had died over the past three months from unknown causes. Medical Center officials had "no comment."

Wonder where they got that number? The more the merrier. I bet the suits are flipping out over this one.

He had decided two days ago that it was time to create a diversion. Plant a bomb. It had worked.

He had learned from a colleague that the powers that be had decided these were isolated and random issues. There was no proof of any unexplained deaths. Legal had put the lid on any further discussion of the causes. When it was obvious that there was to be no internal communication about the deaths, he had gone to a local office supply store, thirty miles outside of his neighborhood, and anonymously faxed the yellow communication brief to the newspaper.

Now they would have to face this issue, or Joint Commission would be down their throats once this hit the press. The hospital could lose its accreditation status, and that would affect cash flow. Physicians would lose money. The political, financial, and public consequences of his little game would be more than he had ever dreamed possible.

He sat back and squared his shoulders. This was his baby. His mission. He was going to make them suffer, 'fess up for their screw-ups. Even with a conscience the size of a pea, he wondered how people in charge could conspire to hide patient deaths. They were covering their own tails. They needed to pay.

In a flash of insight, he considered the irony.

They aren't much different from me. They don't care about patient lives. Why should I?

CHAPTER 42

It was Friday morning. Wendy, having a bad hair day, and lab coat needing a wash, was desperate for a day off. She had slept little the night before and was operating on coffee and granola bars.

Last night, her three-year-old son had come down with an ear infection and needed the comfort of Mommy. She picked up his baby picture from her desk and gave the adorable little face a quick kiss through the glass. Born after years of infertility treatment, he was a treasured gift to both her and her husband, Raphael. Thank goodness, her son had Raphael's head of thick, curly dark hair and not her wispy, fine hair that frizzed in the humidity. She was especially grateful today that they had decided that Raphael would scale back on his job and be part-time day care for their son. Wendy was able to go to work with a clear conscience while Daddy watched over their little Carlos.

Leaving her desk, Wendy went to check for new orders. Scrolling down the list with her back to the rest of the lab, she had the uncomfortable sense that someone was watching her. She turned around to see one of her colleagues busy with a specimen. *What is his name? I should know his name.* She had seen him frequently and never paid him much attention. He always kept to himself. She remembered, with a quick flash of insight that he seemed to be around the CCU when they were meeting to talk about the deaths. *Maybe he's morbidly curious,* she thought to herself. She was glad that the team had made the decision to meet off campus, away from prying eyes. She shook off the mild feeling of paranoia and then looked at the stack of new orders. It was going to be another busy day.

CHAPTER 43

Wendy was getting too close. She was watching him all the time, tracking him. This was his game. He called the shots. They played his game with his rules.

He was particularly annoyed today because he had to float. The census in the hospital was down, blood chemistry was fully staffed, and they were taking turns covering the rest of the house. He had an order to collect a nasopharyngeal specimen from a patient they suspected had the novel H1N1 flu. Just what he wanted to do—be exposed to one of the most highly contagious viruses on the planet.

He knew all about viruses and what they could do. His obsessive-compulsive, disordered mind clicked through the statistics. From one hundred to one thousand times smaller than the average bacterium, viruses were resourceful predators. They could live, unseen, on hard surfaces like elevator buttons, tabletops, or restroom faucet handles for hours to days, where the unsuspecting person might touch them and then rub his eyes or blow his nose, bringing a load into the body. Viruses lived off cells until they destroyed them. Sometimes they could replicate so fast that the body's immune system would not have time to wage war with its army of white cells: lymphocytes, leukocytes, macrophages. By the time the body realized there was a problem, the virus could have taken over the lungs, the GI tract, or even the brain, and death or disability might not be far behind. Yes, he knew about viruses. He was living proof of what a virus might trigger.

Fuming, he took the elevator up to the fifth floor to collect the specimen. His anger masked his viral phobia.

He checked in at the workstation, found the patient's room, and then carefully gowned and gloved. Finally, he put on his mask and walked in. The patient, an elderly man, was coughing, spewing microorganisms into the air by the billions. *Get in and get out quickly,* he thought, holding his breath.

Exhaling, he explained the process, then took the swab out of its container and swabbed the patient's throat and nose. The mucus was thick and green: a definite signal that this was not your garden-variety respiratory infection. Masking his disgust, he carefully placed the swab back into the collection vial. Then he drew a blood sample for anti-body titers and quickly left the room.

Outside, he stripped off his contaminated gown, cap, mask, and gloves, tossing them into a nearby container. Then he walked over to the nearest sink and vigorously scrubbed his hands. As he washed, he shook his head at how many people thought that gloves offered total protection. He was not going to take any chances.

Heading to the elevator, he took a deep breath of relief that this one was over. He was terrified of viruses since suffering from Guillian-Barre Syndrome. He wondered how many people the patient had infected in the thirty-six hours before he even realized he was going to get sick. H1N1 was wildly contagious, killing nearly twenty thousand people in the US during a recent flu season—a season that now seemed to last all year long.

Back in the elevator, he was alone for a moment, and an idea popped into his head. If Wendy was getting too close, why not put her out of commission for a while? *Another flash of genius.* When the elevator doors opened, his mood had done a one-eighty, and he whistled softly as he headed to the lab to process the specimens.

CHAPTER 44

Back in the lab, he scanned the area, checking for witnesses. It was nearly deserted. Most everyone had left to grab a quick lunch or collect other specimens. He moved methodically, logging in, working through the paperwork, starting the analysis of the specimens, waiting for an opportunity to make his move.

He put on a clean set of gloves, swabbed the exterior of the vial with alcohol, and tucked the virus-soaked specimen vial into his lab coat pocket. Slowly and carefully, keeping an eye on the lab door, he moved over to Wendy's computer station. Removing the vial from his pocket, he dipped a cotton swab into the specimen, picked up her telephone and swabbed the mouthpiece and the handset. Then, for good measure, he brushed the swab across her computer keyboard.

In all of five seconds, he had successfully transferred millions of living viruses where Wendy would surely touch them. Unsuspecting, she would likely scratch her nose, or better yet, blow it, transferring the viruses to warm and nourishing mucus membranes where the minute killers could penetrate the blood vessels. Like all great parasites, they would find a new home, feeding on the living tissue of their host and bringing incredible misery to their victim.

He smiled. *Threat disabled.*

CHAPTER 45

From the patient's perspective, hospitals are an introvert's nightmare.

It had started out as a normal Sunday morning with the anticipation of a busy and fun day at home. Tom and Carol Sanders were still in love after three decades of marriage. They had a special weekend routine begun years ago: breakfast in bed with freshly brewed coffee in oversized white cups, whole wheat toast, lingering over the papers. She snuggled warm and cozy under the down comforter they had covered in dark green flannel. They watched the dawn break on an unseasonably cold Houston morning.

Weekends were a treat because they meant no commute for Tom, time for him to spend at home nesting and cocooning far away from the noise and congestion of the city. She was reluctant to emerge from the warmth of the flannel sheets, but with a long list of things to do, she got up, showered, and put on blue jeans, a turtleneck sweater, and a blue plaid polar-fleece jacket.

Carol stood at the kitchen sink, cleaning up the breakfast dishes and enjoying the feel of the warm soapy water on her hands, while Tom went out to wash one of the cars, braving the forty-something-degree weather. The cold did not matter to him; he called washing the cars his "meditation." It was a beautiful morning. She could see the ducks across the pond beginning to assemble for their orderly walk into the brisk water. The sun shimmered on the pond's surface, and the post oaks stood out in dark, craggy relief against the pale blue sky.

I need to call Santos, she thought. It was the one-year anniversary of Marianna's death. *Hope she's doing okay.* Marianna and Carol had been dear friends. When Marianna died, Carol was there for Santos. In many ways, Santos had become an adopted daughter to the childless couple.

Suddenly, everything changed. The pain began sharply in the back of her throat and burned up her jaw, radiating down her shoulders. She stood still, holding her breath, hoping it would pass. Then it continued down through her chest and into her abdomen, where she felt what seemed to be the warm and painful sensation of tearing tissue.

She walked two steps to the phone and picked it up, trembling fingers ready to call 911. She wondered if she could get to the garage door to call to Tom. Her worse-case diagnosis was not a heart attack, but an aortic aneurysm. Her Aunt Ruth had had an aortic aneurysm. Uncle Chips had found her bled out on the floor of their home. She did not want that to happen to Tom. She moved to the door.

Still nearly paralyzed by the intensity of the pain, she opened the door to the garage with phone in hand and said, "Can you come in now, please?"

Carol went back in and sat at the table, still holding the phone, looking at the ducks on the lake, wondering if this would be her last view. She had waited so long for this new house, this time in her life when she was not working, this time when she could notice and enjoy the precious and fleeting moments of nature.

He appeared, looking concerned. "What's wrong?"

"I have chest pain. This is different," she said, and went on to explain her symptoms.

"Have you taken aspirin yet?"

She shook her head and said "No," and he went over to the kitchen cabinet, pulled out two low-dose aspirin, and gave them to her with a glass of water. He waited a few moments.

"I think we need to take you in. We'll go over to the Community Emergency Center."

"I don't want to go." Carol stopped to think. "I will go, if you promise not to drive so fast as to raise my blood pressure."

A former critical care nurse, Carol kept her head, gathered her health insurance card and ID, and headed to the car. Tom drove carefully along the way, asking her on a regular basis if it had gotten any better. The spasm was just a dull ache by the time they pulled into the nearly empty parking lot of the neighborhood center.

Tom took Carol's arm as they left the car, and they walked into the building. Approaching the reception desk, he explained the reason for the visit, and they were quickly ushered into a room. The next few hours were a blur of activity: assessment first by the nurse-practitioner, then by the physician: vital signs, EKG leads attached, blood drawn, saline lock IV inserted, chest X-Ray, CAT scan. The room was an icebox of isolation—no clock or windows, no pictures, just white walls, white sheets, and white cabinets. It was so bone-chillingly cold that not only did she have goose bumps, but the hair on her arms stood at constant attention. Her only comfort was that the attentive staff kept piling warm blankets from the heated warmer that kept her comfortable for about five minutes.

She was trying to go with the flow, accepting the decisions of the health care team, but losing control over her destiny as most patients do. She knew too much, being a nurse. She could almost hear her late mother saying, "Snap out of it." The nitroglycerine tablet she placed under her tongue was at least warming her up a bit, and the headache was not as bad as they usually warned patients to expect.

What am I doing here? She apologized to Tom repeatedly for ruining his weekend.

"If I had it to do over again, we would have just waited at home and ridden it out."

"You know that's not the best thing to do. The earlier we get in, the better it is for you if it *is* a heart attack."

Dr. Fiorenza came into the room, closed the door, pulled up a chair, and sat down so that he was at eye level with her. He leaned in and said, "CAT scan and chest X-Ray were negative, your initial enzymes were negative, but I want to send you to the hospital for observation in the short stay unit."

She felt it like a blow. "Really?"

"Really. The city ambulance should be here in about twenty-five minutes, and they'll take you over to the hospital. You know that your initial enzymes could be negative, and they'll put you on a monitor and check your enzymes round the clock."

"A twenty-three-hour stay unit? Then I can go home?" she said while dreams of a peaceful weekend were dashed to bits.

The last place she wanted to be was in a hospital. She had spent over three decades of her life trying to make hospitals a better place for patients and staff, and it was still an uphill battle. As warm as the hearts were that beat in many of the staff, certain hospital units were as depersonalized as concentration camps. She knew this from experience, from working all over the country. Still, there was hope. Her last two hospitalizations had been positive; she was hopeful that this one would be, too.

While they were waiting for the ambulance to arrive, she gave Tom a list of things she would need.

"From my makeup drawer, bring me lipstick, under-eye concealer, my pick. I will need that small bottle of contact lens solution—it should be in my overnight bag—and my case. Don't forget my glasses."

Tom headed home to pack a suitcase while she waited in the room for the ambulance to arrive. The flurry of activity was over. Business had started to pick up in the Community Care Center, and Carol was alone in the cold treatment room.

What am I doing here? she wondered again. And then a new thought. *Maybe I should call Santos and see if she can help us?*

CHAPTER 46

On that bright Sunday morning, Santos and Patrick had agreed to meet for a late breakfast at Le Madeleine in Rice Village. Later, they would head over to Heather's for their team meeting. She arrived first. The restaurant was already bustling with customers, singles reading the paper or texting, and couples and families hunkered down for a hot breakfast on a cold morning. The delicious smell of freshly baked bread and pastries filled the air. Looking at the food delivered to the tables—omelets stuffed with spinach and mushrooms, French toast piled high with strawberries and whipped cream—made her stomach growl with hunger.

Helping herself to a cup of coffee, she added cream, and sat down at a table by the window where she could watch for Patrick. She had dressed in black slacks and a red fleece hoodie. Her hair was growing longer, and she had tied it back with a piece of red flannel. It was fun to dress warmly for a change; the cold weather gave her more energy. As she sipped her coffee, she saw his car pull into the parking lot.

I like him so much, she thought as she watched him methodically lock the Jeep and stride toward the restaurant. He was wearing a University of Texas burnt-orange button-down shirt and blue jeans. *He is cute,* she thought, *and smart. Such a good man.* And yet, their relationship confused her. The intensity of work kept them together but apart. *Is he the one?* She couldn't deny how good she felt around him. So happy. He was fun, cared about the same things she did. He had a great sense of humor. He challenged her to think, to grow. She took another sip of the steaming coffee. They had deliberately set this date to give themselves time to talk away from the hospital.

"Hi, there, don't you look pretty today. All in red."

He leaned down and his lips brushed her cheek with a quick kiss.

It felt right, respectful, comforting ... a kiss of friendship. Without thinking, she reached out for him. She put her hands on either side of his clean shaven face, breathed in the scent of his soap, and drew his face close to hers, kissing him softly on his lips. His lips were soft and warm ... her heart thawed, defenses crumbled. Frightened by wanting more she pulled back.

"Didn't know I was going to do that," she laughed, covering her face with her hands, embarrassed. "Sorry ...." She looked up at him, questioning, searching for his response.

"I don't mind. Let's do it again."

Before she could protest, he leaned down and gave her a quick, firm kiss with promise.

"What a way to start the day!" he said with a grin as he drew back.

"Patrick, enough is enough. Our first kiss and it's in public?" She looked around the crowded restaurant.

He sat down across from her and took both of her hands in his.

"What are we waiting for, Santos? I think you know I care about you. I hope you care about me. I'm not asking for a commitment or anything at this time. Let's just be together, discover what we might be as a couple."

And there was the confusion again. "Patrick, work is so complicated these days."

"Life is complicated. It isn't going to get any simpler

as we get older."

She looked into his eyes and saw his hopefulness. His strong hands warmed her small cool ones. She felt the connection and the promise of something more. It felt good and peaceful.

"You're right. We're friends. It's a good place to start. I don't know where it will end, though, Patrick."

"I don't think we need to worry about that right now. Every moment is precious. Let's take advantage of every one of them."

"I just don't know if I have the energy for a relationship right now. Work is ... you know how work is. It's tough right now. I always seem to be tired."

Patrick looked deeply into her eyes. She saw complexity and compassion. "Anything worthwhile is going to take energy, Santos. But I truly believe that if we click together, we will create energy, more than we have as individuals. If we are good for each other, it will still be work to develop a relationship, but you will get something back, something wonderful, something that sustains you and helps you grow. And me, too."

She drew back, serious and thoughtful. "Do you believe that we each have a path, Patrick? That though we make choices, we have a path in this life? How do we know if we are on the right path—the path we are meant to follow?"

"Wow, okay, let me see if I can track your thoughts. Yes, to a degree, I believe we have a path. But I don't believe in fate. I believe that we make things happen. That the choices we make open up possibilities."

"Did you ever read the book *One?*" she asked. "It was written by Richard Bach, the same guy who wrote *Jonathon Livingston Seagull.* My friend Carol loves that book."

Patrick shook his head. "No, tell me about it."

"I've talked with you about Carol, haven't I?" she asked.

"A little … why don't you give me the *Reader's Digest* version?"

"Okay. Carol and my mother were friends for years; they met at the women's shelter where they volunteered. When Mom died, Carol took me under her wing. She understood what it meant to lose a parent. And being with her made me feel, sort of, close to Mom. Does that make sense?"

"Yes, it does."

"Okay, back to the book. The book is about a happily married couple who, through some time warp, travels back and sees how the choices they each made could have kept them apart. The book shows where they were actually physically near one another, but the thoughts they had and the choices they made could have kept them apart. They might have never met, fallen in love, and gotten married."

"We've met, Santos. Something has brought us together. Now it is up to us to chart our future. Isn't it?"

"I agree. You must be in my life for a reason." Santos paused and shifted the conversation. "And right now, I'm starving! I saved myself for breakfast with you. So can we go and order?"

He squeezed her hands once more and pushed back his chair. "I've heard that you get cranky when you're hungry. Don't want that to happen."

"Who told you that?" She laughed, and they headed to the counter to place their order.

CHAPTER 47

The root-cause analysis team met that afternoon at Heather's comfortable home in the Braeswood area, not far from the Texas Medical Center. Heather and her husband, Don, had lived in the unassuming, rambling home built in the 1950s for over twenty years. Nick, Wendy, Emma, Santos, Patrick, Chad, and Susan arrived together, a collective of energy, walking and talking, getting caught up with one another as they entered the family home. Santos could feel the flow of teamwork. Their cumulative IQ and synergy was an amazing force to see and feel.

As Santos entered the house, she felt the peace and warmth of the family home, rich in history and memories. Heavy wood beams supported the high ceiling of the vaulted, spacious great room. Scores of framed pictures, chronicling a lifetime of events from Christmas to weddings to christenings, were scattered throughout the room. Piano music played softly in the background. Heather's collections of teapots were carefully arranged on the dark, knotty alderwood shelves that Don had built. The teapots were a combination of gifts, family heirlooms, and treasures collected on their travels. The room was a contrast of dark wood and light walls with warm indirect lighting.

Passing through the rooms, Santos felt cocooned, transported to a safe place, a place of tranquility. It made the traumatic events of the past months seem surreal and her earlier conversation with Patrick more real with a sense of possibility. There was life away from work. For a bare moment, the burden of solving the deaths felt lighter.

"So Nick, what's this I hear about someone by the

name of Nancy?" Patrick asked, jabbing his friend with his elbow.

"Give me a break, Patrick. We just met."

"Well, Nick, tell us about her," asked Emma as the group passed through the great room.

Santos thought Nick looked a little embarrassed, and she stifled a laugh.

"She's an anesthesia resident. Works her tail end off. I met her at Kelly's." Kelly's was a local gathering spot for the medical center and the starting place of more than one romance.

"I heard something else about her," teased Patrick.

"Oh yeah? Tell me something I don't know."

Patrick looked around to make sure he had everyone's attention.

"I heard that she was a University of Nebraska cheerleader!"

"Whoa!" shot Wendy.

"Nick, you didn't first see her at Kelly's," said Santos. "She helped us with the code, remember? She's gorgeous—even in scrubs!"

Nick thought for a moment. "Yeah, you're right. We were all so busy, I didn't even remember."

"Go for it, Nick!" Santos said. "About time you got yourself a life."

"Patrick, you and I will talk later," said Nick with a good-humored laugh. "You can be a real pain, you know!"

Emma smiled, grabbed Nick's arm, and said warmly, "Well, honey, we are going to have to keep tabs on this new romance."

Then Emma turned and looked at Santos and Patrick standing close together. She winked at them.

Patrick leaned over and whispered to Santos. "I think

she thinks there's something going on between us."

"Okay, everyone, enough is enough," said Heather. "Time to get going."

As Heather walked with them through the house, she told them how fortunate she felt to have such a dedicated team. They were truly a group of linchpins—each unique and creative, each committed to giving the best to patients and families.

Once more, Santos let herself feel the throb of connection and energy when the group was together. The team had persevered through the politics and would work together to find out what was going on. She felt blessed and comforted.

Heather had brought home a flip chart, and it was set up in the sunroom facing the huge bur oak in the backyard. She guided the team into the cheerful room, an addition to the original house. The room was long and narrow, painted pale yellow, with tall glass windows that warmed it in the winter and were shuttered to shade in summer. A comfortable sectional sofa, sprinkled with large pillows and vibrant crocheted throws, wrapped around a huge distressed, dark oak coffee table.

Heather had placed a large, colorful Talavera pottery platter loaded with cheeses, crackers, fruit, and olives on the coffee table for the crowd. Santos could smell granola cookies baking in the kitchen. She knew Heather loved any excuse to bake. With the kids gone, she had told Santos in the past that it was nice to have close colleagues to share her home. They were like family to her.

After everyone finally assembled around the coffee table in Heather's sunroom, Susan said, "Now, where are we?" Susan was wearing a loose-fitting, long, crinkle-cloth, deep-green caftan with a hood. Gold hoops dangled from her ears. Her shoulder-length black hair hung free and wavy across her shoulders. Under her direction, the team got organized. Some sat on oversized cushions with notes on the floor and snacks on the table. Others grabbed chairs and pulled them up, while the first to hit the couch staked out territory with comfortable pillows either placed behind their backs or hugged in their arms. A couple of laptops were open and ready to use, just in case research was necessary.

The doorbell rang, and Heather excused herself. She returned in two minutes, beaming her wide smile with Dr. Whiting by her side. The previously noisy group immediately stopped talking. They stood to greet him, surprised and uncertain, looking at each other. Why was Dr. Whiting here?

He took a long look at the group assembled around the coffee table. "When Heather told me that you were going undercover, I couldn't resist coming to join you."

Santos could see the smiles of relief on her teammates' faces.

He continued, "This is very important work. Probably more important than any of you realize … I wanted you all to know that I appreciate your commitment and courage. I'm here to help. May I?"

Nick quickly spoke for the group. "Of course, Dr. Whiting. This is great!"

The team rearranged themselves on the sofa to make room for him.

"When I first saw you in the doorway," Emma said, "I thought we were busted!"

The group laughed, and the tension broke.

"Everyone grab a snack," Susan said, "and let's get started. I want us to work on scenario planning."

"What does that mean? It feels like where're taking two steps back for every step forward." Santos asked the question everyone else wanted to ask.

"Good question, Santos. We need to work on possible concepts, or scenarios, of what might be going on. Thinking it through and creating potential scenario options A, B, C, and D, like that," Susan explained. "We also need to be very sure—that we believe strongly that the scenarios will hold up—to our colleagues ... and administration."

"Okay. The scenario planning sounds interesting. This seems to be taking forever though."

Susan summarized. "We know that the mechanism of death is very likely inaccurate lab data ... we are quite certain that the deaths so far involved potassium levels. Under what scenarios could this be possible? How could a series of lab results be inaccurate?"

Susan looked around the room and asked, "Any more questions?"

Wendy started to speak and sneezed, carefully covering her mouth and nose by tucking her face into her shoulder.

"Not right now," Wendy said, "but I'm sure I'll have some along the way. Gosh, I hope I'm not catching something. Sorry, y'all, I've just started to feel like I've been run over by a truck." The others looked at her with concern. She was starting to look flushed.

"Let me get you some hot tea and vitamin C," Heather said. "If you start to feel worse, I think you should go home."

"Thanks, Heather. I think I'll be just fine. We're all pretty tired right now. But I want to hang in there."

As Santos looked around the room, waiting for Susan to lead, she saw an exceptionally talented group of professionals, some young, some seasoned. Some appeared more exhausted than others. Nevertheless, they all looked expectant, committed, and hopeful, completely focused on the work at hand. Nick looked like he needed a shave badly, but that look was "in" these days—the "five o'clock shadow" of her era now considered rugged and sexy. Wendy, already sleep deprived from mothering a sick toddler, looked pale but determined, cradling a cup of tea in her hands. Patrick was disciplined and "on" as usual. Emma, in her maternal way, was making sure everyone had what he or she needed. Chad was quiet, just getting to know the group. Heather and Richard, as the formal leaders, were sitting back, letting the team begin their work. Susan's job as facilitator was to bring out the best in the group, guide the group in dialogue, and keep everyone on task, always with an eye on the clock.

The doorbell rang.

Heather looked at Richard. "I wonder who that could be. We aren't expecting company. Excuse me for a moment, everyone. I'm really sorry for the interruption."

"Maybe we really are busted!" said Nick with a sly smile.

The group chatted and snacked, waiting for Heather, who emerged in a minute with another visitor.

"Sheila! Great to see you! How did you know we were meeting?" Santos said.

"I thought it might be a good learning experience for her, since she was a part of this from the beginning. I hope ya'll don't mind?" Emma queried.

"Fine by me," said Heather. "Just as long as you agree to stick by our ground rules and keep this confidential."

"Not a problem," said Sheila.

"Sit down and grab something to eat. We're just going to dive in here, Sheila, so we don't lose traction," said Susan warmly.

"I totally understand," said Sheila and found a place to sit.

The group refocused, and Susan began.

"I want to take us back to our work on the fishbone diagram from a week ago." She directed the team to the flip-chart paper she had hung on a blank wall. "When we looked at potential causes, we started talking about errors. I want us to dig deeper and come up with at least three probable, not just possible, scenarios."

"Now, when you say 'probable,' you mean that we shouldn't get all wild and crazy?" Chad said, getting a laugh from the group.

"Yes, every scenario has to be probable, realistic, based in fact," Susan said.

Everyone nodded acknowledgment and continued to listen.

Wendy cleared her throat. "Okay, while I still seem to have a few brain cells functioning here, could I suggest that we look at two probabilities? Since I am the medical technologist on the team, I want to bring up human error in collecting and processing lab specimens. There's also the possibility of processor error." She sneezed, again trying to bury her nose in her shoulder.

Nick moved aside, giving Wendy room so that she could stretch out on the couch. Santos put a pillow behind her.

"You just lay there, honey, and we'll get you what you need," Emma said soothingly. "We need you to hang in here with us for a while longer."

"Did you get your flu shots this year?" Heather asked with a hint of hesitation.

Wendy sighed. "I got the regular flu shot but the combo came out later."

"Well, let's not jump to conclusions right now," Heather said. "Just keep your hands clean, watch your sneezing, and we'll pump fluids into you."

"Sorry, y'all. I hope that if I do have the flu, I won't infect you!" Wendy said.

"Okay, everyone. Let's keep going here. Wendy, your two scenarios sound plausible. What do the rest of you think?" Susan asked.

"I would like to add a third one," Santos added. Then she paused. She knew how awful it sounded, but she just could not let this one drop. "Beyond human and process errors, I think we have to consider that someone might be deliberately manipulating the system. I've mentioned this several times before this meeting and no one really wants to take it seriously."

"You mean—someone tampering with lab results? I hear you now!" Wendy sat up.

The group was suddenly stunned quiet.

"I agree with Santos. I believe that it's entirely possible," said Patrick.

"That's really frightening," Emma said. "Wendy has told us over and over again that seventy percent of health care decisions are based on lab results. The implications are horrific."

"Criminal background checks on staff can do a lot, but they don't screen out everything. And often they're limited to the specific state," said Heather.

"You mean we could be helping to kill patients and not even know it?" said Sheila, quietly shifting to attention from her relaxed position on the floor to her knees.

"We all know that there is a tremendous amount of psychopathology out there. Didn't I just read that at least fifteen percent of the general public may have a mental health disorder?" Nick added.

"I read this book called *The Sociopath Next Door*, and the author says that as many as twenty-five percent of the population may not have a conscience," said Santos.

"After the Wall Street debacle and the Deepwater Horizon's oil spill, I can believe that—not to bring politics into this," said Patrick. Nick made a smart remark back.

"Okay, everyone, settle down now. Let's take this step by step, as Susan has suggested," Richard remarked. "These events have serious repercussions," he glanced at Heather who nodded.

"Remember," Susan began, "we've talked about the fact that specimens could be drawn out of order, and that could lead to a false result."

"And I told you that if a blood specimen was chilled, and it shouldn't be, that could lead to a false result," Wendy added.

"If the specimen was labeled incorrectly—the wrong patient name—we would get the wrong lab result," Santos added. "There has been a huge push to make sure we are bar coding and attaching the labels when we send the specimens down. But there could be a glitch."

"Are there new people on staff, Wendy? Sometimes with inexperience, we see errors," Emma remarked.

"Like we do when a new crop of residents arrive in July?" Patrick said with a look at Nick.

"These days, with the economy, we've had very little turnover. Same group of staff. In fact, we haven't even had students rotating through," Wendy responded.

"Didn't you also tell us that specimens could be improperly diluted or the wrong reagents added?" said Chad.

"Yes," Wendy said. "And if the equipment is out of

calibration, it could also be a problem."

There was sobering silence for a moment as the realization sunk in. This was much more complicated than they had ever realized.

"Oh, and something else," Wendy said slowly and somberly. "Medical technologists check all the results before they're posted on the patient electronic record. It's possible that someone could adjust the lab results when they are recorded there."

"So let me play this out," Santos said slowly. "If I was skillful, knew the system, and was sick, I could tamper with lab results or post different results or the wrong results anytime I wanted to?"

All eyes went to Santos. The only sound in the room was the ticking of the grandfather clock.

"It's worse than that," said Wendy, wiping her eyes after another sneeze. "It would be nearly impossible to trace. Techs can work in isolation on their own specimens. They can access lab results from almost any computer. Plus, they will usually be working with multiple specimens and results."

"Can't you track computer entries like we track staff access to medical records?" Heather asked.

"We would have to trace every single data point with every staff member and hopefully find some link to the patients who've died. And we don't have a clue how many patients might have been affected."

"So this could be much bigger than we ever thought," commented Emma.

"In my case, where potassium was the culprit, you mean someone could manipulate and change almost any lab result?" Santos said.

Wendy nodded. "Some more easily than others."

After a brief pause where everyone kept their thoughts to themselves, Susan redirected the team.

"All the deaths were a result of sudden cardiac death. All were nonorganic?"

"Yes," Richard spoke up. "We ruled out all potential clinical causes of sudden cardiac death." He had been following the conversation intently.

"I think we need to focus on what we know," Heather said. "This is like creating world peace or solving world hunger. Let's focus on what we know and what we might be able to do something about."

"I agree," said Susan. "Let's try to hunker down here and really focus on the lab results that could trigger sudden cardiac death by omission or commission."

"Like what I did when I administered KCL to a patient with a normal-to-high level of potassium," Santos said. "The lab value I reviewed was low, triggering administration of KCL, when in fact, his potassium was really within the high range of normal. The administration could have killed Mr. Gideon."

"Okay, that's commission," Chad said. "What would be an example of omission?"

"If we had an actual low potassium level and the lab result came back as normal, and we did nothing about it. The patient could die either in the hospital or at home," offered Patrick.

"While we're on potassium, let's focus on this one right now," Susan suggested.

"Potassium has been known as the 'Kevorkian killer,'" Chad added.

Santos jumped in. "Yes, you got it. What triggered my response to Mr. Gideon was my time in the OR, when we used KCL to stop the heart from beating during cardiac surgery. I saw the same EKG pattern and knew something was wrong."

"Let me summarize here," Susan began. "There are any number of ways a lab test could be inaccurate, altered, or tampered with—through an error in the way it was collected, being chilled when it shouldn't be chilled, or because of tubes drawn out of order. The test results could be adjusted while posting in the EHR. Tubes could be switched. Samples diluted. We know who has died, suddenly, from sudden cardiac death. We know what has happened in the twenty-four hours before death. What we still don't know is how it was done, who did it, and why." Susan paused to take a sip of water.

"Susan, we may not know the 'why' until we know the 'who,'" added Santos.

"I agree," Patrick said. "The only thing we have, from a criminal perspective, is opportunity ... we don't have motive. I think we need to put aside our fears of blaming someone and zero in on who this might be."

Suddenly Wendy sat up and threw the blanket off her legs.

"I may have an idea who it could be ... I hate to say it. But there is this guy I work with ... maybe you would recognize him. He gives me the creeps. I can't believe it—I don't even know his name!"

CHAPTER 48

While the team was meeting, trying to get a handle on the events at the big house, Carol was on her way to the community hospital, south of town, in the ambulance. Thankfully, there were no lights or sirens. She wanted to call Santos, but she did not want to disturb her on a weekend. She could use a patient advocate. While a patient, it was difficult to be a nurse. Carol was terrified of being hospitalized. She knew everything that could go wrong. Santos would be a great help, especially with her clinical background in cardiology.

The paramedic, young enough to be her son, and the ambulance driver wheeled her into the hospital to the "obs unit," as they called the units where patients stayed for twenty-four hours or less for observation and evaluation to determine if they needed to be admitted. The nursing assistant pointed to a gurney with a cubicle curtain for walls.

"This is your bed," she told Carol. "I'm the PCA and the unit secretary here. We're short staffed. Let me know if you need anything." Then she turned around and walked away.

Carol sat gingerly on the edge of the bed, looked up at the TV suspended from the ceiling, and listened to the drone of the patient behind the curtain next to her watching the local news. Then she looked at the plastic chair where Tom would sit for hours on end and thought about spending the night sleeping with strangers.

I bet they keep the lights on all night long, too, she thought.

She sighed. *All nurses need to be patients periodically,* she told herself. *It keeps us in touch, reminds us how it feels.* Feeling cold and vulnerable, she got in motion and set out to find the bathroom.

She returned to her room a few minutes later. A PCA came, took her blood pressure, pulse, and temperature, placed monitor leads on her chest, gave her a bag and strap to wear the wireless device while she walked, and left. Tom arrived with the suitcase and looked with disappointment at the hard plastic chair by her bed.

"Nice place here. What's going on?"

"I don't have a clue. I haven't seen a nurse yet. I don't know if I want to do this."

"Could we have some water, please?" Tom said to a passing staff member who avoided eye contact. The staff member sighed and a few minutes later brought a Styrofoam cup of water and ice.

"What's the plan?" he said.

"I don't know. Let me find out." Carol went over to the workstation, observed a staff member surfing the web, and asked if she could talk with her nurse. She returned to her bed. Her nurse arrived, introduced himself, and answered their questions simply.

"You will have blood drawn every six hours. The doctor has ordered a stress test. I'm not sure we can get it done today. You may have to wait until tomorrow. I think you can still order lunch—it's served until two. Once the cardiologist reads your stress test, you'll go home or be admitted."

Without another word, he turned around and left.

"I thought that last thing they were supposed to say was, 'Is there anything else that I can do for you before I go?'" Tom said with sarcasm.

Carol, preoccupied, ignored his comment. "I hope my IV holds for bloods."

She had small veins. The fact that her right arm was the only one available for IVs and blood draws compounded the problem: she'd had a lumpectomy and removal of her lymph nodes on her left side for breast cancer some years before. Limiting trauma and fluid in that arm was supposed to prevent the swelling of lymphedema.

"It'll be okay, Honey. Hopefully they're pros here," he said.

She was not too sure. They settled down for a long afternoon of waiting.

CHAPTER 49

When evening came, Carol ordered some dinner. The hospital had adopted the room service feature where patients could order whatever they wanted off a menu from 6:30 a.m. to 8:30 p.m. So far, this was the best thing about her stay. She had not eaten since breakfast.

"Things can really change in a minute, can't they?" She looked at Tom and squeezed his hand. "Here we are ... lovely hospital cuisine," She attempted a smile, "Instead of grilling out and sitting in front of the warm fireplace at home with a glass of wine."

"I'll make it up to you tomorrow," he said. "Whatever you want. Stay home or eat out." He looked at her tenderly.

She reached over to stroke his face. She loved him so much at that moment. Hard to believe after so many years you could still love someone more every day.

"Honey, you look as exhausted as I feel ... go home," she glanced at the clock. "It's after nine ... get some rest."

"I don't want to leave you alone."

"I don't want to be alone either, but I'll be fine. Just come back before I leave for my stress test, OK?" She smiled. "Give me a kiss."

"Move over."

Carol scooted to make room for him in the narrow bed. He wrapped his arms around her and she felt the warmth of his body. Tears formed in her eyes and her heart ached with love.

After Tom left, Carol was anxious and alone with the nightmare of her thoughts. She clutched her cell phone tightly; it was her connection to the friendliness and warmth of the world outside. Surrounded by the hustle and bustle in the halls, the floor cleaned by a power washer at 10:38 p.m., and blood drawn at midnight, she felt isolated and alone.

She knew hospitals too well. Though they were places of hope and miracles, they were also places where bad things happened. Patients had wandered off their units and been found frozen to death. Patients developed septic shock and died. Patients sometimes received the wrong drugs or the wrong dose. Until "time out," a safety net where a nurse stops a procedure and asks to verify, surgeons could amputate the wrong limb or treat the wrong body part. No safeguards in the world were enough to keep all patients safe. The nurse was the first and last line of defense for patients. Unfortunately, Carol lacked confidence in this particular group.

She closed her eyes and tried to sleep. She dozed on and off all night with the lights blazing overhead. She knew that she would wake up feeling jet-lagged, dazed, and exhausted. The unit finally went to sleep around two, and there was quiet.

Chapter 50

The days were getting shorter. Soon it would be dark when he got up and dark when he came home. He dreaded this time of year. Everyone was cheerful, anticipating the holidays. He could not remember the last time he'd gone to a holiday party or a home for a family gathering.

His seasonable affective disorder would soon kick in, triggered by the declining light. Then he would pack on the pounds. Depression would take him down, deep, like an undertow. He had no hope of rescue. The only thing that kept his despair at bay was the intellectual stimulation of the game in play.

He never thought of the kills as murders; most of the time he was able to rationalize why a certain subject became a target. Sometimes it was to test their stamina, like that big guy who seemed so arrogant when he drew his blood. Giving the "I hope you know what you're doing" line. Was he stupid? The man risked his life when he challenged the master.

Or the lady with the chronic heart disease? She was old and frail anyway. Maybe she was tired of living. Maybe that son of hers inherited some money. That would be a good thing.

Then there was always the game of hide-and-seek he was playing with the medical staff, who still had not figured this thing out—-even with the VIP. *Stump the Secret Service. That one was really fun.* It was time to expand the field and the rules of engagement. In finite games, he who launches the game makes the rules and decides how and when it will end.

Tonight he was driving south of the Texas Medical Center. He had a country music channel playing softly on his radio. Normally he drove in silence, concentrating on the road. Tonight, it was a long drive. They were rotating lab staff across the system to increase efficiency and flex the coverage. It was his time to float to the hospital twenty miles away from the big house, as they all called the flagship or main hospital. For his purposes, floating was a good thing. It kept him moving and out of constant sight. He did not mind the drive since it was late on Sunday night and it gave him time to think.

His mind mulled over the kills of the past, thinking it was getting too easy.

Time to widen the net. Expand the game.

He pulled into the parking lot and easily found an empty spot close to the entrance. He was excited to get to work, his mind racing with the details of the possibilities. Once inside, he asked for directions from the security guard posted in the front lobby. Then he found his way down the quiet corridors to the lab.

CHAPTER 51

During the graveyard shift, he analyzed the lab tests that had been coming in all night. Time passed quickly. Looking up at the clock, he noted it was already 4:30 a.m. He decided to take a break before he began the morning lab draws. He walked over to the cafeteria to grab a cup of coffee. The good news about today was that he would be driving home in the daylight.

When he walked on the short stay unit to collect specimens at 5:00 a.m., it was still quiet. The night shift was in the lounge making coffee, most of the patients were sleeping behind curtains, and the brightly lit halls were empty. It was quiet and peaceful on the unit, the calm before the next shift arrived and brought the hustle and bustle of a shift change, admissions, discharges, and transportation to tests. As he walked down the hall, his Vibram-soled shoes made no noise. This was his favorite time, and he had deliberately planned his arrival so that he could come and go relatively unnoticed.

He had spent the night monitoring all the blood tests from the unit, and now it was time for him to "meet the patients," his favorite part of the game. He went from bed to bed and collected specimens, made notes, and labeled them carefully. One of the patients was awake when he came in. She was dressed in blue jeans and a blue polar-fleece jacket. That seemed a little strange.

She looked up.

"More blood?"

He nodded.

"What are you drawing this time? "

"Just the tests the doctor ordered."

"It's okay to tell me. I'm a nurse. I'd like to know. Can you please draw them from my saline lock? My veins are shot."

"Lipid profile, cardiac enzymes, electrolyte panel ... that's what has been ordered for this draw. I'll need three tubes," he replied. "And yeah, I can take it from your port. But I'm good with the needle; I've started IVs on myself with one hand."

She did not comment.

He collected her blood samples, efficiently made his rounds on the other patients, and quietly left before any of the nurses emerged from the lounge. As he rounded the corner in the deserted hallway, he smiled. Playing the game here would be fun. They would never know.

The target was obvious; the symmetry perfect.

CHAPTER 52

It was still dark when Tom got out of his car in the well-lit hospital parking lot. He braced himself for another frigid morning. He carried a thermos of her favorite hot coffee.

"Hey, Tom!" he heard shouted from behind. "What are you doing here?"

Surprised, he glanced around to see who had called him.

He saw Santos, red scarf blowing in the wind, wave to him and head his way. He was surprised how relieved he was to see her. When she reached Tom, they exchanged a quick hug of greeting. Her cheeks were cold.

"What are *you* doing here?" he replied. "Aren't you supposed to be staffing the big house? You're the last person I expected to see."

"I'm down here to do a CE course for the nurses. Came over early to get my bearings, find the conference room, and grab some coffee. I hear they have a great cafeteria here." She spoke in rapid-fire, typical critical-care nurse speak. "Okay, enough of me. Why are you here?"

"Carol had chest pain yesterday morning. I brought her in to the emergency center and they moved her here for observation."

She grabbed his arm. "Is she okay? Why didn't you call me?"

Tom saw concern and sadness in her eyes. Santos and Carol had spent a lot of time together, especially after Marianna's death.

"I'm sorry we didn't, Santos. Try not to worry. We didn't have time. The good news is so far the lab results are negative, CAT scan negative. We're waiting on the stress test this morning. You know how private she is. But if she would call anyone, it would be you."

Santos quickly looked at her watch, then took his arm again, propelling him forward. "I've got time. Let's go in and see her."

CHAPTER 53

While Santos went to check out the conference room, Tom hurried to the observation unit with his thermos of forbidden coffee for Carol. He walked in to find his wife was sitting up in bed, wearing the clothes she'd worn yesterday. She was gray with fatigue.

"Morning, Honey. I missed you," he said and leaned down to kiss her.

"Missed you, too." She managed a weak smile. "Thank goodness you brought me coffee. There is no coffee like your coffee. It will help me feel like I have a piece of home." She unscrewed the top, poured the coffee into the lid, and sat warming her hands, inhaling the rich fragrance. "Tom, I'd love to take a sip now, but I can't risk it with the stress test."

"Oh, I'm sorry ... but, I have another surprise for you ... hmm, maybe not a good choice of words," Tom said. "Guess who I ran into in the parking lot? Your guest should be arriving any moment."

Before he could say another word, Santos parted the cubicle curtain and dashed in. Carol's face broke into a smile. Tom watched them exchange the warm hugs of dear friends. He took a deep breath and thought, *We really aren't alone.* Though he had downplayed the incident while talking with Santos, he was very worried.

"Must be cold out there! Your cheeks are flushed and cold. You look beautiful as usual, Santos." Carol smiled, holding Santos at arm's length. "It is so good to see you."

"I wish you had called me. I would have been here sooner."

"It was the weekend. We didn't want to bother anyone," Carol replied. She hesitated. "I know this is a little out of the ordinary, but would you check my orders and my labs? I think the staff is getting a little tired of my hands-on and need-to-know approach. I know it's hard to have a nurse on the unit, much less a former chief nursing officer. I'd just really like to know how things are looking."

"Let me see what I can do." Santos dropped her purse and notebook on the chair. "I've got a couple of minutes before I have to run to the conference room."

"Oh, don't worry. I'll be fine," Carol said. "I don't want you to be late."

"Not a problem. This will only take a sec," Santos said, giving her dear friend a quick hug and a warm smile. "What are friends for?"

Santos joined a few of the nurses at the desk. They chatted for a few moments, and she scanned the patient record. Then Santos thanked the staff and quickly returned to Carol's cubicle.

"You had your blood drawn early this morning?"

"Yes, a whole battery of tests. This should be the final cardiac enzymes."

"As soon as your results are in, if they are good, when the doctor comes in, you should be good to go!"

"Great! When will that happen?" Carol responded. Tom thought she looked relieved.

"Labs will be up shortly, and the docs usually arrive early to do their rounds. I bet you'll be out of here by noon at the latest."

"Sounds good to me," Tom said.

Carol smiled back at Tom. He pulled up the chair by her bed, sat down, and reached over to take her hand.

Santos glanced at the clock on the wall.

"Got to go! I'm sorry to just drop in like this ... by the time I'm finished with class, you'll be out of here." She leaned over to give Carol one last big hug. Her cheek lingered on Carol's and she whispered, "I love you so much; you know ... Mother loved you so much."

Tom watched Carol's eyes fill with tears. "Yes, I know, and I loved her very much. You look more like her every day ... Now go! You don't want to be late," Carol said, smiling.

"Tom, you'll call me when you know what's going on? You have my cell?"

Tom nodded, and Santos picked up her coat and scarf, then left with a quick wave.

Tom turned to Carol. "I slept awful last night without you."

"I know, Honey. But you were sleeping in our bed, you lucky man." Carol gave him a kiss and quickly changed the subject, on a new mission. "Do you know of any nice single guys? She's so beautiful and so good. She needs to find a boyfriend and get married, have kids, find a life away from work ... that one, I feel like she's running away from commitment. Maybe she doesn't want to be hurt?"

"Honey, Santos will find the right guy when she's ready. But I'll think about it. Let's just focus on getting you out of here."

CHAPTER 54

As Santos rapidly walked down the hall, she was introspective. Tom and Carol really reminded her of the Gideons. They shared the same deep love and commitment. She smiled with a sudden, bittersweet pang. In her heart, she longed for that kind of relationship. *Was Patrick the one? Could they have something as warm and beautiful as this love?*

Deep in thought, Santos headed to the conference room. She saw the lab tech from Medical Center Hospital. *What is he doing here?* They made quick eye contact, and Santos gave him a nod of recognition. Then, recalling that staff sometimes floated to the outlying hospitals, she dismissed the question in her mind. Thoughts of love, Patrick, and the unknowns in her future consumed her mental energy until it was time to get to work.

⌒

Seeing Santos sent a jolt of anxiety through him like a lightning bolt of electricity.

Stunned to see her away from the medical center, he stopped for a moment ... then, acting on reflex, no thinking required, his cold, steel core kicked in. He turned and purposefully lumbered away with his crutch supporting his weight.

She saw me. She recognized me. What if she puts two and two together?

He began to sweat as he walked to the lab, lifting his leg, weight supported by the crutch, and then dragging it forward. His anxiety, always under the surface, began to spill into his consciousness, threatening to distract him from his mission. Anger, held in check for so many years, quickly emerged and replaced the anxiety with the determination and focus he needed to stay on track.

The anger gave him energy.

On autopilot, he continued the positive self-talk.

Just creates a greater challenge, he thought. *I'm going to have to keep a closer watch on her and the rest of the team. Probably time to take another one of them out of the game. Mission accomplished with Wendy; she called in sick for Monday. Time to even the odds. Make it more fun. What should I do this time?* He smiled, considering his choices, turned the corner, and headed to the lab.

CHAPTER 55

Tuesday dawned clear and cool.

While Santos had been giving the CE course and working with the nurses in the community hospital on Monday, a subset of the team met to study the matrix of all patients who had unexpectedly died in the past three months and drill down into the data. Santos was anxious to hear the results.

At the end of multidisciplinary rounds, when the room cleared, the team who had been working under the radar met to study the data in detail. Upon review of all the electronic patient records, they found that every single patient had a blood chemistry panel immediately prior to death. Potassium results up to the last electrolyte study had been normal, and then the last test before death had come back either low or high normal. In some cases, they had done nothing because the results had come back normal. In other cases, like Mr. Gideon's, they had administered KCL to bring up a false low value: omission and commission.

Not only that, but there had been more than four deaths that fit the description. The discovery process pointed to the probability of fabricated lab results in the cases of Mrs. Adams, Mrs. Verona, Mr. Gideon, and four other male patients who Santos did not recognize.

"Mrs. Adams, too!" Santos exclaimed. "I had a feeling. I hoped it wasn't true ... she was such a doll."

"I know. We were all close to her. And there may be even more that we can't find. But seven in three months is significant," Patrick said.

"I hate to say this, Santos, but I have more bad news,"

Emma said. "Wendy does have H1N1, so she's going to be out for a while. Her husband told me that she's really sick and feels awful that she may have exposed us. She's also upset that she can't be with us, solving this case."

"This could be a real setback for us," Santos replied.

"Oh Santos, I do have some good news," said Patrick with a smile.

"I could use some good news right now."

"Remember the code we responded to on Jones 6? The VIP?"

"How could I forget?"

"Well, she finally went home last week. Isn't that great?" Patrick smiled.

"You're kidding ... that's amazing! Such wonderful news!" Santos replied. "Thank God. I thought for sure she wasn't going to make it. Her husband must have been terribly worried. I bet Dr. Whiting is relieved."

Santos paused for a moment, thinking. She saw Patrick look at her quizzically.

"Patrick, remember during her code, what Whiting said about the INR? He said it couldn't be right. It was normal and she was hemorrhaging. Remember? Is it possible that whatever this is, this 'killer,' dare I say it, has moved outside of CCU and is targeting patients outside of CCU?"

Santos felt her cell vibrate and pulled it out of her pocket to check who might be calling her at work. When she saw Tom's name, she looked at the group and said, "I probably should take this call. Excuse me. This conversation *has* to be continued."

Santos left the conference room and headed to a quiet alcove of the hallway.

"Hi, Tom. What's up? How's she doing?"

There was silence on the end of the line.

"Tom? Are you there?"

"I'm here."

"Tom? What's wrong?"

After a long, drawn-out sigh, Tom said, "I have very difficult news." He paused. His voice was a whisper.

"Carol's gone … she's dead."

Santos felt as if something had slammed her in the chest. She leaned against the wall for support.

"What? What happened?"

After a moment he said, "I would have called you sooner, but I was so caught up in what happened yesterday, her family, my feelings …." His voice trailed off into sobs.

Shocked and drained, Santos could not contain the tears that spilled from her eyes and trickled down the side of her face. Glued to the phone, she mindlessly hunted in her pocket for a tissue. Deep devastation rocked her. She thought she might faint she was so lightheaded; overcome by dizziness, she leaned against the wall.

She did not see Emma until the older nurse was standing right in front of her.

Tom continued, "We thought that everything was fine. But they were concerned about her blood work. Something about her blood chemistry. They gave her a dose of KCL, I think they said. She seemed fine, but right before they took her off the monitor, she started having these bad heartbeats."

He paused. Santos could hear him breathing hard.

"They couldn't stop them. So they called a code, did CPR, but they couldn't bring her back." His voice cracked. "She was strong and healthy. I should never have taken her to the hospital. It's my fault."

"Oh, Tom … oh my God, I'm so sorry." In shock and

pain, words of comfort escaped her.

"Listen, I've got to go. I just wanted you to know. She loved you so much. You were like a daughter to her. I hope you know that," he said.

He hung up.

Santos stood in the hall, immobile, stunned by the news.

"Oh, Emma!"

Santos let Emma take her by the arm and walk her to the staff lounge. Thankfully, no one was there. Santos sat down in shock. She could only stare at the glass of water Emma had placed on the table in front of her. Stunned, her mind and emotions were reeling.

"Drink," Emma said softly. Santos looked at Emma, seated beside her, and looked into gentle brown eyes filled with compassion and sorrow.

Santos took a sip and tried to hold herself together.

"Talk to me … what happened?" Emma asked.

"My friend, Carol, died." She paused. "I just saw her yesterday at the hospital. She was fine, ready to go home. She died. That was her husband, Tom, calling to tell me what happened."

"Oh honey, I'm so sorry. This has been such a hard time for you, hasn't it?"

"It seems like it's one thing after another. I feel so powerless to do anything … for anyone. I'm wiped out. Look at me. I'm a wreck! First Mother, then this … why is this happening to me?"

Through eyes blurred with tears, Santos looked at Emma. *Always a rock, always present.* She was unflappable. But Emma had a family to support her. She had Leon, the love of her life, and her children at home. She had kids to hug and kiss, baseball games to watch, hopes of grandchildren. Santos felt empty. Her life, up to this point, revolved around work. All that work. Was it worth it? She needed someone to hold her, love her, and never go away.

The door to the lounge opened. Santos looked up. Embarrassed by her tears, she was anxious that no one see her. Her nose was running, and she blew into the tissue that Emma offered.

Patrick came in. He stood in the doorway looking confused. She saw his vivid blue eyes quickly change from cool with confusion to warm with concern.

He walked over, pulled up a chair, and sat on her other side. She turned away from Emma to face him.

"What's wrong? Santos, baby, what's wrong?"

"Oh, Patrick, I can't believe it!" Without hesitation, she threw her arms around his neck, clung to him and sobbed into his shoulder. "Hold me ... I can't believe all of these terrible things ...."

After a moment, Emma pushed back her chair and got up. "You need me anymore?"

Santos pulled back from Patrick. Her nose was running and the tears continued to flow.

Emma reached down and passed Santos another clean tissue.

"Blow your nose," Emma said.

Santos blew into the tissue. "Thank you, Emma. I'm sorry for losing it like this."

"Honey, better to get it out of your system. You're safe here." Emma smiled and headed for the door.

A thought popped into Santos's head.

"Emma, stop, don't go."

"What's wrong?" Patrick looked at Santos with concern.

"*Por Dios!* I may be crazy ... but what if ... is it possible that Carol's death … I don't know how to say it. But could Carol's death be another one? Oh, Patrick, what do you think?"

"Santos, I can check on it. I don't know what Tom said to you."

"He said they gave her KCL and she had some bad heartbeats. And everything was fine before that."

"That's enough for me." He quickly pushed his chair back, then reached over to brush her hair from her face. "Will you be okay if I leave you alone right now? I can start working on this."

"Yes. We have to find out if she was another victim. If I ever find this person …." Santos's sorrow gave way to galvanizing anger. "We must find him, whoever, whatever he is. We must find him."

Chapter 56

Anonymous, cloaked in his white lab coat, he observed many things while collecting specimens and drawing blood in the CCU that Tuesday. He saw the team of "super heroes" meeting in the conference room after multidisciplinary rounds, and he thought he heard something about a "chart matrix" and then heard the name "Adams" cried out by Santos, obviously in dismay.

Then he saw Santos come out of the room into the hallway to answer her cell phone. He did not want her to see him hovering, so he backed off. Looked like bad news. She was cute, he thought, even when she cried. Made her eyes get even bigger and darker. They sparkled with her tears. He bet she was feisty, though. And smart. *I need to keep her close.* Keeping her close would have its rewards.

He had a sense that they were beginning to put the pieces of the puzzle together. He was pleased that Wendy was out of the way, probably for as long as he wanted to play the game. She would get over the flu, but it had gotten her off his back. Maybe the next time he needed to collect a specimen from an infectious patient, he would find another use for it. Viruses were created for a reason!

After seeing Santos at the Community Hospital, he'd thought a lot about who on the team should be next. *Just put a few more obstacles in the way of their chase.* He had made his decision, and now, it was merely a matter of timing. Timing was everything.

CHAPTER 57

Santos and her sister, Camilla, went to the Funeral Mass for Carol at St. Anthony of Padua Catholic Church in The Woodlands. Everything in life seemed to be spinning out of control. Santos felt as if she had lost her balance.

Camilla, with her sixth sense, had called the day after Carol died. Santos was riding the bus home from work when she got the call. She started to cry as soon as she heard her sister's voice. Though Camilla could at times be overbearing, if there was a problem, her compassion and sensitivity came online in full force. Camilla had wanted to be a nurse, but she had married young and focused all of her efforts on raising their three sons, now grown men. With her maternal instincts, she knew exactly what to do and say.

Today, Santos was very grateful for her older sister. She could not imagine facing the funeral of her dear friend alone. Patrick had wanted to come, but the unit could not spare him with Santos off. It was such a comfort to have her sister sitting solid and warm next to her.

The beautiful church with its dark, polished wood pews and large, round stained-glass windows was full of mourners. The sun streamed in through the colored glass, casting purple, blue, and yellow tones on the people at prayer. Since Carol had been adamant about immediate cremation, there was no wake or viewing before Mass ... and no autopsy. Though Santos emotionally understood Carol's wishes, it meant that the family might never know what had caused her unexpected death.

From their vantage point in the middle of the church,

Santos saw Tom come in with Carol's father and his elderly parents. She could think of nothing worse than a parent losing a child. Now Carol's father, at eighty-six, faced this sorrow. Since Tom and Carol had no children, Tom would be alone. Overwhelmed with emotion, she felt the tears seep uncontrollably from her eyes.

She felt Camilla shift, then put her warm arm around her and squeeze. She took the handkerchief Camilla passed her and blew her nose, now red and sore. The song "I Will Raise You Up on Eagle's Wings" began, and they stood with the congregation to begin the service.

CHAPTER 58

The next day, he knew Santos was off, so he took his time, lingering in the unit. The scene of the crime called to him, drawing him in. With every fiber of his being, like an obsessed lover, he yearned for being close to the experience. Live and breathe it. He knew that being visible was dangerous, but he was powerless to stay away. More and more, he needed to be there to watch. He hungered for the smell and bitter taste of their failure and the exhilaration of his victory. He wanted to enjoy their pain. No longer satisfied with being a puppeteer behind the scenes, he longed for the rush of a real-time experience.

The next step of his ultimate plan was to watch them scurry around, powerless to save their patient, during a Code Blue of his design. Then he could witness his expert handiwork from start to finish. He would make sure they could not change the outcome of the next kill. But that would come later. Today he had another purpose on the unit. As he walked, he smiled, remembering his field trip the day before.

Yesterday, he had stood in the shadows in the back of the church, unseen by Santos. He had slipped away to the funeral for two reasons: to see Santos, and to extract as much flavor as he could from the experience. His hunger was insatiable. For the first time, he saw the devastation one of his kills had caused. It was doubly sweet since he had killed not only a nurse, but also a nurse who was close to Santos. He had the power to change people's lives with the elegance of a simple keystroke. He was becoming addicted to his feelings of *schadenfreude,* taking great pleasure in the misery of others.

From his vantage point at the church, he could clearly see Santos. He discretely adjusted his phone to photo and snapped a few pictures. Dressed in black, she looked like a tragic heroine in a play. She had the carriage of a victim. His victim. He had transformed her. She was no longer the perky, confident nurse, always smiling. Crying, eye makeup smudged, she moved as if she were in a trance.

My Little One. Look where you are now. Look what I did to you. I can never have you, but I can own you. He left the ceremony before it was over. He could not resist stopping to get her a bouquet of fresh fall flowers. *Something to comfort her.* He drove to her home and parked a block away. He watched and waited, then seeing no one, slowly walked over and left the flowers at her front door. No card. She would never know. He would always remember. He took a picture with his phone of the flowers at her front door. They would make another great addition to his electronic trophy wall. *Great day!*

He allowed himself a moment to gloat, secure in his success. Yet, he knew that success could lead to complacency. Complacency could lead to discovery. He would have to be vigilant. The game was his to win.

It gave him energy, a challenge, enjoyment, and a feeling of satisfaction that made life worth living. He felt alive and potent with purpose.

After the funeral, he found working on the game wall deeply satisfying. Studying the storyboard, he decided on his long-term strategy for the game, making a few adjustments with tactics. He felt no remorse. The wall provided an opportunity to chronicle the details. He posted everything from lab reports and pictures to obituaries of his victims. Too bad he had missed with that VIP. The newspaper coverage would have been stunning! *Good tactic; worth it to try again.* Each night, after work, he would add some new piece of data to the collection of deaths. It gave him a sense of accomplishment and allowed him to savor the experience in the privacy of his home over and over. He could safely study this altar, the legacy of his power, anytime he wanted.

The game would continue, at least for a little while longer. When he chose, it would end. Then he would go on, someday, to create and play another perfect game with unsuspecting people who became players, then pawns.

He had read in *The Chronicle* that morning the front-page article entitled, "People Are Getting Away with Murder," about the backlog of unsolved crimes in Houston. *You bet people are getting away with murder.* The best way to get away with murder was to kill without discovery. That was his goal. Play it until he tired of it. Then end the game until he was ready for more. This game of Solitaire was for his enjoyment only.

In the meantime, he had a mission for Wednesday. All the beds were full, and staff was working short. The unit bustled with EKG techs, lab techs, doctors, nurses, PCAs, medical students, and nursing students. He had observed the rhythm of life on the unit; he knew the work routines and the patterns of human behavior. Emma always brought her own lunch. *She must cook up a storm,* he thought. Staff rarely found time to leave the unit for food.

He did not want to kill Emma, just get her off track for a while. He decided that giving her a case of mycetism was a good way to go. Doing his research, he learned that thirty-two varieties of mushrooms had toxic consequences. Houston had suffered through some recent soggy weather, and mushrooms were popping up all over his lawn. The mushrooms commonly found growing in grass were *Chlorophyllum molybdites*. He checked out his, and they looked just about right. He gathered some, chopped them up into fine little bits, and put them in a small plastic bag. He knew that these particular mushrooms would cause her some stomach upset, but would not kill. She would think she'd just picked up a GI bug somewhere. His conscience came alive for a moment, and he felt a little bad, because he too had sampled some of her cooking during a unit potluck last year over the holidays. She was a great cook. She would live to cook again.

He opened the lounge door and looked around. It was empty. He opened the refrigerator and easily found the green, insulated food tote embossed with her name on top. He quickly opened it, took the bag of mushrooms from his pocket, and stirred them into her container of black beans and rice. Then he replaced the lid, zipped up the tote, closed the refrigerator door, and left the lounge. It took all of about fifteen seconds, and he was gone.

CHAPTER 59

On Friday morning, Santos and Patrick were in the lounge, standing at the counter grabbing a quick cup of coffee before rounds. The lounge was festive, like much of the unit, decorated with autumn leaves and pumpkins for Thanksgiving. Heather, baking again, had brought in some of her famous banana-walnut bread. It was sliced and placed on a brown pottery plate near a stack of orange and yellow fall napkins. The coffeepot was full of fresh coffee. Someone had brought in cinnamon potpourri. The combination of warm coffee, banana bread, and cinnamon made the hospital lounge smell like a bakery, an oasis from the hectic pace of the unit and the traumatic events of the past few months.

The joys of the holiday were lost on Santos, who felt as if she were moving in slow motion. Still dazed, she focused on stirring cream into her coffee.

Patrick leaned in close, carefully took the coffee mug from her hand, and put it on the counter. Then he gently but firmly tucked both of her hands in his. "I'm very, very sorry about the loss of your friend, Santos. I don't know what to say or do to comfort you."

Santos looked down at his large hands cradling her small ones. They felt warm and safe. She let the tears slowly fall.

"Thank you. It's been really hard recently. And I realize I've not been myself. Carol's death has stopped me in my tracks. I feel battered by everything … numb."

Patrick took a tissue and tenderly dabbed the tears

away. "When you lose someone you love, you lose a part of yourself."

She managed a quick, bleak smile. "I feel like I've been carved out inside … like that pumpkin over there." She pointed. "I wonder if I'll ever be the same."

"Probably not."

His words were so far from the clichés she'd been expecting that they caught her off guard. Wondering where he was going, she listened intently.

"The experiences we have change us, if we want them to, for the good. Just think about the empathy you have since you lost your mom, for people who lose their parents. You lived through that. You'll live through this," he said warmly.

Looking thoughtfully down at their two joined hands, she spoke from her heart. "You know, I've always liked that quote by Martin Luther King that goes something like, 'The real measure of a man is not what happens to him, but how he responds to the experience.' I believe in that, don't you? It's not what happens to us, because bad things happen. It's how we grow or lean in to the experience."

"I believe that, too. You can either be bitter about something for the rest of your life or move on and learn from it."

He squeezed her hands, let them go. Then he picked up their mugs and coffee cups and nodded toward the door. "Time to go."

She saw a twinkle in his eyes, a bit of a smirk on his face, and wondered what was coming.

"You are a strong woman, Santos," he paused. There was a teasing tone in his voice. "Sometimes maybe too strong."

She crossed her arms against her chest and waited for

him to finish, poised to retort.

"After all these years, you're still resisting me!"

The door opened, and Heather leaned into the room. Santos looked from Heather to Patrick and back to Heather. *Busted,* she thought.

Heather smiled at them and said, "I've been looking for you two. Rounds are ready to start. Let's go!" Then she turned around and headed out, obviously looking for more strays.

"'Resisting' you?" Santos jibed back, pushing him away from her and nearly spilling their coffee. She couldn't help laughing. "I wouldn't call kissing you in public resisting you! Still can't believe I did that. Or sobbing in your arms! Whatever happened to taking it slow?"

He smiled at her. "We have to stop meeting like this. When are we going to have another real date? Like dinner or something?"

"Hmmm, let me think about that."

She paused for a moment. "I've got it. A real test for you. How about coming with me to Camilla's for dinner? We have a family dinner scheduled in a week or so, I think."

"Your sister Camilla? Will your dad be there?"

"What are you thinking?"

"Oh, nothing, just wondering who all is at these dinners so that I can be prepared."

Santos grinned. "Nothing, Patrick Sullivan, could possibly prepare you for the noise and chaos of one of our family dinners. You will be deluged with questions."

"But I'll bet there will be great food. I'll do just about anything for great food. Besides, it will be fun to meet your gene pool!"

"Fun for them, I think, to run you through the ringer."

"Okay, we'd better go," he said. "Keep me posted."

They laughed, and she realized her mood had lightened. She grabbed her mug, and they headed out the door to rounds.

Santos stopped in the doorway and turned to him. "Patrick, did you send me flowers?"

"Probably would have been a good idea ... no, I didn't ... why?"

"Someone left flowers by my front door. No card."

"Maybe the card blew away ... maybe someone from your family?"

"No, I asked."

"Maybe wrong address?"

"Patrick, it felt a little creepy. They were just there—-when I got home."

"Probably someone's kind gesture, try not to worry so much."

"You're probably right. I'm getting jumpy about everything these days." She managed a brief smile.

They started to walk toward the conference room and Patrick stopped.

"Oh, I meant to tell you." Patrick's tone turned serious as they approached the door to the conference room. "Emma is out sick today with what she thinks is food poisoning. And Nick, too. Seems they shared Emma's lunch yesterday and both got sick."

Santos turned around and looked up at Patrick.

"This is ... weird."

"What's weird about it?" Patrick asked. "People get sick all the time."

"But these are all people on our team, just when we're starting to get somewhere. First Wendy, now Emma and Nick. Something is going on here," she said with concern. "I can feel it."

～

Ten feet away, he overhead a bit of their conversation about Emma and Nick. *Brings new meaning to the term "kill two birds with one stone,"* he thought. This had been fun so far. He watched the two walk down the hall and felt the sharp stab of jealousy as he watched her look at the tall blond and smile. He would have to continue to watch Santos and Patrick. "Nothing will get in my way," he muttered under his breath as he moved away.

CHAPTER 60

The following Monday morning, Santos sat behind the raised counter of the workstation doing a quick review of the patients who had come in on Sunday, her day off. She looked up and smiled seeing a joyful Emma sauntering down the hall toward her. Light on her feet, Emma twirled around in front of Santos and struck a pose, hands on her hips.

"Looky, looky, looky," Emma danced around in a circle, swaying her generous hips. "I lost five pounds! Can you tell?"

Santos quickly caught herself from saying what was on the tip of her tongue. Something like, "With the scrubs, it's pretty difficult to see the loss of five pounds." Diplomatically she said, "Yeah, I can see it in your face! How do you feel?"

"Like a new woman. Little discomfort, great payoff … might even start myself on a diet. Get ready for the holidays."

Nick, pale, stooped with exhaustion, walked down the hall and approached the counter with less exuberance. His rumpled scrubs were a testament to his sleepless night on call.

"Hey, Nick. How are you doing?" Santos asked with concern.

"Obviously not as well as Queen Latifah here." He gestured to Emma, then rested his elbows on the counter and dropped his head into his hands.

"Well, if you'd left more of the beans and rice for me, young man, maybe you wouldn't have gotten so sick!"

Nick raised his head to look at Emma, elbows still on the counter. "Emma, you know that no one can resist your food. For us starving residents, your food is like the nectar of the gods!"

"Oh, you sweet boy. Wait till ya'll see what I brought in today!"

"Emma," Nick stood up and groaned, placing both hands on his stomach. "I think I'm still on clear liquids for a while."

"I thought of that. Brought you some gumbo in chicken broth, no spice, lots of rice."

Nick beamed. "If you weren't already married, I'd ask you to marry me. That Leon is a lucky man."

"What about Nancy?" Emma asked.

"Cut me some slack. I'm running on empty!"

Santos laughed at the interplay.

"Hey, folks, time for rounds. Let's get going." Santos got up from behind the desk, and placing her hands on her colleagues' shoulders, nudged them down the hall toward the conference room.

They found three seats in the nearly full conference room. Always consistent, Heather and Richard were comparing notes, waiting for rounds to begin. The unit had had several admissions on Sunday. Staff would need a briefing on the new patients. Everyone seemed to get sick on the weekends, when doctors' offices were not open. Urgent care centers had exploded into a billion-dollar business, taking the place of emergency room visits for many patients who needed care in the off-hours.

Janet, charge nurse for the night, began the chronicle of updates and welcomed dialogue from the multidisciplinary team. There were three new patients: Mr. Aaron Dowd, a sixty-five-year-old chronic obstructive pulmonary disease with R/O MI; Mrs. Mary Simpson, a fifty-four-year-old mother of six in with atrial fibrillation, a potential cardioversion if medical management did not convert the rhythm; and Mr. Anthony "Tony" Tucci.

Mr. Tucci was a bit unusual for the CCU since he was only ten years old. He had cystic fibrosis. Nurses from the CF unit would team with nurses from the CCU. Tony was in the CCU for evaluation for either a double lung transplant or a heart-lung transplant. Santos knew that lung transplants were a last resort for children like Tony. A recent gastrointestinal virus that produced severe dehydration compounded his complicated and fragile clinical case. Still recovering, he would require close monitoring. His hospitalization for symptom management would move him up on the transplant list if a donor match became available while he was in the CCU.

Santos was assigned to Tony because she had the most experience with pediatric patients, having completed a pediatric intensive course at the Texas Children's Hospital, right down the block in the Texas Medical Center. Tony would be quite a challenge, not just clinically, but psychologically.

"Isn't cystic fibrosis the most common lethal inherited disease in Caucasians?" Santos asked.

"Yes, most carriers of the gene are asymptomatic— they pass it on to their children without knowing," replied Richard. He looked at the students in the room. "For those of you not familiar with CF, the disease involves many organ systems but primarily affects the lungs. In CF, the mucus secreted in the lungs is stickier than normal, attracts bacteria, and results in chronic respiratory infections. Children in Tony's age group with end-stage lung disease comprise thirty-six percent of all lung transplants."

"Wasn't the first heart-lung transplant done here in the TMC?" asked Patrick.

Richard replied, "Yes, way back in 1968."

Assignments made, the night shift signed off, and the 7:00 a.m. to 7:00 p.m. shift took over. Santos headed directly to her two patients to check in. She wanted to meet her new patient first. It would take more time to assess him, build trust, and create a relationship where he could be a partner with her in his care.

CHAPTER 61

Tony Tucci was sleeping as Santos approached his bed. She paused to watch him. He was one of the most beautiful children she had ever seen. His long, black eyelashes rested on alabaster skin. His dark head of thick, curly hair was tousled from sleep. His cheeks flushed with a hint of rose. He looked like an angel, a perfect model for the Italian artist Botticelli.

Looking closer, Santos noted smudges of blue under his eyes, probably from exhaustion. He had some circumoral cyanosis, a clue to his poor oxygen saturation. He was on oxygen via nasal cannula; she would have to determine if that was enough. His heart was in normal sinus rhythm, rate was normal, blood pressure normal. Santos observed that though he was small in frame, he appeared well nourished, with good muscle tone. She assessed the amount and color of urine in the collection bag at the side of his bed and noted the small amount, still dark from dehydration. She made a mental checklist of things to talk with him about when he woke up, including drinking fluids. His lips were dry, and there was some crusty, dried blood in his nose, probably from where the cannula rubbed on the tender mucous membranes.

"Wait until he wakes up," a voice whispered.

Startled, Santos turned around to see a petite, well-dressed, beautiful woman with shoulder-length, thick raven hair. Santos thought the woman looked familiar, then quickly put two and two together and recognized her as Angela Tucci, the popular anchor for a major Houston TV network. Santos had often admired her clothes and jewelry on the air, wondering how anyone could always look so perfect.

"Angela Tucci," she said, reaching out her hand to shake Santos's. "I'm his mother."

Noting the striking resemblance, Santos smiled. "He looks so like you."

"Thanks, I'll take that as a compliment."

Angela paused to look at her son, still at peace.

"Isn't he a sweetie? He can be quite a handful, though, coping with his illness and growing up ... but he is as beautiful inside as on the outside." She spoke like a mother in love with her fragile child, a child who might not live to see adulthood. "We were really worried about him this time."

"Mom, are you talking about me again?" came a sleepy voice from the bed.

When Tony opened his eyes, they held the weariness of experience and the worry of wondering what the day might bring.

"Good morning, sweetheart."

Angela acknowledged his knowing look with a hopeful smile and bent down to kiss his forehead. "I wanted to stop in and see you before I headed to work." She paused. "And I've met your new nurse. I think you'll get along together just fine."

The little boy looked up and noticed Santos for the first time. "Hi, I'm Anthony. But you can call me Tony."

Santos knew that Tony had been in and out of the hospital since he was diagnosed at two with cystic fibrosis. As a child of CF, he would know the routines of hospital life. She wondered if his illness had required that he grow up more quickly than healthy boys do. *I bet you get everything you want,* she thought to herself. Such a beautiful child. He probably knew how to manipulate the hospital system. Chronic disease had been his way of life, the only life he knew.

"What's on the schedule for him today?" Angela turned to Santos.

"He's scheduled for a comprehensive workup by the transplant service. Looks like we're going to draw some baseline blood work. And I want to check his oxygen saturation."

"Yes, I see the circumoral cyanosis. That worries me a bit," replied Angela, her forehead wrinkled with concern.

"We need to keep an eye on his dehydration." Santos pulled back the sheet covering the urine collection bag to show Mrs. Tucci the small amount. "We need to give him fluids without overloading him."

"You're talking about me like I'm not here again, Mom."

"Sorry, Tony," Santos replied. "That won't happen again." She walked over and stretched out her hand to her new patient. "Hi, I'm Santos. I'm going to be your nurse for today, and perhaps for most of the entire time you're here."

He smiled, shook her hand, and looked past Santos to his mother. "She's prettier than most of the nurses, Mom. You can go now. I'll be fine."

"Smarty," his mother said. "I'm glad you're in good spirits. This may be a long day for you. I'll be back around two. In the meantime, be good to your nurse. Do what she says."

Angela ran her hand through his hair, unsuccessfully trying to arrange the chaos of curls into a semblance of order. Her hand lingered on his head, mindlessly stroking. She looked at Santos, and her eyes suddenly filled with tears. Santos watched the highly trained professional's mask crack as Angela's face crumbled with grief. *She's first a mother ... she must be so worried,* thought Santos. Santos reached over to grasp Angela's free hand and squeezed warmly, hanging on tightly while Angela continued to talk with her son.

"You know you can get me on my cell anytime," she said over the top of his head, not making eye contact. She quickly turned her back so that he could not see her tears and hunted through her purse for a business card to give Santos and a tissue for her nose. Santos watched the woman struggle to regain her composure.

After giving her son a hug and a kiss, Angela walked away from the bedside with Santos. They briefly talked about her work. As a TV anchor, her days were long and demanding, but the news schedule allowed for breaks during the day and evening. She told Santos that she and her husband, with her mother, who had moved in with them, rotated care of Anthony and his sister, Marissa. Marissa was just six months old, and there was no sign yet that she had inherited the disease that was crippling their son. Tony's illness was a constant source of sorrow tinged with joyful experiences and bits of hopeful news.

Angela explained that after Anthony's diagnosis, they had thought long and hard about having another child. Eternally optimistic, they had felt called to be parents and yearned for another baby. Marissa was the result of their choice. She brought such joy to their family. Anthony loved his little sister dearly. Their daughter helped balance out the emotional roller coaster of their lives. Santos found herself with tears in her own eyes and the knowledge that she had just received a gift in hearing the intimate story of the life of a family. Santos gave Angela a hug before she left.

"I'll take good care of him," Santos said.

Santos returned to Tony's bedside to talk with him about his coming day and the plan of care. When she was finished she asked, "So, Anthony, we have our agenda for the day. What would you like to accomplish?"

He looked back at her with huge chocolate eyes that twinkled with mischief.

"How about we play a little with my snap circuits? Or we could play cards?"

He paused, looking down thoughtfully.

"Or just get me out of here," he pleaded. He looked up at her with fear in his deep brown eyes. "I'm really tired of this, being sick. Just for once, I'd like to spend the holidays at home."

Chapter 62

He was up on the unit drawing specimens for the morning orders. He scanned the environment for opportunities and threats. Emma and Nick were back at work. He could handle that. Wendy was still out with the flu. Good. She was the most important player to eliminate from the game, since she had the most knowledge and access to the lab.

He had made the decision that this would be the last kill for this particular game. They seemed to be closing in. It was too close for comfort. Discovery was not an option. But he was starving for one more intense, rich experience of his choosing. This would be his *piece de resistance,* his finest hour. He would not fail.

He wanted to savor this from the beginning—target selection, method of kill, kill in progress, and death. Just one more for the record. Then he would have to be content with watching them try to figure out what had happened. He wanted to see and feel their impotence when they were stumped, unable to untangle the intricate trap of death he had woven. It would brush away like a spider web when he was done. Not a trace of the complexities he had woven would remain. No evidence, no trail. It would remain his secret pleasure.

He saw Santos leave the bedside of the new patient. She looked tired and preoccupied. He had already made the rounds of all of the patients in the unit, circling for the kill selection. This was the last one to go. The coast was clear.

Oh, aren't you a pretty boy, he thought to himself as he looked down at the child. *You would be a heartbreaker.*

Tony looked up.

"More blood?"

"Yep, more blood. I bet you've had your share taken, huh, buddy?"

"Yeah. More than you know."

He bent over to check Tony's ID band. Then he began laying out tubes and labels, a fresh vacutainer, butterfly, tourniquet, and gloves. He made conversation to gather information as well as create a connection with the young patient.

"Your ID band says you're ten. Just ten?"

"Ten, going on forty."

He frowned. "Why's that?"

"If you'd been in and out of hospitals since you were two, you might feel the same way!"

"Well, I haven't. But during the war, I was in the hospital for a long time."

"What war? World War II?"

"Do I look that old?" He smiled, realizing that all adults looked old to children.

"Sorry, I didn't mean anything."

"It's okay. I was in the Vietnam War. I was a pilot. A helicopter pilot."

"Really?" Anthony perked up now, interested in the conversation. "Did you see any action?"

"Lots of action. Too much action. Things I never want to remember. Things you don't want to know about." He patted Anthony on the arm. In the midst of their conversation, he finished drawing the blood and began to pack up. He stripped off his latex gloves and threw them in the wastebasket by the bed.

"Will you be back again? Maybe we can talk some more?"

"Maybe. I'll keep a close eye on your lab results. Take care, kid."

He walked away from the bed deep in thought.

Poor kid. I'll take a look at his record, but he seems tired. Not much of a life spending most of your time in the hospital. CF kids were like that.

He shook his head, stopped, and turned around once to look at Anthony in the bed. The little boy had already drifted off to sleep, another morning nap in the making. As he shuffled down the hall to the lab, his choice was clear.

CHAPTER 63

"I win! Again!" Tony said loudly, slapping his cards down on the bed.

"I give up. You're too much. No one warned me that you were a card shark!" Santos retorted.

"Okay, you two," Angela interjected. Santos looked up. She remembered that Angela had said she would be back at 2:00 p.m.

"What's going on here, Tony? Are you playing fair with Santos?"

"Mother, of course. She's just not very good," he said, cocking his head toward Santos.

"Excuse me?" Santos said to Anthony. He ignored her, and she smiled at Angela. "Hi, welcome back. Have you been here long?"

"Just a few moments. Watching you both have fun," Angela said, smiling. She walked over to Tony, leaned down, and gave him a kiss on the top of his head.

Though Santos did not have a lot of time to play with Anthony, she would make time for a few minutes here and there. His condition was stable for the moment, and he would be heading down to radiology for more tests later in the afternoon.

"Hey, Mom ... what did ya bring me?"

"I brought you myself. I've been at work since I saw you this morning." Angela turned to Santos. "Anything new?"

"I was about to check on his blood work from this morning. Why don't I give you two some alone time, and

I'll be back in a few minutes." Wagging a warning finger at Tony, Santos left for the workstation.

CHAPTER 64

He sorted through the labs of the morning, saving the boy's for last. The lab would clear out over lunch, giving him relative quiet and privacy. It took about an hour to review the tests and complete the profiles to his satisfaction. All the time his hands worked, his mind was active.

The kid's INR, the measure of how long it takes blood to clot, was high. Under the right circumstances, the boy was at risk for a major bleed. He wheeled his chair over to the second computer station. He scanned the electronic patient care record, noting the history of GI flu, nosebleeds, and the treatment for dehydration. That would make sense. Loss of fluid and nutrients from the GI tract could deplete Vitamin K levels, reducing the blood's ability to clot normally. There were orders for a nutrition consult and additional snacks to increase Anthony's caloric intake and hydration.

All blood chemistry levels were within normal ranges. He considered using K+ again, but thought it was time to try the INR again. Might be messy, but this time, he would make sure it worked. *Need to add some insurance.* There could be no trail on this one. He completed the work and electronically transmitted the results to Anthony's patient record.

He looked up at the clock. It was almost 2:15 p.m. Time to go for a walk and then put the final play into action. He rolled his chair over to the crutch propped against the desk, positioned it on his forearm, and heaved himself out of the chair. He then placed the crutch in the corner of the lab. The next step in the plan had to be completed without the crutch in evidence.

As he slowly and carefully ambled down the hall toward the cafeteria, he wondered, *Chocolate or vanilla? What flavor would best disguise the bitter taste? All kids like ice cream. Don't they?*

CHAPTER 65

Santos ducked into the lounge to grab a glass of water and found Emma sitting at the table staring into space, the food in front of her growing cold.

"You okay?"

Emma pushed her plate away.

"I'm worried. Can't get over what has happened here on this unit." She looked up at Santos and said firmly, "We can't let our daily work distract us from finding out what is happening here."

"You're right. We've kind of gotten off track these days with Wendy being gone—and then you and Nick sick. Patrick and I are working different shifts, so there hasn't been any time to talk."

"Let's get back on track."

"Emma, I've been thinking. This might be a lot of work … but we know the labs that were drawn on the patients within the twenty-fours before they died. Can we start looking at staffing—who was on duty when the lab results were processed and posted? We may never be able to trace them electronically. But if the same name starts showing up, we might have something. Remember before Wendy got sick, she had a feeling about one of the guys in the lab? I've got her phone number. Do you have a moment to give her a call at home?"

Emma nodded. "No time like the present. We need to be careful though, about jumping to conclusions about one person."

Santos pulled out her cell, scanned her directory, and

quickly called Wendy's home number. Wendy picked up after two rings.

"Hi there, it's Santos. How're you doing?"

"I am almost human again. How good of you to call. I miss talking with you. I have cabin fever!"

"Okay if I put you on speaker? Emma is here with me, and we'd like to pick your brain, if that's possible, for a few minutes."

"Absolutely. I just put Carlos down for a nap. I have a few minutes of peace where every sentence doesn't begin with the word 'Mommy.'"

Santos switched the phone to speaker and nodded to Emma.

"Hey there, girl, how ya'll doing? Feeling better?"

"Emma! Great to hear your voice. It gets a little lonely here just talking to a toddler."

"Wendy, Emma and I have been talking. We really need to continue our work. We still don't know what's going on with the lab tests. Things have been quiet here for a few weeks, but we're worried that we could be blindsided again."

"I agree. What do you need?"

"Wendy," Santos began, "can you run some sort of electronic trace to determine who ran the labs on the patients who died and on Mr. Gideon?"

"Oh, wow, that would be huge. There are hundreds of labs ordered on all of the CCU patients ... let me think, we could narrow it down to blood chemistry."

"What about staffing? We need to identify who was working in the twenty-four to forty- eight hours prior to the deaths," Santos countered.

"You know, I don't think that's going to help us much. Staff in the lab is pretty consistent. I can track who was staffing blood chemistry, though." Wendy paused. "I've thought about this, too. You know we don't have any new staff in the lab. Everyone who works there has been there for years. Why would someone start doing this all of a sudden?"

"I don't know. Maybe there's been some sort of trigger," Emma piped in. "Who knows what causes someone who seems healthy to suddenly crack? Think about those kids who shoot their classmates or kill their mothers. There is usually something that pushes them over the edge."

"Wendy, remember, right before you got sick … you had a gut feeling about one of the MTs?" Santos added.

"Santos, I've told you, we need to be careful about jumping to a conclusion about one person," Emma reminded.

"Regardless of the trigger, we can't stop until we find out what or who is causing patients to suddenly die." Santos paused. "I've been saying for weeks now that we have a killer at work, and I think … now, don't think I'm crazy … but with members of our team suddenly getting sick … I think this person may know we're on his trail. He knows what's going on and he is trying to slow us down. Derail our efforts."

"Santos, that gives me the creeps," Emma rubbed the goose bumps on her arms. "You think someone deliberately made me sick? My God, my lunch is always in the fridge. Anyone could see that. You think someone gave Wendy the flu?"

"That makes me nauseous," Wendy said. "It's way too easy for someone in the lab to take a viral sample and spread it. The outbreak could be incredible!"

"OK, let's get back on track," replied Santos. "Wendy,

can you get going on the staffing? Can you do it from home? Can you find the name of that MT that made you suspicious?"

"Sure, I have computer access. Just need to pull up the staffing and cross-check it with the patients in the window of twenty-four to forty-eight hours before death."

"Sounds good," said Emma. "How can we help?"

"Let's make sure I have all the names, admission dates, things like that. I'll put together a staffing grid. I'll call IT and we'll do a search of the labs, and we can see if there's a pattern." Wendy paused. "Santos, we probably need Heather or Richard to get us priority with IT without raising all sorts of red flags."

"Done," Santos replied. "I'll talk to Heather as soon as we hang up." Santos stood poised to leave.

"I'll feel a lot more like celebrating the holidays if we do something about these senseless deaths," said Emma.

"Me, too," replied Santos, placing a hand on Emma's shoulder. "Why don't I send you an e-mail with all the info?"

"Perfect. I'll get on it as soon as you send it to me."

"I'll get it to you this afternoon."

"Breaks my heart, all those families who lost someone this year. Now they're living through their first holidays," Emma said soberly. "This is a really tough time of year to be alone."

CHAPTER 66

Hopeful that they were back on track again, Santos left the lounge, found Heather in her office, and quickly briefed her. Heather would get their "QI project" high priority with IT. Then Santos hurried back to the Anthony's bedside to talk with his mother before she left to return to work at the TV station.

"Glad I came back in time," she began. "All of his labs look pretty good." She stopped and caught herself. "Anthony, sorry. I need to include you in this conversation."

"Forgiven," said the voice from the bed. "Just let me beat you at cards again!"

Santos grinned. "Anthony, I have to get back to other patients and other things. Let me finish up this discussion with you and your mother, and we'll talk again later, okay?"

"Got it."

"Right now his blood looks good. But his INR is up. Do you know what means?"

"Yes, it's how fast or slow his blood clots. Some sort of international comparison. Right? Is that something we should worry about?"

"No, not yet. But we need to watch it. We'll order it daily for a while. It's probably a result of his dehydration from the GI virus. But we will want to get it back to normal. We don't want it to stop him from having surgery if a transplant becomes available. I've ordered a nutrition consult. We also want to make sure he's not getting too much Vitamin K in his diet, at least not right now." She paused to include Tony in the conversation. "And you'll like this, Anthony … snacks between meals for you!"

"Oh great, probably something like that disgusting green Jell-O, yuck, yuck!" Tony said, sticking his finger down his throat pretending to retch.

"Anthony, stop it!" said his mother with a stern look.

"I think we can do better than that," Santos said. "You just wait."

Silenced by his mother's disapproving glance, Anthony pantomimed zipping his mouth closed, crossed his arms across his chest, and closed his eyes. With a sly grin on his face, he said, "Bye, Mom."

Then he paused, eyes still closed, and said, "Santos, I'm resting up for round two."

CHAPTER 67

When he returned to the CCU late in the afternoon, patients were trying to rest or were off the unit at tests. The nurses were busy charting. Medical staff were nowhere to be seen, either busy with patient appointments or in surgery. He slipped into the unit unnoticed.

He went directly to Anthony's bed. As he approached, the young boy's head was turned away from him. Coming in closer, he saw Anthony brush a tear away and blow his nose into a tissue. The little boy clearly did not hear him.

"Knock, knock," he said.

"Oh, you're back." Anthony quickly balled his tissues and tucked them into the folds of the sheet. "More blood already?"

"No, no blood. I brought you one of your snacks."

Anthony looked at the large cup and straw he held out to him.

"For me? A shake?" He took off the lid to look inside the container. "Chocolate! My favorite!"

Anthony unwrapped the straw, slipped it into the slot on the plastic lid and took a long sip. "This is great! Wow!"

"Glad you like it."

"Does my mother know?" Anthony asked.

"It's on your orders. Don't worry." He looked around. "How about we keep this visit our little secret?"

"Sure, sure ... will you bring me another one later?"

"I'll try. Gotta go now. Back to work."

"Thanks, thanks a lot!"

He tucked the sheets around Anthony, who beamed

back at him. It was if a light had gone on in the kid, he was so excited.

He turned around to leave without remorse. The maneuver was slow and difficult, as he was walking without his crutch. He did not want the kid to remember that about him.

He was confident and pleased that the first phase of the mission was complete. Obviously, Anthony did not taste the five aspirins he had crushed and mixed with the ice-cold drink. The ice cream would mask the texture, the chocolate the bitter taste. He was taking double precautions with this one. If internal bleeding did not kill him, then Reye's syndrome could.

CHAPTER 68

Slammed with admissions for the rest of her twelve-hour shift, Santos paid little notice to the clock as the hours flew by. Anthony was on and off the unit all afternoon for tests. When she stopped in to see him and assess his vital signs at 5:30 p.m., he was fast asleep. She saw some blood on a tissue in his bed and wondered if he'd had a nosebleed. She quickly assessed for bruising, another symptom of an elevated INR, and noticed he had a few bruises on his right arm. That might have been from his blood draws. He was stable, so she let him sleep and went to check on the other new patients and complete her charting.

She planned to check in on him again at 6:15 p.m., right before the end of her shift. She would settle him in for the night, do her final assessment, and introduce him to the new graduate nurse assigned to him for the night shift. Kathleen Florence, a graduate of Saint Mary's College in Notre Dame, Indiana, had moved to Houston six months ago and had just completed her rigorous orientation two weeks ago. She had been a quick study and was a perfect fit for the unit team, bubbly and curious with a great sense of humor. Yet she was inexperienced in so many ways. It usually took well over a year for solid critical-care nurse preparation. In Santos's opinion, she could not be in a better place to learn.

Santos had the day off tomorrow. Tonight was the family dinner at her sister Camilla's home in the Heights. This would be Patrick's introduction to her family. Camilla was excited and had told everyone about their special guest. Each of her siblings would bring a favorite dish, and after dinner, everyone would draw names for Christmas gifts. Santos was exempt from bringing a dish since she was coming directly from work. She had volunteered for cleanup and would stay overnight. Camilla and Santos planned to do some much-needed Christmas shopping in the morning. It was a miracle that Camilla was able to corral the entire family for dinner, especially so close to the holidays. Santos was looking forward to great food and seeing everyone—a healthy escape from work. She hoped Patrick would enjoy it as much as she did. They had agreed to drive separately and meet at her sister's home.

Approaching Anthony's bed, Santos saw a tall, fair-haired man wearing a long taupe trench coat standing by his bed. Immediately on guard, she walked over to question him.

"Santos, where've you been?" Anthony said. "Come here—meet my dad!"

Santos looked back and forth between father and son, searching for a resemblance. She found none. Fabio Tucci noted her confusion.

"Obviously, Angela has the stronger gene pool." He smiled and extended his hand. "Fabio Tucci. Thank you for taking such good care of our son."

Santos extended her hand. His grip was warm and firm. "Hello, Mr. Tucci. Now I've met the whole family. It's good to meet you."

"You haven't met Marissa yet!" called Anthony.

"That's right," Santos remarked. "Can't forget her!"

"Angela told me that Tony has given you a run for your money at cards. Unfortunately, one of the pitfalls of being hospitalized so much is that he's picked up some bad habits." Fabio reached over to tousle his son's hair.

"Dad, stop it. You're embarrassing me!"

"It's almost time for bed, Anthony," Santos said. She

explained to him that she would not be back until Wednesday. She would drop by later to introduce him to his night nurse, Kathleen. Emma would be his nurse tomorrow.

"Oh no! Not her! I heard she has kids!"

"Yes, that's a good thing. She'll know how to handle you!" Santos sparred back.

"You're no fun!"

Fabio's voice grew a little stern. "Anthony, settle down. Time for bed. I can stay a few more minutes, but I have a business meeting tonight. I'll be back first thing in the morning."

"Anthony, did you have a nosebleed today?" Santos asked with concern.

"Yeah, when I was down in radiology. They had to press *hard*. They packed my nose and it stopped."

"Let us know right away if you have anything like that again. Okay?"

"Don't all kids have nosebleeds?" Anthony asked, confused.

"Lots of kids have nosebleeds, but we need to be a little more careful with you. So let me know, okay?"

"Sure."

Santos finished up with Anthony and bid Mr. Tucci a good evening. After completing her charting and reporting, she quickly took Kathleen to meet Anthony. They hit it off immediately. Kathleen had four siblings and was great with kids. Santos was reassured when she saw them interact.

Finally, she was ready to go. She took the elevator down to her car in the nearly deserted parking garage. She was really looking forward to getting away, being surrounded by people she loved, and sharing her family with Patrick. She could hardly wait. She was starving!

Chapter 69

The drive from the medical center to the Heights was quick, about twenty minutes. For once, she hit every green light on the way. The historic Heights district, first designed by O.M. Carter in 1891, was built to be a community with first-class residences and businesses. Today, only a handful of the original Victorian homes still stood, but the community remained close-knit and true to its roots.

Santos saw Patrick's silver Jeep already parked out front. She pulled in directly behind him, all the while wondering how he was faring with her boisterous family.

Camilla, with her husband and two children, lived in an original Sears catalog 1920 Craftsman-style home. Over the years, they had updated everything from plumbing to wiring but maintained the original dark wood finishes of the era. They had added on to the kitchen and built a guestroom downstairs. Their long, wide, screened-in front porch was full of white wicker furniture and lush green ferns, hanging from the ceiling, still thriving in the cool of early winter.

Every window in the house blazed with welcoming light. She smiled with anticipation and curiosity as she walked up the uneven sidewalk to the house. She noticed that Camilla had already planted her winter pansies along the sidewalk and wondered, *where does that woman get her energy?*

She bounded up the three steps to the porch. Knowing that no one would hear the doorbell, she turned the doorknob of the heavy oak door, found it unlocked, and smiling, walked right in. Immediately she felt the warmth of the room. Her senses were bombarded by the sound of laughter and noisy conversations in both Spanish and English. The pungent smell of peppers and spices wafted in from the nearby kitchen. She quickly left the world of the hospital behind, enveloped in the abundance of home and family.

"Santos, you're here!" called her father. He was waiting for her by the door.

"Hi, Papa! It's been too long." She threw her arms around him and hugged, smelling Old Spice and soap, such familiar, comforting smells.

He pulled back, holding her at arm's length.

"He seems like a nice young man," he said, nodding his head in the direction of Patrick, who was deep in conversation with Santos's brother Santiago.

"Now we can finally eat! Ma, Tia Santos is here! Let's eat, let's eat! I'm starving!" yelled Santos's six-year-old nephew, Alfonso, as he ran into the kitchen.

Santos saw Patrick look toward the front door at Alfonso's announcement.

Camilla emerged from the kitchen, wiping her hands on her red-checked apron.

"Santos, welcome! I've had a pack of animals here chomping at the bit for food. Thank God you're here! Can you help me in the kitchen? Wash up—use our bathroom upstairs if you need to."

"Be right with you. I just want to say hi to Abuelita."

Santos wove through the maze of people and connected with Patrick. She reached for his hand and gave it a reassuring squeeze. He gave her a quick kiss on the cheek.

"How are you holding up? Have they given you the third degree yet?"

"Santos, you have a great family. Lots and lots of questions, but everyone has been great. I'm glad I recognized the names from our conversations or I'd be lost here."

"Got to check in with Abuelita. You're okay? We'll eat soon. That will quiet everyone down."

Patrick nodded.

Santos spotted her grandmother, wearing a beautiful, Saltillo-striped woolen shawl of gold and burnt orange. She looked regal, tucked back in a comfortable chair in the corner of the living room where she could watch everything, and with her hair pulled tightly back in a braided bun. As Santos approached, her grandmother's lean, deeply lined face, an older but still beautiful version of her mother's, lit up with a broad smile, and she reached out for Santos. Santos kneeled down next to her grandmother, leaned in and hugged, rubbing her warm cheek against the dry, weathered cheek.

Her grandmother pulled back and held Santos out at arm's length. *"Tu eres muy bonita."*

"Thank you, Abuelita." Santos sighed and nestled close to her grandmother. The sandalwood scent of her grandmother and her warm, soft touch brought back a flood of sweet memories. "I have missed you so much." Abuelita was the only grandmother she had ever known. Her father's mother had died when Santos was little. She had a few memories of forbidden candy and a warm, ample lap, good smells always coming from the small kitchen. But all other memories were of this woman who had so recently suffered the loss of her daughter.

"Beautiful Santos, my precious girl, I am so proud of you. You look more like your mother every day … I know that you are working hard. Your sisters keep me up to date," said Abuelita as she stroked Santos's hair and hugged her tight.

As Santos held her grandmother, she felt that she had lost weight and seemed frail. Her voice was still strong. She leaned back to sit at her grandmother's feet.

"He seems like a nice young man." Abuelita paused, looking at Patrick. "Time for you to have someone in your life, take care of you, you take care of him. I saw the way he looked at you." She smiled, then gently tapped her finger on Santos's nose. "He's in love with you."

"Oh, I don't know about that," said Santos with a glance toward Patrick. "We're really good friends and have worked together for a number of years. It feels good to be with him ... safe."

"Well, that's a good start," said her grandmother with a smile.

"I think so. It's probably time for me to find a life outside of work. Sometimes I feel as if I'm missing so much. But I love my work. Guess there are trade-offs to any choice."

"You can have both. Love between two people makes them better, stronger. Life is richer with love. What would food be without spice? Life is the same with love. Love makes life worth living. Respect between two people makes anything possible."

"You're right. I need to create the space for that possibility. Or it may never happen to me."

"Oh, I think it is already happening." Her grandmother smiled and looked deeply in Santos's eyes.

Santos felt herself begin to blush. Or maybe it was the heat of the room.

"Oh, I made you a special treat. Your favorite," her grandmother added.

Santos pulled back. "What?"

"My secret. You'll have to wait for dessert."

241

Santos smiled. "Okay, I'll wait. But I'd better quick wash up and help Camilla. I'll be in big trouble if we don't eat soon."

"Go, go." Her grandmother waved her away. The gold bracelets on her elegant, slender wrists softly jangled with the motion of her hands. "I want to talk to Patrick some more. Send him over, please."

Santos wove back through the crowd to Patrick.

"Abuelita would like to chat with you again, when you can get away."

"Great. She's a wonderful woman."

"Got to run. Help Camilla."

Santos ran up the stairs to use the bathroom, change, and clean up, and she thought how blessed she was to have this family. It was extra-special to share them with Patrick, weaving a new memory into their relationship. Though she did not see her family as much as she would like, they were the foundation of her being. Even with their disagreements common to all families, they were her family. She loved them all.

Safe here with them, for a few hours, she could let the stresses of work fade away.

CHAPTER 70

That night, Santos was deep asleep in her sister's comfortable and quiet guestroom. She was peacefully snuggled in soft, lavender-scented sheets under a fluffy down comforter in the antique brass bed. Patrick had stayed to help clean up, leaving the party at 10:30 p.m. He had warmly kissed her good night on the front porch, the only moment of quiet they'd had together all night. She collapsed into bed forty-five minutes later, after they finished washing and drying the last dish and vacuuming up the crumbs left from the family dinner.

Her cell phone rang shattering the tranquility of the night, jarring her from sleep. Disoriented at first, she did not remember where she was. She reached over to pick up her phone from the nightstand and glanced at the glow of the digital alarm clock. It was 11:45 p.m. She had been asleep for only thirty minutes. Who would be calling at this hour?

"Hello?"

"Oh, Santos. This is Santos, isn't it? I have the right number?" asked a highly anxious female voice.

"Yes, this is Santos. Who's this?"

"Santos, I'm so sorry to bother you. I probably woke you up, didn't I? This is Kathleen. I'm calling about Anthony."

Santos was suddenly wide awake.

"Kathleen, what's wrong? What do you need?"

"Santos, Anthony is coding. The Code Blue team is with him now. I can't find his parents' contact information. I thought you might have it."

Santos threw the quilt off the bed and sat up.

"I'll be right there. And I'll call them. Get back to Anthony. I'll be right there."

Santos abruptly ended the call, turned on the light, and found her wrinkled scrubs on the chair. She dressed in a flash. Then she went to the kitchen, wrote a quick note to her sister, and rushed outside to her car, parked in the chill of a dark, moonless night.

CHAPTER 71

He could not believe his good fortune.

When his supervisor asked him to work a double shift, he knew it was predestined. In spite of the late hour, he was full of anticipation, charged and alert. At 11:30 p.m., he had been up in the CCU drawing the bloods of the day and collecting specimens. Though he was in reconnaissance mode, he stayed clear of Anthony's bed, stopping only to wave and then move on. Anthony appeared to be sleeping. When the young nurse went to check on the boy, he moved quietly down the hall.

"Code Blue! Call a Code Blue!"

Could it be his? This was too good to be true. He lumbered down the hall, the first on the scene.

"Need some help?" he asked. The young woman was obviously distressed.

"I need the crash cart!" she ordered.

He started down the hall, limited by his gait, only to see one of the residents pushing the crash cart rapidly down the hall. The resident passed him as if he were invisible and continued to Anthony's bed. As he watched, he saw a stream of white coats on the run. They entered the unit from all points. Double doors swung open and stairwell doors slammed against walls as clinicians from all parts of the hospital converged on the CCU.

He moved to the side of the hallway to avoid the stampede. In the blink of an eye, the CCU transformed from dark and quiet to a unit pulsing with energy, charged with action and light. Clinical crises made an immediate, palpable, impact on the environment.

Euphoric, he moved in more closely to the room to watch. This was his moment. It was like watching the birth of his child. They had no idea of the power of his manipulation. He was drawn in, totally absorbed by the drama unfolding before him. Minutes passed. He watched, drinking in every detail, as clinicians heroically struggled to save Anthony's life. The bedside was utter pandemonium. Equipment moved in and out. People came and went. Trash from supplies piled up on the floor. Sweat poured off the brow of the brawny resident doing restrained pediatric chest compressions.

His obsession, his dream, was achieving complete fulfillment. Watching this was as deeply physical as a long-awaited sexual release. He wanted more.

Time passed quickly, and CPR continued. This was a child. They would not give up easily. The one attending physician who happened to be in-house barked orders. He watched the clinicians, once strangers to one another, fueled by a common cause, forged into a team. Trying to save the life of a child most had never met.

He was completely enthralled by the life-and-death scenario unfolding before him. He was in it. He felt it. He gleefully inhaled their sweat and felt their frustration. They were tired. Anthony remained lifeless. They were powerless to save.

The double doors to the CCU flew open, and he was surprised to see Santos race in on a controlled run. She stripped off her coat, threw it into a chair, and went directly to Anthony's bedside. She looked like she had just crawled out of bed. Her scrubs were wrinkled; her hair was a mess. *So unlike Santos,* he thought smugly. She always seemed so perfect, scrubs pressed, not a hair out of place. *Wonder how she found out about this? Just makes it more interesting.*

Perfect ... I can keep her close.

"Can someone give me an update?" he heard Santos ask.

He ventured closer. No one noticed him. They were rotating who did chest compressions and ventilating. The chief resident was focused, intent on counting chest compressions. Dr. Nancy Nathan was the anesthesiologist on call for the code team; she was bagging Anthony through an ET tube. A unit of blood hung from the IV pole, dripping into his vein, and a unit, already administered, was in the trash. There was blood everywhere, on the sheets, the floor. He looked at the clock in the room. They had been at it now for forty-five minutes.

"I walked in and he was unresponsive. I saw that he had been bleeding from his nose. No pulse, no respirations, so I called the code," he heard the young nurse tell Santos. "I'm so sorry." She looked ready to burst into tears.

"I've got to get to his parents," Santos said to the nurse. "They need to be here." She turned around quickly to leave in search of a place to call.

Hovering close, he was unable to move fast enough to step out of her way, and she bumped right into him— hitting him squarely in the chest.

CHAPTER 72

"What are you doing here?" she challenged him sharply.

"I came to help."

Santos's brain quickly clicked through the series of times she had seen him, remembering locations, recalling him outside of the conference room. He usually worked days. *What was he doing here tonight?*

"Excuse me. I know you. You don't belong here." Frustrated and exhausted, Santos lost her cool. Her anger rose white-hot as she thought, *this is too much.* He was standing there like a bird of prey, a vulture, watching a helpless child die. Santos did not get angry often, but this pushed her over the edge. Protecting and caring for patients was her life. Anyone who would find pleasure in watching the dying struggles of a child deserved to be fired.

She saw his name badge and pulled it off his jacket, stuffing it in her pocket.

"Get out of here. In the morning, I'm going to call your supervisor. Leave before the family arrives and sees you."

She looked him squarely in the eyes. What she saw chilled her. They were dull and black, flat, deep wells, empty of emotion. She felt a flutter in her gut, and she briefly felt fear rise up in her chest—alarm bells of impending danger.

Pushing the strong feeling of intimidation aside, she strode away from him to find a quiet corner. She pulled out her cell phone to call Anthony's parents, stopping for a moment to gather her thoughts and compose those first few words. Then, full of sorrow and dread, she punched in Angela's number. The phone at the other end rang.

CHAPTER 73

His first reaction was complete and utter humiliation. He was speechless.

She had spoken to him as if he were a child, in front of all of those people. Some of them even stopped and stared at him as he backed away. His mind, on reflex, traveled back to his childhood, resurrecting long-buried but never forgotten memories. Bullies. The mental tapes were as fresh if they had happened yesterday. He felt reduced to the small, helpless, and beaten boy of his youth—insignificant under their taunts. And then the long, long days in the hospital after Guillian-Barre, in rehab, reduced to a child again, helpless and angry ....

He saw her ignore him and walk down the hall to make a phone call.

His feelings of humiliation quickly shifted, erupting into rage.

Who was she to tell him what he could do? *The little bitch ....*

Years of hatred and anger, smoldering and searing him on the inside, spewed up from his gut into his consciousness. He was delirious, consumed by emotions that washed over him, threatening his self-control.

His hands balled into fists and his jaw set with determination, he found the poise to collect his gear. Then he stood as straight as he could, leaned on his crutch, and began the walk back down to the lab. Livid with purpose, he knew what he had to do.

CHAPTER 74

The only sounds Santos heard as she pushed the lightly loaded, shrouded gurney to the morgue were the squeak of the wheels and the soft squish of her shoes on the linoleum. At 2:00 a.m., the pale green, tiled basement corridors were quiet and dim.

She felt like a train wreck. She put one foot in front of the other, leaning on the gurney for support. Her body was on empty, her mind dull, floating aimlessly. As she approached the morgue, her mind drifted back to the horrific events of the day.

Anthony's parents were devastated to find their son dead. They were confused, in a daze, full of questions without answers. When she left them, they were sobbing in each other's arms, overcome by grief. There was no way to console them, and Santos did not even try. One moment their child was alive, playful, and mischievous, a typical ten-year-old; the next moment, he was dead. They were unable to say good-bye. From this wound, this loss, they would never recover. Though the pain would fade, their life path was changed forever.

Her heart was heavy with sorrow. She was crushed by his loss and consumed by guilt. The wound left by her mother's death a year ago was now open and raw. First the patients who died, then Carol, now this. The layers of grief cloaked her, eroding her spirit. *What have I done to deserve this?* Barely able to see straight, she gently and carefully pushed Anthony's body to the morgue. *If I had been there, would he still be alive?*

She did not blame Kathleen. This was her usual self-talk, the thought processes of the nurse who felt accountable. She knew in her heart that she would never be able to save everyone. But she could not help herself; she would forever be the rescuer. She had bonded quickly with Anthony. Fallen in love with him the moment she laid eyes on him. Caring made it more difficult. Yet for her, it was impossible not to care.

Santos had not slept for nearly twenty-four hours. She felt the fatigue around her eyes. Her contacts scratched her eyes as if crusted with sand. Her knees trembled with weariness.

She looked down at the small form on the gurney and choked back a lump in her throat. She was taking the boy's soulless body to the hospital morgue to await the arrival of the funeral home. She had offered to do it for Kathleen, who was paralyzed by the experience. Santos had sent her home at midnight with instructions to take the next day off.

Walking to the morgue at night gave her the creeps. The corridors were shadowed; she had seen too many horror movies in her lifetime. Her vivid imagination and nurse intuition, fueled by fatigue, had her nerves on edge. She scanned the hallways but saw no one.

She shook it off.

You're done. Buck up. Put him to rest.

Death for adults, who may have lived a full life, was one thing. Death and children sparked the deepest sorrow in Santos. The pain she saw in parents cut right to her heart. She remembered why she had not chosen pediatric nursing as her specialty. She could never have dealt well with this on a regular basis.

The cloud in her brain cleared for a moment, and she

reflected back on her angry exchange with the med tech. She had probably overreacted a bit on that one. She made a mental note to return his ID and have a more professional talk with him when she returned to work. She owed him an apology for her outburst. At the same time, she still felt that he had been out of line. And not just then—other times. Something about him put her on edge. Every time she saw him, he seemed to be brooding. He looked angry. And those eyes, they were so cold. She shivered with the memory. *Got to talk with Patrick.*

Santos began to tally the number of times she had seen him. *Didn't I see him at the Community Hospital, too? The day before Carol died? Did I imagine that?*

When she reached the morgue, Santos noted that security had already unlocked the door. She flipped on the bright fluorescent lights, pushed her body weight against the gurney, and maneuvered it through the door. Then she pushed the gurney across the room, heading for the large refrigerator where Anthony's little body would be stored.

Though she had done this many times, it still made her anxious—just like taking showers in strange places conjured up memories of the movie *Psycho.* Trips to the morgue reminded her of the movies she used to watch on *Creature Features* and of the Edgar Allen Poe books she had read as a child.

I've DVR'd one too many NCIS *and* Bones *episodes,* she said to herself.

Santos pushed the gurney past the stainless-steel dissection tables with their fluid drains. Even though the area was spotless, the smell of death and formaldehyde lingered. She opened the big walk-in refrigerator door, took off her shoe, and propped the door open. She knew that she should be able to open the door from the inside, but she never took any chances.

The temperature in the refrigerated room was set at about four degrees Centigrade, designed to cool bodies down in twenty-four hours. Important for the preservation of human tissue, the low temperature could be deadly for her. Hypothermia could set in quickly, resulting in death in a matter of hours. Besides, no one would remember where she was. Her mouth twisted at her own morbid thoughts. *Some day off,* she thought. She would call Camilla, ask for a rain check on the shopping, drive home, and crawl into bed.

She pushed the gurney into the refrigerator and noted that there were three other bodies inside. She quickly found a space for her charge. Then she heard a noise in the room outside. *Was that a door closing?* She paused for a moment to listen. Nothing.

As she leaned down to lock the gurney wheels, she felt the air shift in the room. Santos stood up. Before she could turn around, she felt a crushing blow to the back of her head.

Her knees buckled. She blacked out before she hit the frigid, hard floor.

The lights in the freezer flicked off, plunging the room into darkness. Her shoe was removed from the door. The hydraulic seals of the heavy door slid shut with a soft whoosh.

Chapter 75

At 6:30 a.m., the day shift was arriving in the CCU, among them, Patrick. At rounds, the night shift was unusually talkative as they described Anthony's death. *He was such a beautiful child. It was such a gruesome death. His parents took it very hard.* Grief and depression were palpable. The wounds from the previous deaths were torn open by this one. The nurses gave their reports quickly and hurried out the door, craving sunlight and warm hugs from their precious children before the kids headed off to school.

"Hey, do you know when Santos left?" Patrick called out to a staff member walking off the unit. Emma had mentioned that she'd come in the night before when Anthony was coding.

Walking backwards while talking, the PCA said, "Don't know. Probably left hours ago. She was beat."

"Okay, thanks."

Patrick went to the computer and began to review his patient assignment as well as the labs and goals for the day, but he was preoccupied. He was worried about the impact of Anthony's death on Santos. She had really liked that kid. He knew that Santos was strong and stoic. That made her difficult to read; she kept things inside until they finally gushed out. Concerned and distracted, he thought he would give her a call, even if he woke her up. His gut told him that it was the right thing to do. Besides, he wanted to hear her voice—the sweet, warm voice that he loved to hear. Talk with her. Make sure she was okay.

CHAPTER 76

Santos opened her eyes. Was someone calling her? She could see nothing; it was quiet and dark. Then she heard a new noise, a soft mechanical hum. She was freezing. She was lying on her stomach on the floor. Her head pounded with pain.

Where am I? She got up on her hands and knees and sat back on her heels. The floor was ice cold.

After a few minutes of foggy confusion, Santos remembered where she was.

I'm in the morgue refrigerator with Anthony.

Claustrophobia created panic. She shivered. Her teeth chattered uncontrollably. She fought back tears. The only thing she could see was the face of her watch. It read 6:30 a.m. She pulled out her cell to call for help. No bars. No service. And her battery was nearly dead. The flashlight app would run it dry.

On her hands and knees, Santos began her blind search for the door. She crawled slowly, searching for a wall. Her head-splitting pain made her dizzy. Her fingers were numb from the cold. Moving blindly, she bumped into a piece of equipment. It crashed with a loud metallic clang, the sound reverberating against the stainless steel walls and tile floor.

CHAPTER 77

Patrick found Emma checking the electronic patient record before seeing a patient.

"I tried Santos on her cell phone. She isn't answering."

"She has the day off today. Remember? Probably has it on vibrate or off. She must be suffering, terribly ... and she needs to rest, recharge her batteries."

"I don't think her cell is off ... she has a hard time weaning herself away from constant communication. Have you seen how many times she checks her email?"

"What do you want to do?" Emma asked, turning around. Her dark eyes narrowed. "Do you want to check on her at home?"

"I wonder. She was spending the night at Camilla's. Do you think she went back there?"

"Worth a try, Patrick. Call Camilla first before you run all over Houston. And make sure she actually left. We don't know that for sure, do we?"

"Will do," Patrick said. He started to walk away when Emma called him back.

"Patrick, come talk with me for a minute." She guided him to a quiet corner. Emma looked around. His curiosity piqued. She whispered, "Wendy, Santos and I had a conversation not too long ago ... we're concerned that someone is actually attempting to take the team out—take us out of commission. I think we may all be getting a little overly dramatic, but ...." She paused, grasped his arm and looked deeply into his eyes, her forehead creased with concern. "What if we're right? What if someone has her?"

CHAPTER 78

Santos struggled to remain calm. Hold her anxiety in check. Every time she moved her head, she was hit by a wave of nausea and dizziness.

She pulled down the sheet shrouding her former patient and wrapped it around her.

Sorry, Anthony. I need this more than you do now.

Still on the floor, she continued to crawl on her hands and knees, feeling for the walls and the door to the refrigerator. Her toes were now numb from the cold. Her brain was cloudy. Her mind was shutting down, and her search became clumsy, moving in circles. She hurt all over, particularly her head. She touched the back of her head and felt the stickiness of clotted blood.

Did I fall and hit my head?

She sat still for a moment.

I need to rest.

The slow, steady creep of hypothermic drowsiness would soon come to its inescapable conclusion.

CHAPTER 79

Patrick, always a rock with patients in crisis, found himself working to control his panic—it was different with someone you love. He knew now for sure. He loved her. He could not live without her. He had to find her.

He quickly called Camilla, struggling to keep his tone even. He learned that Santos had left a note saying she was coming back to the hospital. They had not seen or heard from her since.

"You'll call me when you find her?"

"Yes, Camilla. Thank you so much for dinner last night. It was great. Sorry to make this quick, but I'm worried, too. This is so unlike Santos—not to be in touch."

He tried her cell again. No answer. It went immediately to voice mail. Where was she? He felt certain that something was terribly wrong. He paced the hall, trying to think. If she had gone home, that would be fine. He would focus his search where she could be in danger—here, in the hospital, the parking garage. What if she had been attacked in the garage? Security would have found her. His mind raced, but he needed more information. He knew that his search might involve waking up a few staff members, but his intuition was strong, and he had rarely missed the mark. He could feel her fear. Something was terribly wrong.

He went back to the workstation and rapidly checked the assignments for the day shift the day before. The new graduate nurse, Kathleen, assigned to the patient who had died, went home at midnight. He looked at his watch. It was 7:30 a.m. Maybe Kathleen would know something. He dialed her number on his cell.

"Oh, Patrick. She was so wonderful with the family. But I was a wreck, and she sent me home. She offered to take the patient down to the morgue for me when they were finished with last rites and the final bath."

Kathleen wanted to go on about the experience, but Patrick conscious of time, quickly ended the conversation and began to retrace Santos's steps. If she was still here, her car would be in the parking garage. He knew pretty much where she parked when she drove and was hopeful he could find it.

He dashed out of the unit with a wave to Emma and took the elevator down to the parking garage. Luck was in his favor. He found her car, parked in its usual place, close to the elevator.

She was still in the hospital.

He quickly ran back to the elevator bank and pushed the up button. He looked at his watch: 7:45. When the elevator did not arrive in five seconds, he impatiently headed for the stairs. He raced up, his long legs taking them two at time. His next stop, following her trail, would be the morgue.

When he arrived five minutes later at the hospital morgue, staff was just beginning to filter in. He abruptly approached the first staff member he saw.

"Have you seen a nurse down here? Her name is Santos Rosa. She brought a patient down in the middle of the night."

"Haven't seen her," the staff member said, turning her back. She began to make coffee for the day crew.

Patrick's mind raced with options. His heart filled with worry.

If she isn't here, then where is she?

He quickly scanned around the autopsy suite. It was

clean, but cluttered with equipment and carts tightly wedged together in one corner of the room. None of the autopsies had started for the day. He started to leave but was unsure of where to go next. Desperate with worry, out of the corner of his eye, he saw something out of place.

What was that on the floor? Curious, he walked over. By the large walk-in refrigerator, he noticed that pieces of equipment and tables had been pushed against the refrigerator door, wedging it closed. The room was relatively small, and the space was crowded with equipment. Looking closer, he saw a small white shoe—a female shoe.

CHAPTER 80

Patrick launched into action heaving aside equipment and tables blocking the entrance to the refrigerator door, oblivious to the noise and chaos he created. Tables slammed into gurneys, glass shattered, and metal bowls hit the floor, all the while his heart pounded with dread.

Was she in there?

Hearing the crash of equipment, a staff member called out, "Hey, what're you doing?"

"There may be someone in there. I need help!"

The two men pushed and shoved, moving equipment until finally Patrick could reach the door. *What if I'm too late?* Sweat trickled down the back of his scrubs as he felt an overpowering fear of failure. His brain raced, thinking ahead.

He grabbed the handle and pulled the door toward him. Light filtered into the cold, dark space. He could see three shrouded gurneys.

"I need light!"

The morgue staffer reached in, flipped a switch, and flooded the refrigerator with light.

Patrick saw her. She was on the floor, wrapped in a sheet, curled into the fetal position.

He rushed over and quickly knelt at her side.

"Santos! Santos!"

She did not move. He shook her. She did not move. He shook her again—harder.

"Come on, Santos, wake up!"

He tore the sheet off her body and ran his fingers under her jawline, feeling for a pulse. She was cold to the touch, her skin alabaster, her lips cyanotic blue. His eyes began to fill with tears.

A pulse; he felt a pulse. It was thready, and he could hardly feel it, but it was there. He saw dried blood on her scrubs and rapidly searched for the source. He needed to get her off the cold floor and warm her fast, but he did not want to hurt her more by moving her. He gently turned her head and found that her hair was sticky with clotted blood. Had she fallen? He added head injury to his assessment and decided he had to risk it.

"Do you want me to call a code?" The staff asked from the doorway.

Patrick, still on his knees, scooped her up in his arms and stood up. "I'll get her to the ER. They'll know how to handle hypothermia."

Cradling her in his arms, Patrick rapidly navigated out of the refrigerator and through the morgue, quickly covering the twenty yards to the back door of the ER.

"Stay with me now," he said to Santos. "Stay with me. I'm not going to lose you."

He approached the entrance of the emergency room, where a bright red-lettered sign announced, "DO NOT ENTER. ALARM WILL SOUND." Ignoring the sign, he turned around, pushing open the lever on the door with his right hip. The door swung into the ER, and the siren blared.

Everyone in the hall looked up, alert to the sound.

"I need some help here!" he shouted over the noise to one of the trauma nurses. "Severe hypothermia and head trauma. Her breathing is shallow. We need the warmer and probably a CAT scan ...."

He followed the nurse into a trauma room, carrying the unconscious Santos.

CHAPTER 81

The only light in the room was the dim glow of the computer screen. The heavy curtains, drawn close, blocked out the brightness of the early winter day. Hunched over the keyboard, he took a sip of hot black coffee. He was busy, intense, as he added the finishing touches to the storyboard on his firewalled private website. He had won the game, his solitary game, hands down.

Ruminating as he pointed and clicked with the mouse, he realized that he had flirted with discovery when he lost it with Santos. But he had done his homework. There were no security cameras in the area. No one saw him come or go. He had clocked out prior to waiting for her, watching from the janitor's closet off the morgue hallway.

When his gloved hands crushed her skull with the stainless steel pitcher, in his fury, he had not cared if she lived or died. If she died, she would have been his forever. She would never belong to anyone else. When she lost consciousness and crumpled to the floor, he quickly removed his ID badge from the pocket of her scrubs. He picked up the stainless steel pitcher and dropped it into a sink of disinfectant with other equipment. No trail.

The next day, there was a lot of chatter about Santos's accident. Despite the late night, he had made sure that he was at his post early. It was important that he be visible. He could not disappear simultaneously with her injury. Rumor had it that she had slipped and fallen, hitting her head. She was admitted and under observation. Evidently, she did not remember what had happened. It needed to stay that way.

He would lay low for a while. The holidays would help. Staff, caught up with family, friends, and parties, would be distracted. Almost everyone took some time off during this period. He would make sure that he was friendly and appeared happy during the holidays. Actually, it would not be that hard this time. He thought he might offer to help plan the lab holiday party. That would throw them off. The temporary happiness, the sense of fulfillment, would fade as the days went by. The secret website, his alone, would always be a monument to his success, his brilliance. He would always have that.

CHAPTER 82

Patrick sat by Santos's hospital bed, watching her sleep, cradling her cool hand in his, absentmindedly brushing his thumb across her wrist. He could not stop touching her.

"Please be the one. Please be the one ...." Who wrote that song? Was it Karla Bonoff? He couldn't get the melody out of his head.

Her dark hair, fanned out on the pillow, created a stark contrast to her skin, which was still very pale. She looked small and fragile buried under mounds of blankets. When he'd found her, her body temperature was ninety-three degrees. No wonder she still felt cold. She was so near death.

What if I'd been too late? The thought wrapped bands of pain around his heart, squeezing, filling him with dread and despair. Already, he had so many hopes and dreams of life with her, waking up with her every morning, their children ... so many hopes and dreams. They had so much to talk about. The only way to purge his fear and feel that she was safe was to find out what had really happened.

Her eyes closed, she asked, "Are you still here?"

She opened her eyes and smiled at him. He loved her smile. His heart fluttered.

He picked up her hand, kissed it, and rested it against his cheek. He had almost lost her.

"I'm afraid to let you out of my sight."

"Patrick, I'm going to be fine. Just need some rest. This will heal." She paused. "How does anyone sleep in the hospital?"

"You're so funny!" He laughed with relief.

After a few moments of silence he leaned back into his chair and spoke soberly. "When you're ready, we need to talk about what happened."

"Now?"

"When you're ready."

"We might as well get started."

Patrick cleared his throat. He would have to choose his words carefully ... balance his emotions with objectivity, try not to let the conversation add to her trauma. He had already come to his own conclusion.

He dialed back his urgency and spoke quietly and gently.

"Santos, what if you didn't fall? What if someone hit you? They hit you and left you in a refrigerator where you could have died. We're talking about attempted murder. Why would someone want to do that to you?"

There was silence for a moment.

"Why would someone want to kill me? I don't know anyone who would do that ... what are you thinking, Patrick?"

"I may be getting paranoid, but my gut tells me this could be connected to our search for the cause of our patients' deaths ... think about it ... put the pieces together. Wendy gets sick ... Emma and Nick get sick ...."

"That's terrifying ...." Her eyes were dark with worry and she grew even paler.

Patrick nodded.

"If you're right, if this is connected to our unsolved deaths, we must be getting very close. We're obviously becoming a huge threat."

Santos sat up in bed.

"Oww, headache ... probably shouldn't move that

fast." She paused to get her equilibrium, clear her head. "Okay, think about it. Think about what we already know. We believe that someone may be tampering with lab results. We just had another death, little Tony." She started to cry. "Oh, it's all coming back. I feel so bad. It's so awful."

Patrick moved over to sit on the edge of her bed. She pushed him away. "I'm sorry that I'm so emotional!"

"Come here; let me hold you for a minute." She hesitated for a moment. He reached out and wrapped his arms around her small shoulders, tenderly drawing her close. She smelled of shampoo and the lingering scent of antiseptic. His cheek gently grazed the top of her head. He was filled with tenderness and a fierce sense of wanting to protect. *I've never felt this way about anyone.*

He felt her relax, and they sat together for a moment, holding each other tightly.

Suddenly, she backed off and sat up straight.

"What's wrong?"

"Patrick, when I came in … when Kathleen called me to come in … I ran into this guy from the lab … physically bumped right into him. He always seems to be around … sort of stalking. I let him have it … it ticked me off because I caught him watching the code. It didn't seem right. He didn't belong there … disgusting!"

She paused.

"And?"

"Well, I got mad. Grabbed his ID badge—ripped it off his lab coat, and put it in my pocket. I told him that I would talk with his supervisor in the morning."

"Where is it? Do you know his name?"

"I don't know where it is. But I'm sure that Wendy knows his name."

She looked down at her hands and frowned, then

looking up and reached out for Patrick's hand.

"Patrick, I looked him right in the eyes. I stared him down. And what I saw there was something I've never seen before ... in anyone's eyes. They were deep pools of black ... cold, hard ... empty. It startled me ... scared me."

She was silent for a moment, then, "Oh, my God!"

"What's wrong?"

"I just remembered something else. I saw him at our Community Hospital ... when I was there for the CE course. He was there when Carol was in the hospital! Right before she died!"

Patrick sat up straighter and pushed himself away, adrenaline connecting the dots. "Okay, Santos, you may have something here. Did he see you?"

"Yes ... he did. I think we need to get all the records together, add Carol and Tony. We need to get the staffing data from Wendy. If his name shows up—over and over—on the days of the deaths, then we might be able to do a back trace of their labs, see if we can't find his trail."

"I think we're going to need more than that." Patrick shook his head.

"Like what?"

"From what Wendy has told me," Patrick explained, "MTs leave their computer stations without logging off. Anyone could change lab results ... even remotely. The staff is stable. The same people work nearly every day, same shift. So linking an MT with a death would be like linking us to the deaths. We were here, so were the same lab staff."

"But I saw him at Community Hospital! I've seen him at nearly every death." Santos paused, grabbed Patrick by the arm and continued. "Okay, what about tracking his computer access? Even at home. Doesn't every computer have an IP address? Do you know any computer whizzes?"

"Yeah, we could talk to Hal in IT."

"Oh, I know Hal. I like him! He would be great."

"Santos, so far, we're still searching for links. Wouldn't the evidence we have so far be just circumstantial?" He fought the urge to give in to her train of thought, realizing that they would need proof.

Santos leaned back and crossed her arms across her chest. "Are you going to night school to study law? First, you use 'attempted murder,' then 'circumstantial' … not that you aren't smart, Patrick Sullivan."

"No, I'm not going to law school. But I did grow up with an attorney," Patrick said slowly.

"Who?"

"My dad was a prosecuting attorney for decades. He died a few years ago."

"Oh, I remember that. I'm so sorry. I think I had just started and you were away at his funeral. I guess we've both lost parents. Is your mom still alive?"

Patrick nodded.

"Enough about my law background. Let's keep going here."

"So, we'll do the back trace on the labs, check his IP address and see what we find … I don't know exactly what we could find. But you know that guy, McGee on *NCIS*— he finds all kinds of things. We need a McGee!"

"Keep going. You're on a roll."

"We need absolute proof that he took a result, tampered with it, and a patient died. Until we do that, all the evidence may be considered circumstantial," Santos responded.

Patrick leaned in closer. "It's going to be very difficult to find a trail … nearly impossible. This guy is obviously smart, has covered his tracks. Created an elegant crime."

"We can't risk another patient dying!"

"So what do we do?"

"We need to catch him in the act. Prevent the death before it happens," Santos replied.

"What are you thinking?" Patrick paused. He could see her mind at work. "I don't think I like that look in your eyes."

"We need to set him up. Make him want to kill again. Bring him out in the open."

"Play our game instead of his?" Patrick replied.

Santos nodded.

"How are we going to do that?"

Santos leaned forward, her eyes focused and intensely serious. "I volunteer."

CHAPTER 83

"Santos, you've crazy!"

"I don't think you should do this!"

"This is dangerous!"

Patrick, Emma, Nick, Yasmin, and Wendy all huddled around Santos's hospital bed, where she was shaking her head.

"Come on, ya'll, we don't have a choice. It's either a patient or me. At least we know I'm a target." Santos reached over and grabbed Wendy by the sleeve of her lab coat and pulled her close. "Wendy, you need to be careful. You work with him."

They had learned his name. It was Hadrian Blair.

"Should Heather be in the loop?" Nick asked.

"Wait a minute, Santos, we've got to figure out how we're going to do this ... *if* we're going to do this," responded Patrick.

"Heather would be helpful, but we can't involve her," Emma said. "We could be putting her job at risk."

Santos looked up at her fashionable friend, who was perched on the edge of the bed. "Yasmin, maybe you should leave, too. We don't want to get you into trouble."

"I'm not worried."

"What about our jobs?" offered Nick.

"Depends on how we do this." Santos thought for a moment. "Help me, guys; let's just talk it out. Then we can decide if it's feasible. Humor me!" She smiled at all of them. "Come on, please?"

"Well, the first thing we need to do is the electronic traces, the back traces on the lab work, and then see if we can track his work from home. I'll talk with Hal," Patrick offered.

"And I have the list of all the patients who may have been victims, plus their labs. As best as possible, we've linked the labs with the tech that ran them or posted them. But it's possible that he used other computers or logged in on someone else's ID and password," Wendy offered.

"If we work the electronic traces from angles, home IP address and work, we should have a greater chance of finding some matches or suspicious coincidences," Patrick said.

"There you go again, Patrick, 'suspicious coincidences.'"

"Innocent until proven guilty, Santos," replied Patrick. "Wendy, why don't you and I go talk with Hal? You're the MT expert, and I have some ideas. Who knows what we'll be able to find if we can get his home IP address?"

"We can find his IP address. Hal can help us if we can come up with the serial number. Every computer we have, home or here, we have the serial number. The serial number is linked to an IP address," Wendy added.

"Whatever we do," said Emma, "we need to stay under the radar."

"We could get in trouble for this, you know," said Nick.

"And more people could die," Santos shot back.

"Let's think of this as a QI project, not a witch hunt," said Emma. "We've had some issues in the ICU, we are the designated team ... we're looking for patterns, potential errors."

"Good point, Emma. Patrick, can I join you and Wendy?"

"Sure, Nick. Glad to have your brainpower on board."

"Is it time to talk about Plan B?" asked Santos.

No one replied.

"Plan B?" she repeated.

"Santos, you're pushing it. We need to see how we can set him up, other than using someone—you—as a target. Catch him before he executes. We can talk about it, but I don't think it is a good idea. It's way too dangerous. He could come at you from any number of angles," said Patrick.

"Well, let's think about it. First of all, we have to make her a target," said Emma.

"Aren't I a target now?"

"We don't know what he knows or does not know about you," Nick responded.

"And we don't know if or how he would come at you. That's what worries me," said Patrick. "If we make him anxious, who knows what he'll do? He could mess with your car in the garage. He could poison you, inject you with a virus, tamper with your lab results ... we already think he does that. He has many choices with you here in the hospital. He's on the inside. Don't ever underestimate this guy. He's proven he can kill."

"Patrick, I had no idea you had such an imagination!" laughed Santos. "Sounds like you missed your calling. You should have been a detective ... or a mystery writer!"

CHAPTER 84

Hadrian Blair stood outside of Santos's room. He hesitated, thinking things through.

It was still dark outside. This was the quiet time of the morning between change of shift. Everyone was in rounds or charting. How much did she remember? He took a couple of deep breaths to steady his nerves. His mouth was dry. He had to know. And the only way he would find out was if she saw him. His palms were sweaty. He pulled out a tissue from his pocket and wiped them dry. Then he leaned on his crutch, grasped his equipment with his other hand, and ambled into her room.

Santos was sleeping. She was so still and pale she could have been in a casket.

He quietly approached her bed.

Little One, you must die. Then I can stop worrying. This loose end nagged him. He liked everything neat, clean. If she died, she was his, and he was free.

Hadrian stood watching her, and the seconds ticked by. He resisted the urge to stroke her hair … he longed to touch her … too risky. He had an excuse to be there: draw routine blood work. He would have to wake her. He had to know. He could deal with what he knew.

CHAPTER 85

Santos's heart hammered in her chest.

She kept her eyes closed. Sensing his presence, she was terrified. An electric current of fear rippled through her body, warming her. Shift change was underway, and she knew she was vulnerable. Her mind raced with the possibilities. *What did he want? What would he do?* She knew that in dangerous situations she had two choices: confront or flee. Fleeing was not an option. She had to face him.

"Why don't we let her sleep for a while longer?" whispered a voice from the doorway.

Santos's eyes shot open, and she saw Hadrian turn around to face Emma. She let out an imperceptible sigh of relief.

"I've got a doctor's order here for three tubes," he replied.

"I know that," said Emma.

"Emma, it's okay. I'm awake."

"You sure, honey?"

Emma walked over to the bed and reached down as if to assess Santos's pulse. Santos watched as Emma searched her face for clues. Santos's frigid, clammy hand reached for Emma's. She squeezed. Emma's warm, dry hand squeezed back.

Santos looked straight at Emma and nodded.

"I'm not sure you'll find any veins. I'm still cold," she said to Hadrian.

She made a snap decision: no confrontation. She would pretend she did not remember him.

Emma, play along with me, she thought. *Play along with me. Follow my lead.*

Emma gave her a long, appraising look and arched her eyebrows. Then Emma turned away from the bed to face Hadrian. "She's had a head injury and is having trouble remembering. Be gentle with her, okay?"

He nodded.

Emma picked up some trash, threw some dirty laundry in the hamper, and appeared to be gathering towels for Santos. Lingering.

Santos let Hadrian tie a tourniquet around her arm, palpate a vein, clean the area with alcohol, and smoothly insert the vacutainer needle. It gave her the creeps to let him touch her. She fought back the nausea of disgust and looked away to mask her feelings. He efficiently drew the blood, swabbed her arm with alcohol, and placed a cotton ball with pressure on the injection site.

"Press down on this for a few minutes," Hadrian said.

Santos reached over to apply pressure. She used every ounce of her stamina to retain her composure. Her stomach churned. She wanted to throw up.

Hadrian gathered up his supplies.

"How are you feeling?" he asked.

She hesitated for a moment. "Very foggy. I have a splitting headache most of the time. But hopefully I'll be able to go home today."

"Well, feel better," he said.

Santos watched him turn around and walk out the door.

Emma closed the door tightly behind him.

Santos sat up in bed.

"Oh, Emma, I was terrified! I'm dripping with sweat. Thank God you came in. I didn't know what to do. Emma, please come here, I need a hug!"

Emma crossed the room and sat on her bed.

"Come to Mamma, honey," and she wrapped her arms around Santos. "Well, that warmed you up a bit!" Emma smiled and Santos lay back on the bed pulling the blanket up to her chin.

"I came up to see you. When I saw him down the hall heading to your door, I followed … but he didn't see me. I saw him hesitate outside your door. I wasn't sure what he was going to do, so I followed him in … he stood and watched you for a few seconds. I think he was considering what to do."

"And I thought I could let myself be the target! No way. I need to get out of here. Home safe … before he makes a move … if he's going to make a move."

"That bought us a little time, but the trail will get cold if we don't get going." Emma paused. "You going to be okay?"

"Yes. Guess we'll have to consider another Plan B. I don't even know if there should be a Plan B. I'm way too exposed here in the hospital. He could come at me from any direction."

"I think that's what Patrick was trying to tell you."

"He was right. I've got to get out of here. I don't feel safe." Santos paused. "But what are we going to do, Emma? Before he goes after someone else?"

CHAPTER 86

"She's doing really well," Sheila said to her lunch buddy. They were sitting in the busy hospital cafeteria. "She should be going home today."

"Does she remember what happened?"

Sheila leaned over and whispered. "She remembers. She remembers everything and more. They think they know who may be responsible for those deaths. They're collecting data as we speak."

"Is it someone on the inside?"

"I can't say right now."

∽

Hadrian, at the next table, his back to the two students, heard every word.

So she lies, too. She does remember. Little girls, you had better be careful who overhears your lunch gossip. He sat, waiting, until they got up, cleared their table, and walked away.

He would not fail.

CHAPTER 87

Hadrian waited until midnight to make the drive. He had missed his opportunity while she was in the hospital. Then again, killing her remotely by adjusting her lab results seemed too cold and clinical for his Little One. Besides, they would be watching. He had decided to change his *modus operandi* and move outside the hospital.

He parked a block away, around the corner from her house. The heavily wooded area was gloomy, illuminated by only a few streetlights that cast shadows across the manicured yards. He was dressed in black; the darkness made great cover. Slowly, he made his way to her patio home, continuously alert to traffic and sounds. The area was quiet, a few porch lights lit, no lights on in the houses. That was good.

The evening was cool, and though air conditioners still hummed, he could see windows open to catch the evening breeze. He approached her house. All her lights were out. The clouds parted, and the full moon illuminated the landscape. He stopped to get his bearings. Then he continued to the back of her house. The moon slipped behind the clouds, and he melted into the night.

This was his lucky day. He saw a patio door cracked open to take advantage of the cool evening. He pulled out a pair of new lightweight black gloves and put them on, making certain they fit snugly. Then he quietly slid the screen door open. He listened and waited ... no sound, no movement, no light. Then he slid the glass door open, just enough so that he could slip inside, careful to maneuver as gracefully as he could. He hugged the wall for a moment, listening for movement ... waited ten seconds. Nothing.

This *was* his lucky day. It would be a clean kill.

Santos was sound asleep in the double bed. He would need to move quickly before the opportunity passed. He reached for the pillow next to her. She would die in her sleep. He would have her all to himself.

Chapter 88

Santos screamed.

Patrick jumped off the coach in the great room and ran. In the darkness, the black hulk of a man hunched over her, holding her down, crushing a pillow to her face. It was Hadrian Blair. Her feet kicked out, and her hands thrashed helplessly as she struggled to stop him.

Patrick reacted without thinking. He grabbed Hadrian from behind, wrapping his right arm around the thick neck of the attacker. He jerked back, trying to get Hadrian off Santos. Hadrian reacted quickly, sharply jabbing Patrick in the ribs with his elbow. Patrick doubled over in pain. Clutching his chest, Patrick remembered the man's disability, and drove his knee hard into the back of Hadrian's leg. Hadrian roared.

Patrick jumped on Hadrian's back, circled his arm around Hadrian's neck attempting to knock him off balance. Hadrian leaned forward. Patrick held on tight. Then the bear of a man shook him off, and Patrick flew across the room, knocking over a lamp. The lamp crashed sending shards of glass across the room. Patrick landed hard and fell back hitting his head on the tile floor. He fought waves of blackness, and sucked in deep breaths of air.

"You bastard!" Hadrian screamed and hurled the full weight of his body down on Patrick.

Patrick quickly rolled, avoiding the body slam and powerful arms that could easily pin him.

How do I stop this guy? He had to get up. His head was spinning. He knew he could not compete with Hadrian on the ground. His advantage was on his feet. He pulled himself up, adrenaline pumping. Galvanized by anger, he kicked Hadrian in the ribs once, then twice.

Hadrian groaned and rolled, protecting himself. He lunged at Patrick's leg, grabbing it and pulling him down. Patrick lost his balance and fell again, hitting the floor on his side, cracking ribs, unable to move, the wind knocked out of him.

How long could he hold out with this guy? Where was Santos?

Helpless to resist, Patrick felt Hadrian flip him over on to his back. Hadrian straddled him, crushing Patrick's chest with the full weight of his body. He was unable to draw in a breath. Then Hadrian's strong fingers wrapped around his neck, choking. Hadrian's grip tightened.

Patrick was suffocating. He had seconds to live. He struggled, reaching up to push Hadrian off him, but he was outmanned. Blood pounded loud in his ears. He heard a siren in the distance. Hadrian pressed harder, strangling.

The last thing Patrick saw was Hadrian's face contorted in rage. He started to black out.

From a distance he heard a metal thud.

Hadrian fell forward, a dead weight on top of him.

Gasping for air, heart pounding, Patrick sucked in a few deep breaths. Then he rolled Hadrian off his body and looked up.

Santos stood over him in her long flannel nightgown, cast-iron skillet in her hands, tears running down her face.

CHAPTER 89

After the police left, Santos and Patrick sat on the couch in the great room where Patrick had been sleeping. Wrapped in an Irish mohair lavender throw, she snuggled close to Patrick. The room blazed with light. The curtains were closed, every door and window locked. Patrick had seen to that, double-checking to be sure.

Mrs. Banks walked out of Santos's bedroom. She had heard the sirens and rushed over in time to see the police drag the cuffed Hadrian, screaming obscenities, out the door.

She immediately took charge of the young couple.

"I put clean sheets on the bed. It's ready for you now, Santos."

Santos shuddered. "I don't think I'll be able to sleep in there for a while."

Mrs. Banks turned to Patrick. "Keep some ice on those ribs." She paused, leaned over, and pulled his shirt collar away from his neck. "And we'd better put some ice on your neck. You're going to have some bruises there, pretty bad."

"I'll be okay." Santos looked at him with concern. "But I'll take the ice."

Mrs. Banks shook her head, walked into Santos's kitchen, and rummaged around in her refrigerator. She pulled out a bottle of white wine and some cheese. She fixed a plate of cheese and fruit, and then carried the food and wine into the living room. She put the tray on the coffee table in front of the quiet couple.

"Eat a little. Have a glass of wine. It will help settle you."

"Thank you, Mrs. Banks. We'll be fine." Santos was drained and shaken while at the same time wired and wide awake.

"Do you want me to stay with you? Do you want me to call your family?"

Santos managed a weak smile. "Oh, no, we'll be fine. But I'd better call them before they hear about it on the news. What time is it anyway?"

Patrick looked at his watch. "About 5:15."

"Already?"

"Maybe I should make coffee," Mrs. Banks offered.

"Thanks, Mrs. Banks. Thanks so much for being here. We'll be fine now."

Santos got up and gave her neighbor a warm hug. She was grateful for the maternal presence. "Thank you, thank you! You have been such a comfort."

The older woman just smiled. "Glad to be able to help, Santos. Not often that I feel needed these days."

"Just because your kids are grown doesn't mean they don't need you." Santos gave Mrs. Banks another hug and walked her to the door.

"I'll come back and check on you later today."

"Thanks. I'd appreciate that. We can have a cup of tea together ... I'm not sure that I want to be alone here."

Mrs. Banks nodded and gave Santos a parting kiss on the cheek.

"You'll be fine. You're strong, you're alive. You are safe."

Santos closed the door behind her neighbor and locked the deadbolt. She turned around to face Patrick, who was standing behind her.

"I thought I would get more sleep here than in the hospital. And be safer! Was I wrong."

Patrick laughed with her then doubled over in pain clutching his ribs.

"Guess this night is going to be with me for a while."

"The ibuprofen should kick in soon." She smiled at him and gently touched his ribs. "Well, our relationship has certainly been interesting—never a dull moment ... I'm all for some less exciting times." She paused. "Well, I guess we're even."

"What do you mean? Oh, I get it ... you mean I saved your life and now you saved mine?"

"Yeah. Isn't that what a couple who cares is supposed to do for each other?"

He pulled her close to him and winced in agony.

"Yes, Santos, that's what I believe, too."

He leaned down and kissed her. The warmth from his lips flowed through her, tingling down to her toes, and she clung to him, drinking in the pleasure of his kiss. She would never get enough of this.

She pulled away and looked up at him. He was pale and bruised. But his eyes sparkled with tenderness, eyes that had turned deep blue with warmth.

"Thank you, Patrick. Thank you for being in my life. You are a gift."

"I love you, Santos. I think I've loved you from the first moment I met you. I felt that you were something special. I wanted you in my life. Now more than ever."

Happiness swept through her, and that, coupled with the memory of what had just happened, threatened to overwhelm her. "When I saw him choking you, when he looked like he would win, I was terrified. I was scared to death that I would lose you. Then I got mad. He had hurt too many people that I cared about ... I had to stop him."

She paused, smiled at him, and continued. "Amazing

how something like this sort of crystallizes everything—makes it very clear."

"Makes what clear?"

Her eyes glistened. "I love you, too, Patrick. I didn't want to admit it to myself, admit that I wanted someone in my life, that I needed someone … I didn't realize how lonely I was. I love you, Patrick."

She wrapped her arms around him, gently put her head on his chest, and sighed.

Epilogue

The mountain valley village slept, tucked under a blanket of new snow. The long-awaited white powder had arrived quietly in the night. Steam rose from exhaust vents on the roofs and hung suspended, nearly frozen in the cold, gray light of predawn. The sun had yet to cast patterns of light and shadow on the distant mountain peaks. The scene was still and so breathtakingly beautiful, it might have been a canvas painted with pinks, grays, and blacks.

Bundled up in a thick white terry robe, with a steaming mug of coffee warming her hands, Santos stood on the balcony high over the village. The fire burned brightly behind her, taking the chill out of the morning air. She took in the wide vista of sky, mountains, trees, and ski village below. Santos took deliberate deep breaths, filling her lungs with the fresh, cold mountain air.

From her vantage point six stories up, the village seemed to be in miniature—tiny colored lights twinkled beneath trees flocked heavily with new snow. The multi-colored lights strung on pine trees around the ice rink were still bright in the early dawn. The scene inspired a joyful feeling in Santos—childlike anticipation of the holiday season. *If we stop amidst the chaos and busyness of life, the child in every adult can still feel the magic of Christmas.*

The ice rink below was covered with at least eight inches of snow. It would create a challenge for the Zamboni yet to arrive. Glancing to her left, she saw the majestic pink Dale Chihuly glass chandelier ablaze with light. It dominated the huge window of Pismo, the glass gallery. Shops decorated with red ribbons, fragrant fir, and pinecones, awaited holiday shoppers below. There was no one yet in sight in the village, and the quiet brought peace to her soul.

Her bruises were more emotional than physical, but she was mending. Santos's heart still ached with sorrow over the senseless loss of her patients and her dear friend, Carol. And she would never get over the loss of Anthony. Though none of them had deserved to die, Anthony left a jagged hole in her heart. Though adults entered the hospital with a certain naïveté about what they might experience, children were innocent bystanders to their fate.

She shivered when she thought of what might have happened to her if Patrick had not found her. That was indeed God's work. She was thankful to be alive. She was grateful to Patrick for following his gut—in every way. The day she had left the hospital for home, he had insisted that he spend the night. Though she had protested, he would not budge. Said he was worried that she might have residual effects from her head injury. How had he known she would be in danger again? Thank God for him.

Though she longed to see him again, she needed this time alone to think, to heal. She would not be a victim. The fragile sense of vulnerability she felt early on was starting to fade. She was choosing to recover and move on. Make the experience one that made her stronger, not weaker.

She had kept in touch with the team over the past week, and Patrick called every day. The hospital IT department had been able to track Hadrian electronically and match him to at least five patient deaths. Hal had found Hadrian's private website and was able to penetrate his firewall. The team was shocked to learn how his twisted mind had created a virtual trophy case of his work. When analyzing the computer, they were also able to track his searches. It looked like he might have poisoned Emma and Nick with mushrooms. He had also posted the story of swabbing Wendy's computer and phone with a virus. They found traces of Santos's blood on the pitcher in the morgue. He was sick. The Harris County district attorney's office was still putting together the charges; the FBI, and the Secret Service were all now involved.

Taking another deep breath, she felt grateful, grateful to have such wonderful friends, family, and colleagues. This week away gave her perspective. She was thankful to Yasmin's parents, who had given her this week at their place at the Park Hyatt Beaver Creek, far away from the recent traumatic memories of Houston. Santos felt cocooned in the safety of this mountain home. She built back emotional and spiritual strength through solitude and reflection, writing daily in her journal. A breast cancer "thriver" had told her once many years ago, "Healing is not passive. Healing is active." She was doing her part to heal, physically and emotionally.

The phone rang, shattering the silence. She wondered who would be calling this early in the morning. She looked at the clock. It was only 7:30 a.m.

Worried, she hurried to the phone, nearly tripping on the coffee table, thinking that perhaps something had happened to her father. Her father was healthy at seventy-five—very active, but he was seventy-five.

"Hello?"

"Good morning sleepyhead!" said a warm male voice. "Greetings from Houston where it is a balmy eighty degrees and the Christmas decorations are up."

"Patrick, it's so early. Is everything okay?"

"Fine … fine … everything is pretty much fine … did you see that the Gallup Poll for Honesty and Ethics in

Professions rated nurses number one again?"

"No, that's great … what is that, the tenth year in a row?"

"More than that, I think."

"Okay, Patrick, what's going on … you didn't call this early just to make professional small talk."

"I wanted to catch up with you before you headed out for the day. See how you're doing. Are you sleeping yet?"

She sighed, "I *have* started to sleep again. I feel safe here. There's a lot of security and I'm not on the first floor." She paused, "I'm a little anxious about going home. I haven't slept in my bed since that night. The couch feels safer."

"I understand …"

"Enough about me … how are you doing? Bruises healing?"

"Haven't been thrown like that since high school wrestling. My neck is bruised, and my ribs still ache … and I thought I was in shape!"

Santos laughed. "You said everything is 'pretty much fine.' Talk to me. What's going on?"

Patrick's voice sobered. "I wanted you to hear this from me … not read about it in the paper or hear it second-hand from someone else."

"Hear what?"

"Hadrian tried to kill himself … in his jail cell."

Santos closed her eyes. "Oh, Patrick, he is such a tortured soul."

"He deserves to face the consequences, Santos. What-ever they may be. He ended people's lives, and he didn't care."

"Yes, you're right. I'll always wonder, though, why he did it. What drives people to do such terrible things?"

"I don't think we'll ever know. I hope he won't be able to plead insanity. His 'game wall' as he called it, showed a lot of deliberate planning. We'll see."

"It seems like I've been gone a month, and it's just been a few days. I'll be home on Saturday. Back to work on Monday."

"That's one of the reasons I'm calling. How about I pick you up at the airport? Maybe we can go out and catch some dinner together? I miss you, Santos."

"Patrick, I'm still a bit raw," she said thoughtfully. "I don't know how much fun I'll be." She paused. "But a big hug from you and some good food will do wonders."

She heard him laugh and in her mind could see him smiling.

"It's a date, then. I'll check what concourse you're coming in. Meet you at baggage claim, private car exit. Will you check bags?"

"No, I just have my carry-on. Don't like to check bags. Too much hassle."

"We can go somewhere to eat in The Woodlands, and then stop by a grocery store so you have food for Sunday."

"And half-and-half for my coffee."

"Oh, before I forget, I wanted to be sure and tell you that Heather changed the date of her holiday party to make sure you could be there."

"That's really sweet! It will be great to see everyone away from work."

They talked for a few more minutes about holiday plans and the unit. Nick and Nancy were quickly becoming an item. The census was going down. Staff were relieved that the killer had been caught.

After she gave him her flight number and ETA, she hung up the phone.

Santos stood up and went to the window. The sun was rising, and the snow on the mountains sparkled. *What a beautiful day,* she thought. *I wish Patrick were here to share this with me. Maybe next year.* She smiled with joy at the thought. It was just the beginning, and she remembered her promise to Patrick at Kimberly's wedding. It seemed so long ago. So much had happened, so fast. She was blessed.

THE END

Watch for the next book in the series, *The Imposter*,
where Santos and the team from Medical Center Hospital
face a killer who is one of their own.

Acknowledgements

Debut novelists face a steep learning curve with a unique set of challenges that can only be met with a great deal of support. The people who gave of their time and talents over the years were transformed into a virtual team with the common goal of creating a good book. This work has a piece of each team member imbedded into the novel. I am most grateful that you crossed my path and chose to be a part of this journey.

This book would not have been possible without the hundreds of dedicated clinicians, patients, and colleagues that shared and shaped the path of my nursing career over these past three decades. In so many ways, I wrote this book for you. It was my vision that the public might get a glimpse into the world of the hospital, value-driven leadership, the importance of inclusion in work and on teams, and the crucial role of the nurse. It is my hope that the right people might read this mystery novel, find challenge and intrigue, and choose to serve others in a health care career.

Many thanks to the clinical content experts: Theresa Kaplan and Tricia Lewis, RNs, and Medical Technologist, Wendy Matthews. A special thanks to Karen Foltz and Cindy Wigglesworth for marketing advice, and to Debbie Sukin for opening the doors to the lab for me at St. Luke's The Woodlands Hospital. Thanks so much to family and friends who read the book or portions of it in all stages of its development and provided feedback and encouragement: Charity and Maria Aschenbrener, Katie Gibbs, Melanie McEwen, Ann McKennis, Carol Mouring,

Marsha Nelson, Andie Pizzo, Gale Pollock, Elaine Scherer, Cherie Triolo, and last but not least, my dearest sister, Kamy Sullivan.

Learning the art and craft of fiction writing began early in life but in the most meaningful way at the University of Iowa International Writer's Workshop with Max Allan Collins, my first teacher in mystery writing, where I learned the importance of feedback and reading out loud. A very special thank you goes to author Leonard Tourney, who served as teacher and first editor for this book, focusing on elements of a great mystery. Rachel Starr Thompson helped me most importantly breathe life into the characters. And Karen Kibler with her clinical and editing expertise helped me step back, put it all in perspective, and do the final editing for publication. Thank you Eleanor Sullivan for holding my hand during a tough time in my life and guiding me to Nancy Cleary and Wyatt-MacKenzie Publishing who made this dream a reality.

Where would an author be without good friends and family who became the inspiration for some of the characters? Many thanks for your support and guidance. Special thanks go to Santos Castro and Gary Beadle. Please excuse the elaborate fiction that I have created with your characters. You are each one in a million and dear friends.

Though there were many nonfiction books I reviewed to develop this book, some were particularly helpful: *Snoop: What your Stuff Says About You* by Sam Gosling; *The Birth of The Texas Medical Center* by Frederick Elliott; *Cardiac Nursing* edited by Susan Woods, Erika Sivarajan Froelicher, Sandra Adams Motzer, and Elizabeth Bridges; *The Sociopath Next Door* by Martha Stout; *To the Limit: An Air CAV Huey Pilot in Vietnam* by Tom Johnson; *The New Personality Self-Portrait* by John Oldham and Lois Morris, and *Chickenhawk* by Robert Mason

Before closing, it is important to acknowledge the two men I love most in the world: my father and my husband. My dear father wisely encouraged me to choose the nursing profession over a degree in music. "Every woman needs to be able to take care of herself," he would say. He was right. And finally, this book as well as the deep fulfillment I found in my career would not have been possible without the love, support and valuable feedback from my best friend and husband, Peter, who believes that I can do anything. He is waiting for book two. This book has been in the works for a long time, and I'd like to finish with a quote that inspired me all along.

> *Your journey has molded you for your greater good,*
> *And it was exactly what it needed to be.*
> *Don't think that you've lost time.*
> *It took each and every situation you have encountered*
> *To bring you to the now.*
> *And now is right on time.*

Asha Tyson